High Praises:

"A compelling, cinematic novel that unders[...] weirdness often goes hand-in-hand with 'Mid[...] tion of greats like Carl Hiaasen and Elmore Leonard, Moffett combines his love of a place with a keen eye for the strange and the beautiful, bringing us a cast of unforgettable characters who don't mind causing a little chaos as they navigate the complicated relationships, communities, and landscapes that sustain them."–Dean Bakopoulos, author, *Summerlong*

"Well, what do we have here? A murder mystery that is also a ghost story; a rural homily with real-world eco concerns. We find characters: an environmental crusader in a pig suit falling in love; a triad of trophy wives delighted to be shet of their rapacious husbands, all of whom die in circumstances whimsical and grisly at once. Of course, we have foolish politicians. We see a lovely pastoral landscape threatened by the stink and slop of corporate meat production. In short, we have a story—a tale, a yarn! We have a lot!"—Jon Kelly Yenser, author, *The News as Usual and Walking Uphill At Noon*

"Who wouldn't love a mystery in which the governor's portrait goes missing and a bottle of Viagra fails to do its trick? Someone sneaky might very well replace your ED drug with an anti-inflammatory. Talk about the blues! Murder abounds in this laugh-out-loud novel, which tears into the business—the big business—of destroying Iowa's environment. Sandy Moffett writes like H.L Mencken in a cornfield."—Ralph James Savarese, author, *See It Feelingly* and *Someone Falls Overboard* and *When This Is Over*

"You're in for a pungent treat of a read. With pitiable, adorable, and deplorable characters that pop off the page, Moffett creates a fantastical riddle of a story that socks you square in the funny bone one minute but blooms into a painful bruise the next. Craven Snuggs'll stick with you, sitting achingly close to home as it exposes the tragedies of Iowa's rampant confined-animal meat farm—big ag practices that are so environmentally destructive and so inhumane we keep wondering why policymakers are still looking the other way. Despite the sobering subject matter, Moffett spices his Midwestern mystery with humor, sass, compassion, and candor—along with wintry mists of the supernatural, a shimmering reverence for the vestiges of true Iowan beauty, and even the addicting heat of forbidden love. Sure, it's a cliché to say, 'There's something in it for everyone!' But there is. Now, if we could just get our elected officials—and the industry—to absorb the message and see the big picture, we might stand a chance at our own happy ending."–Meredith Siemsen, Associate Editor, *The Iowa Source*

"Part ghost story, part trophy wives' revenge fantasy, and part eco-warrior tall tale, Sandy Moffett's *The Ghost of Craven Snuggs* is a joy ride of a read. This Midwestern whodunit pits a ragtag army of geriatric pig farmers, hapless sheriffs, and dreamy academics against the deep pockets and abundant manure of corporate agriculture. Deliciously written, Craven Snuggs gets dished up with wry humor by an author who clearly knows his way around the fields of Iowa, including the best places to bury the bodies."
—Todd London, author, *If You See Him, Let Me Know*

"In this fast-paced, tongue-in-cheek thriller, Moffett has given us a timely indictment of Big Agra that is also a rollicking yarn. It's a rare accomplishment: an urgently fun read."—Bryan Crockett, author, *Love's Alchemy: A John Donne Mystery*

"I can't decide what Sandy Moffett's book ought to be called. A murder mystery? A diatribe against agribusiness's cavalier treatment of the natural world? A blistering comedic send-up of heartless corporate culture? Whatever you call it, you should put *The Ghost of Craven Snuggs* on your 'must read' list. You'll never look at bacon the same again."–Mark Baechtel, Editor, *Rootstalk: A Prairie Journal of Culture, Science and the Arts*

"A delightful amalgamation of satirical crime fiction, political and societal commentary, and fairy tale phantasm. Though strictly entertaining, at its core it is an enlightening, educational exposition of the large-scale degradation of the environment and political corruption that is taking place in the world today (in this case, in Moffett's beloved state of Iowa) jeopardizing the existence of human society, plant and animal habitats, rivers, streams, and the very air we breathe. The story is playfully alive and an easy read, filled with intriguing characters and vividly theatrical scenes. This is fun stuff … but not for one moment does it lose sight of the very serious matter it is tackling: the ravaging of our precious environment by big business and political corruption, and the desperate moral effort and will that is needed to put a stop to it."
— Isabelle Kralj, Monologuist, Co-Director Theatre Gigante, Milwaukee

"*The Ghost of Craven Snuggs* is a very funny novel about a very serious situation. Moffett is addressing the collapse of our civilization through the eyes of ordinary mid-westerners. As you read you will recall the voice of Edward Abby. It deserves a broad readership."
—Dan O.Brien, author, *Buffalo for the Broken Heart*

THE GHOST OF CRAVEN SNUGGS

A Midwestern Murder Mystery

Sandy Moffett

Ice Cube Press LLC
North Liberty, Iowa, USA

The Ghost Of Craven Snuggs: A Midwestern Murder Mystery

Copyright © 2022 Sandy Moffett

ISBN 9781948509398

Library of Congress Control Number: 2022XXXXX

Ice Cube Press, LLC (Est. 1991)
North Liberty, Iowa 52317
www.icecubepress.com steve@icecubepress.com

The paper used in this publication meets the minimum requirements of the American National Standard for Information Sciences—Permanence of Paper for Printed Library Materials, ANSI Z39.48-1992.

Made with recycled paper. Manufactured in USA

This is a work of fiction; therefore, the novel's story and characters are fictitious. Any public agencies, institutions, or historical figures mentioned in the story serve as a backdrop to the characters and their actions, which are wholly imaginary.

To Betty.

IT was the biggest fire in Nachawinga County since the great autumn and spring prairie fires of a hundred years earlier. That was before the prairies had been plowed under and replaced by endless rows of corn and soybeans, stretching from river to river, smothering all of central Iowa that wasn't paved or untillable. Pickup trucks and cars filled with gawkers lined the gravel road for nearly a mile on each side of a driveway leading to the burning farmhouse and out-buildings. Clumps of orange and blue flame fled straight skyward and the rising smoke, and graying cumulus clouds blocking the sun, turned the landscape below an eerie green. The county fire truck along with several from neighboring counties, unable to get within a hundred yards of the house because of the heat, had resorted to spraying adjacent fields and hedgerows hoping to stop the blaze from spreading. Volunteer vehicles of all sorts, flashing lights attached to the roofs, were parked in adjoining fields, lending a red glow to the blowing grass. Even the high-school show-offs and town bullies, trying to look brave and tough, couldn't get closer. The hissing of the flames, the shouts of the firemen, and the yelling of the onlookers gave the whole scene a feeling of apocalypse.

When a small, dark man stepped through the wall of smoke onto the curling grass between the burning house and the crowd, voices dropped to a whispered murmur—then stopped. Wrinkled and thin, he was wrapped in an oilskin tarp with an old felt hat pulled down to his ears and a five-gallon bucket in his hand. He glared from one side of the silent crowd to the other, then hurled the bucket at them.

"Stay away God damn it, all of you, stay away."

His shrill voice cut through the gloom like a siren. He straightened his wiry body and raised his arms like some Moses on a mountain.

"There ain't nothing here for you to look at, there ain't nothing you can do, and there ain't gonna be nothing left for you when it's done. I told you over and over this was gonna happen but there was too much money out there for you to listen around. But I'm saying again, you ain't gonna see any of it. You ain't gonna get enough to keep your tractors running, let alone what you need to pay off what you owe on all your little farms. And them promised jobs ain't gonna be worth signin' up for. You people better wake up. Your beautiful county, your little towns, your old home places, every one of them is in more trouble than you can imagine. And I can tell you one more thing—you ain't seen the last of me."

He looked as if he was going to continue but an outburst from the spectators stopped him as the tall brick chimney collapsed into the house roof. The fire, as if it had been holding back for this chance, arced out of the crumbling house like a flaming rainbow onto the only unburnt building that remained, the old-fashioned hip-roofed wooden barn, that exploded into flames like it had been waiting to be lit. When a horse screamed, the old man turned, threw off his tarp, and sprinted to the barn. He paused for no more than a second, flung the door open, and stepped into the blaze. As the door opened, four horned goats shot out and ran into the crowd, scattering frightened people in all directions. The goats were followed by two huge Clydesdales. Moving side by side, like they were in harness, they trotted down the driveway. Finally, a tall, gaited horse stepped out, head high, lifting its hooves as if it was entering a show ring. It broke into a fast gait and raced through a lane formed by the onlookers. All eyes turned back to the blaze when the barn imploded, roaring and releasing a twisting hundred-foot ash demon into the sky.

For ten minutes there was no sound but the crackling of the fire and the crash of falling timbers. An old man and his wife, likely farmers, walked toward their truck.

"Let's go, Merle. I can't stand to see no more. There's nothing we can do," the woman said. "They're not going to be able to get in that barn for the next two, three hours." She took his hand. "You don't reckon Craven could have got out somehow, do you?"

"Don't think so. You saw that whole roof fell in on him," he said.

"How do you think it got started?"

"That fire wasn't no accident, I can tell you that. Can't tell you who struck the match. Most of us around here know them who are behind it though. Nobody'll come out and say it. With the kind of money them big boys are throwing around, any of them yahoos up there showing off woulda been happy to spill some gas on the back porch and light it. Trying to suck up. Make um feel like somebody."

"He was a good man, Craven Snuggs," she said. "Did a lotta good things around here. Maybe what he was fighting so hard against is just what's gonna happen. Nothing any of us little folks can do about it."

"I know Sheriff Townsend ain't going to do nothing about it. The big boys got him in their pockets just like all them other politicians. Licking their boots." The old man shook his head. "Everybody else hoping they'll get to feed out of the trough."

They walked on, silent for a while, not wanting to look back.

"Did you see that big flock of crows come out of that plume of ashes when the barn caved in?" the old man said. "Musta been fifty of um. Kept going straight up till I couldn't see um no more."

They reached their truck. They sat for a couple of minutes, catching their breath, bathed in a red-orange glow. Then the old man cranked the engine and turned around in the field. They drove slowly toward their farm.

Fourteen years later.

The imposing white house is off Highway 264, two miles west of Wilson, North Carolina. It is set in tall oaks and hickories a quarter mile off the highway—far enough away for quiet and privacy but near enough to make sure it is seen and envied by passers-by. Its style is nouveau plantation. Twelve three-story columns, a third-floor balcony. An ostentatious stone arch and black iron gate front a circular driveway bordered by manicured late-blooming shrubs and towering white pines. *Wooten Plantation, Since 1875* burned into an ornate metal sign hangs from the arch. Under this is a smaller sign that reads, *Home of Compassionate Family Farms, LLC.* Garages are in back, kennels and stables behind them. A black Camaro with a smashed front fender is parked in the bushes to the side of the driveway. It is 11:17 AM on an early November morning.

In the 'mistress bedroom' on the second floor, Misty Wooten stretches under high-thread count magenta sheets on her king-size bed and turns like a waking feline toward the man lying beside her. She pokes him.

"G'won downstairs, hon, and get my coffee and a couple of Mona's big old chocolate chip cookies. And move that stupid car of yours to the back. It's eleven o'clock and there's no telling when one of Hubert's cronies might come around to see if he wants to play golf or talk about the stock market or them damn pigs or some other shit." She grins at him. "Oh, don't worry about Mona. Her lips are sealed with enough hundred-dollar bills to shut up Hedda Hopper, near about many as I've given you. Ha! And she knows what I've got you here for. By the way, when you get home why don't you burn those damn camo briefs you got on and get something with a little clayass, like a blaze orange thong." Misty's laughter at her suggestion is not unpleasant but shows the influence, as does her voice, of many years of expensive Bourbon and cigarettes. Her accent flows like warm molasses onto a hot buttered biscuit.

Man-In-Bed groans under his breath, trying to maintain some shred of dignity, pushes himself into a seated position, and sighs. As he stretches, the tattoo on his back of a whitetail buck with grotesquely oversized antlers twists out of shape and becomes totally unrealistic, looking as if it has just been gut shot and is in the final stages of a horrible death. He steps stiffly into a pair of designer jeans, stonewashed, with a number of holes and tears to make them look as if they have been used for something useful at one time or another, and slips on his Sperry Topsiders. Holding on to the railing to steady his hangover balance, he descends the right side of the double staircase that curves around an enormous crystal chandelier, as big as a mid-size SUV. He disappears toward the kitchen in back.

Misty slithers out of the sheets, tosses her hair, and poses, imagining she is being looked at and glad of it. She pours herself into a white silk dressing gown adorned with a discreet number of blaze pink flamingos, leaves the front unclosed, lights a Salem, and crosses to the full-length mirror behind her enormous collection of beauty products. Straightening her chemically enhanced henna hair, she smiles at her image. Not too bad, she thinks. Not too bad. She lifts her breasts and as she drops them there is a bit of a frown. Another trip to C. Wiley Hill, MD, 'Cosmetic Surgery as Magic,' Suite A-3, 22 Second Avenue East, Cary, NC may be in order. She has made quite an investment in that business over the years. Still…not too bad.

She hears Man(formerly)-In-Bed discreetly hiding the Camaro on the beige pea gravel in back of the garages just moments before a candy apple red BMW roadster navigates the front-drive and stops.

"Mona." Misty shouts down the stairs to her live-in maid. "Tell him, what's-his-name, to come up the back way with my coffee and cookies." The doorbell rings. "And answer the door. That'll be Wayne Gillam who's standing there in his stupid golf outfit, hoping to see me in my nighty. Tell him to have a seat. I'll be down in five or twenty minutes. Give him a cup of coffee if he wants one. You can tell him Hubert's not here, but he'll come in anyway."

"Yes, Ma'am," Mona, short, café au lait, and smiling to be in on the joke, answers from the bottom of the staircase. "Want me to bring out some cookies?"

"Gawd, no. Then he'll stay forever and eat um all. Oh, by the way, Mona, you remember I'm flying tomorrow to the condo at Seaside for a little boogie and booze with a couple of new girlfriends. Don't know when Hubert's getting home—don't care really. Supposed to be today, I think. Tell him I'll be back when I get back."

Misty takes her time putting on border-line-tasteful morning makeup, decides to keep the flamingos on with nothing under, loose-ly ties her sash, arranges her neckline like she is going to an Academy Awards ceremony, steps into her slippers, and checks the mirror one last time. Not too bad. No. For fifty going on forty-nine, pretty damn good.

Man (who used to be)-In-Bed arrives with her coffee and big fat cookies and makes to sit down. She waves him off. "You go on now. Go sit in your car until you see that red Beemer turn onto the high-way. Then you can go on home. Don't call me, I'll call you—if I need you. You know you were a little limp last night. Better take two or five of those pills next time."

Man (who probably won't be allowed back)-In-Bed shrugs on a Buffalo Wild Wings sweatshirt, tries again for dignity by saying something smart but can't think of anything, and sulks out the door.

Wayne Gillam starts to stand up when Misty reaches the bottom step, but she motions him down.

"What are you doing up this early, Wayne?" she chuckles. He manages a lopsided grin, eyes focused with laser intensity on her cleavage. "Why, didn't Mona bring you any cream and sugar for your coffee—you want cream or sugar?" Wayne Gillam never takes cream or sugar but hopes that Misty might lean over to serve him. He grins. "I sure would love some cream." She knows exactly what he has in mind.

Wayne tips so far forward he almost loses his balance as Mona comes in with the cream and Misty, taking it from her, leaning forward much more than necessary, pours it. He's having a hard time concentrating on any conversation and she and Mona are enjoying his discomfort immensely. "Uh...Hubert not back yet? I, uh...I um...thought we were entered for the scratch tournament at the Long Breast...uh...I mean Long Pines Golf Club in the morning. Been um...trying to call his cell but can't get any answer." He licks his lips. "Just thought I'd stop by and see...uh...what's up." He finally tears his eyes away from the widening gap in Misty's dressing gown and looks around the room. She demurely adjusts it and tightens her sash. Wayne's attention goes to a bare area of the wall under the stairs. "Where's his picture. You're not gonna put it someplace else?"

Misty looks where she has avoided looking for weeks. She yells, with some surprise, "Mona. MONA. Where's Hubert's portrait?"

Mona sticks her head out the kitchen door. "I ain't seen it, Ma'am. It was there when I left yesterday but was gone when I come in this morning. Thought you'd took that thing down."

Two years earlier, Hubert Wooten had commissioned a large four-by-six-foot portrait of himself by the Italian artist, Francesco Giardi, posing with his favorite English setter, Beau (Beauregard of Wooten Plantation). He is standing stiffly in front of what seems to be the weathered wall of an old barn, with an English, bespoke, double-barreled shotgun cradled in his right arm. He made it very clear to the artist that the make of the gun, Purdey, was to be immediately obvious to the viewer. He wears a tweed shooting jacket, leather patch on the right shoulder, jodhpurs, and knee-high wellington boots. He spent $2,300 on lighting to show the portrait to its best effect. Two weeks after the portrait was finished, Hubert backed his Hummer over Beau in full view of his hunting buddies. Beau did not survive.

Misty hates the portrait. For her, it is the emblem of everything despicable about her husband—his arrogance, his smug self-satisfaction, his total lack of concern for anyone but himself. She thinks he looks even dumber in oil than he does in person; he's never dressed like that on any hunting trip he's ever gone on (he'd have been laughed off any quail field in North Carolina if he had) and he can't hit shit with his $125,000 shotgun. Still, even though she has wanted the picture gone ever since he hung it there and would be perfectly happy to see it hanging with the used reproductions at the Good Will, she is alarmed that it has just disappeared. The thought that Hubert will be beside himself when he finds out his portrait is missing, however, is deeply calming.

Fifteen minutes later and 1,000 miles away, a pearl-white Lexus roadster skids to a stop in front of the Chip Shot Room at the Ames Country Club. James J. Schittman, Jr. tosses the keys to the attendant, adjusts the crotch of his light tan golf pants, and smooths his yellow cashmere vee-neck. A man in a hurry, he takes the steps two at a time into the front door of the Members bar as if he were entering his own house. Schittman has close-cropped dirty blonde hair—courtesy of Cool Men-Grey Away—steel blue eyes, and a chiseled jaw. At 74 years old he is vain enough about his looks to spend an hour in his basement weight room at least five days a week. He would be perfectly cast as a Nazi SS officer in a WW II movie. In the bar, an obviously nervous man in a wrinkled powder blue suit walks toward him and holds out his hand.

"Mr. Schittman?"

"JJ."

"Uh, oh. JJ."

"Wooten?" Schittman shakes a cold damp hand.

"No… Uh, no. Albert Moose…uh, Al. I'm Hubert's…uh, Mr. Wooten's attorney."

"Wooten in the john? He is here, isn't he?"

"Well, no…to tell the truth, Mr. Schitt… uh, JJ, he, he, I…" Moose looks around hoping Hubert Wooten might miraculously appear. "To be honest, I don't know where he is."

"You what?" Schittman barks, unused to this kind of situation. "You don't know where he is?"

"I, uh, I don't. We got in from Raleigh yesterday. He wanted to know how in the world he could kill a whole day in Des Moines, Iowa. Then he said he'd like to see some of the hog lots he owns. CAFOs, he likes to call them, whatever in hell that stands for."

"Concentrated animal feeding operations," Schittman helps him out.

"Right," Moose goes on. "He said he'd never seen one in Iowa. Don't think he ever went to the ones he owned in Carolina either. Wanted to see what they looked like—what all the fuss was about with the PETA freaks. He rented an Escalade at the airport, uh, black I think, and I gave him a list of lots and addresses. He didn't get back to the hotel last night. I thought maybe he'd got up with you or, umm, hooked up with some, you know, one of those women or something. Don't know if you can find that kind of woman in Des Moines or not. He don't tell me anything when we travel."

Schittman with growing irritation, "He knew about today, didn't he—the time and all? I got a shit load of other stuff to do this afternoon." He exhales a gruff sigh. "Oh, what the fuck. Sit down. Al, did you say? Let me go over some business with you—don't want to waste the trip. Tell him he god damn better be here next time."

They order. Iowa chop, waffle fries, onion rings, cheesecake for Moose, house salad for Schittman. Moose has a Bud Light; JJ, Perrier. Between bites of arugula Schittman continues:

"You can tell Wooten everything's cool. He can move all his Carolina confinements here and build all the new ones he wants. I know they've gotten touchy down south since all those spills from his CAFOs in NC"

"Yeah. Those fat cats down at Morehead City and Wrightsville Beach started seeing rings on their yachts' water line and found out it was pig shit, and they were smelling it from their beach houses. They got in touch with their favorite legislators," Moose says. "They came up with some inconvenient rules in Raleigh, so I suggested to Hubert that moving the lots to Iowa would be a good idea."

"Well, it's all smooth sailing in here. Just like I said to your boss on the phone the other day, 'We don't have less regulation, we don't have no regulation.' Those protests? Well, let's see, Cerro Gordo County Board of Supervisors, that 'Fight for the Creeks and the Prairie' group in River City, and that bunch of Nachawinga County whiners, they'll get denied. The EPC? Oh yeah, that so-called Environmental Protection Committee, more like the CAFO protection committee if you ask me, is not going to be a problem. The only person on the committee who might even read any of the protests is that little gal schoolteacher the Guv thought they ought to put on it for show. And that idiot that's been raising all the stink at our meetings, the hot-headed prof they fired at State, nobody's paying any attention to him anymore." He goes on. "Oh, by the way, who do you think the Guv appointed to the last open seat, huh? My boy. My own son. They voted him in as vice-chair. Keep it in the family I say. He might as well do his old man some good for a change. Good-for-nothing scoundrel's done nothing so far except spend my money. So, that takes care of the DNR."

Moose is impressed. "And the Ag Bureau?"

"Are you kidding me? No problem. Never has been, never will be." He pats his back pocket.

"Supervisors? Zoning boards?"

"Same. They spend all their time with their county attorneys poring over the regulations in that joke they call the Master Matrix, but there's nothing there. Hell, I helped write the damn thing. We can confine almost as many porkies as we want."

In 2002 the State Legislature, in their infinite wisdom, adopted a piece of legislation that put a 'Master Matrix' into the Iowa Code. It was touted as a way to regulate the astonishing proliferation of CAFOs in the state. It is a pretty good guess that less than half of the lawmakers at the time knew what matrix meant, but it seemed like an impressive word and some of them had seen the movie. The main intent of the legislation was to put an end to an outcry from citizens who were not profiting from these hog and chicken factories and were alarmed at the harm these operations were doing to the environment, the value of neighbor's homes and property, the quality of people's lives, and the economic prospects of rural Iowa. A committee was put together with a majority of members who were closely associated with the industry—so-called 'stakeholders.' They were to create a collection of regulations that would appear to mitigate the harm these animal factories were causing without upsetting the meat industry cash cow. The regulations are almost meaningless. A CAFO that confines less than 500 animal units (12,050 piglets) is completely unregulated. JJ Schittman chaired the committee.

Schittman continues, "so you tell that fucking client of yours I'm not too happy about him blowing me off—he better show up early next time or our deal is off, and I'll stop managing his business up here and taking care of all the so-called public servants. He won't be able to raise a pet pig in Iowa." Schittman picks a bit of arugula from his front teeth. "Oh, by the way, that merger with Freebird Poultry out of Colorado, you know, the chicken people, is in high gear. It's gonna be chickens and hogs, eggs and bacon—that sounds pretty good, doesn't it? We'll have it sewed up top to bottom—hog lots, chicken shacks, and my big packing plant where the wet-backs can kill um, cut um up, wrap um up, and ship um out to feed the hungry American public. But you tell…"

He's interrupted by the opening strains of Beethoven's Fifth Symphony coming from his cell. Looking at the screen, he answers, "Oh, hi hon."

Pause. "No, no, I didn't look this morning."

Pause. "What? What do you mean, gone?"

Pause. "No, I told you I didn't look this morning. But it was there yesterday."

Pause. "Well, it damn well better show up and it better not have a single scratch on it. You have no idea how much I paid to have that portrait painted. You're sure it's gone?"

Pause. "OK, OK, I know you told me. I'm coming right now."

He blurts another expletive and bolts for the door.

Schittman ignores the spots of uncleared mid-autumn snow as he spins the Lexus up the ramp and onto I-35 heading north, forcing the mini-van school bus in the left lane to do a hard swerve to miss him. He keeps the accelerator on the floor until the car reaches 90 and is pulling off the exit ramp five miles from Ames in three minutes. Another three miles on the county road at 80 and he is steering through a huge cathedral gate and skidding to a stop at the door of 1000 JJ Farms Drive.

The house is stone, two-story; two ostentatious Greek-style columns support the extended roof over the entrance porch. There are extensions on either side fronted by porticos that afford views of the large fountain, covered for the winter, in the center of the circular entrance driveway. The heated swimming pool in the back, half indoors and half out, is, on this 25-degree day, overhung with a cloud of fog.

A tree-lined concrete extension off the drive curves several hundred yards up a gentle rise to the stables, each topped by two large running horse weathervanes. White rail fences stretch in both directions almost as far as you can see.

"Connie. Connie! Goddammit, Connie. Where the hell are you?" Schittman is yelling before he gets the car door slammed. He bounds up the porch stairs and swings the front door open, "Connieeeeee!"

A woman walks slowly out of the library and looks directly at her husband with a decidedly unwelcoming expression on her face. "Shut up, Jimmy. I'm not in the barn."

Connie Schittman gives the impression of being even taller than her five feet eleven inches. It could be her high cowboy boots or the rest of her tack: tight designer jeans, white western shirt, and barn jacket. She looks as if she has just gotten off a horse or is getting ready to mount one. Her black hair is softly cut, long enough to spill along the ridge of her shoulders, her eyes deep and almost as black as her hair, and she has eyebrows that Frieda Kahlo would have been proud to paint—or wear.

"You're putting me on about that picture?" His inflection makes it a question. "I know you don't like it, but this is some kind of sick joke, isn't it?"

"I hate that stupid thing almost as much as I hate …" She decides not to finish this thought. "But I'm not going to move it or do anything else with it. That's part of our deal, isn't it? You stay out of my barn and don't screw with my horses, or me, for that matter, and I don't mess with your stuff, no matter how dumb it is."

"Then where the hell is it?"

"No clue. Even though I try not to look at it, I did see it last night. This morning in its place was a lovely blank space. All I could think of was how beautiful my bull riding pictures would look there."

"You know how much I paid for that thing? Not to mention what it cost to get that English artist over here. Everybody in the state thinks it's a major work of art. Check with the cleaning woman and all the other illegals that work for you in the barn. That portrait's gotta be around somewhere. I'll be at the DNR making sure those Grundy County lots get approved, then I got an EPA meeting."

"You check with them yourself. I'm packing for Florida, remember? Misty Wooten, I think that's her name, invited me and that chicken woman from Denver to a little waterfront get-away when she found out our husbands were cooking up some sort of merger. I think we gals might have something in common. It seems we got about as much interest in your businesses as George Dubya has in classical music. A little beach and booze might do us all good. Leaving in the morning. You'll see me when you see me. "

JJ, Jr. starts to reply, thinks better of it, and is out the door. He doesn't see the manicured middle finger extended toward his exit.

The Lexus splashes melting snow going out the gate and fish-tails onto the blacktop. Connie watches it disappear and hisses, "You shit," after him, and wonders how in the hell she got stuck with such an asshole. Then she looks at the barns that most of the people working for her would be overjoyed to live in and thinks of her dozen or so prize-winning quarter horses there in their heated stalls, and she knows. But still, she thinks, is it worth it…there's got to be something more I can do with my life.

The Guv's mansion sits on a rise overlooking the Beaver River in an otherwise marginally seedy commercial neighborhood. It is really just a large Victorian house, a "mansion" only by mid-western standards, that could be mistaken for almost any governor's house between the Mississippi and the Rockies.

It's nine on Friday morning and the place is in a state of panic. One of the assistant chiefs-of-staff is yelling. "Just find the damn thing. He's as proud of that thing as he is of anything in this house. Who took it down in the first place? Call housekeeping. Call security. Call HR. Just find out where it is."

Housekeepers, janitors, carpenters, plumbers, secretaries, receptionists are running around like little ants on a kicked anthill. Someone yells back, "It ain't in this house. We been all over. They ain't no place else to look."

A man with a broom in a loud whisper, "Oh shit! He's coming out." Everyone looks up—then freezes.

The governor, a short, soft man with a small mustache and combed-back black hair wearing a midnight blue velour bathrobe steps out of his second-floor apartment and looks down at the chaos in the main room below. "Has the whole place gone bughouse? What the hell's going on?"

Assistant Chief-of-Staff: "It's...it's gone, Sir...gone."

"Who—what's gone?"

"The picture, Sir."

"What picture?"

"The governor's picture. I mean your portrait, Sir."

"What the ... ? What about the rest of um?"

"Just yours, sir. The rest of um are still here."

"Mine, just mine? The one of me?"

"Yes, sir. The one of you."

"My god. Well, go find the damn thing. Can't be that far away. Some pretty little gal probably took it to put on her bedroom wall. Ha, ha," (smirk) "that was a pretty good one, wasn't it? Do you know how much of my own money I spent to make me look a little bigger than all those other governors up there? If you let anything happen to that picture, I'm gonna feed you all to the Democrats, understand?"

"We're trying sir."

"Don't try. Find it. And get Tim in here."

"He's in the south room, Sir."

The governor, still in his bathrobe, walks into an intimate conference room overlooking the river and slams the door behind him. Tim Taylor, Chief-of-Staff and general factotum, immaculate in his dark blue suit, black shoes, and silk tie embroidered with the state seal of Iowa, rises from his seat at the table and stands at casual attention. As the Governor speaks, Tim notices his fuzzy slippers—maroon and gold, with 'Go 'Clones' printed on the right foot, gold and black, with 'How 'bout them Hawks?' on the left.

"Sit down," the Governor yaps. "You know anything about this portrait business? They probably took it down to clean it, huh? Show it to some school kids or something. You need to find somebody to locate the damn thing. Right now, I'm more worried about my annual pheasant hunt."

"Working on that," Taylor says.

"This is a big deal, ya know, TV, newspapers, but ever since I got the ex-vice-president to commit to taking part, people have been dropping out like ladybugs off a sprayed bean field. (Smirk). That was pretty good, wasn't it? I just got a message from what's his name, you know, the governor over in Madison. Can't make it. He's got to go to his kid's eighth-grade musical, for Christ's sake."

"JJ and that hog lot man from North Carolina, Wooten, are coming," Taylor says, "and the chicken guy from Denver."

"They damn well better come—we're giving them enough tax-payer money for their damn animal factories—don't tell anybody I called um that."

"No, sir."

What about the Senator?"

"The Senator says he can't leave Washington for the next two weeks," Taylor answers.

"Well, you can get some people from the State House—Senators will be better than Representatives. Just make sure we have eleven or twelve guys. Why don't you invite a couple of Democrats? Let the Veep put some birdshot in their asses." He chortles. "That was pretty funny, huh?"

The Governor rises to leave, "And make sure they let enough pheasants loose. Last year it was a half-hour before we found a single one."

"Yes sir. I'll try, sir."

"Don't try, just do it."

"Yes sir."

Taylor walks out the door as the Governor yells, "And get that fucking picture back where it belongs." Tim Taylor, amused at the Gov's irritation, rolls his eyes, exhales, and trots down the majestic staircase.

"JJ was totally frustrated the first night. He said, 'I took those little blue pills, three of um, and nothing's happening. I'm gonna sue Pfizer for all they're worth.' He had no idea I had flushed the Viagra down the toilet and filled the bottle with Aleve." Laughter.

"Hubert's trouble was something did happen—about ten seconds after I stepped out of my nightie. He went off like his million-dollar shotgun. Didn't even make it into the bed." Giggles. More laughter.

"Donald didn't even try anything, just licked his lips and grinned. I guess I'm the only lucky one in the bunch. I'm just around for looks." Gales of laughter.

It's Saturday.

Three women are sitting in a steaming hot tub on a condominium balcony looking through a line of palm trees over the silver water of a moonlit Gulf of Mexico. Late middle-aged but a long way from over the hill, all three are still attractive with a little apparent help, but no desperation. Each is holding a drink—Bourbon for Misty Wooten, martini for Connie Schittman. Lizzie Birdseed, wife of Donald Birdseed the owner and CEO of Freebird Poultry, "Eggs from your Grandma's Henhouse," holds a pina colada. From the tears running down their cheeks, it is clear they have been laughing for a long time.

It's been a great day. Arriving from Raleigh, Des Moines, and Denver, they met at the Panama City airport, and Misty drove them to her Seagrove Beach condo. A couple of hours dozing in the sun, a shower in one of the Condo's five, dinner at the Hurricane Hibachi, *The Best Sushi in West Florida*, and drinks at a lovely bar, listening to a pretty good acoustic country singer who was gorgeous and flirted with them during his whole set, like Keith Carradine and Lily Tomlin in *Nashville*.

Now they are creating a small wave storm in the hot tub celebrating the good things they have in common, bemoaning the bad, laughing loudly at both, thoroughly enjoying each other's company and their newfound connection.

"I guess I got nobody to blame but myself, getting into this mess." This is Lizzy Birdseed, the shortest of the three but perfectly proportioned, very blonde bobbed hair, an infectious laugh, and a truly mischievous smile. "When I was waiting tables at Perkins in Grand Junction, some loser pinching my ass every time I turned around, I thought if I just had everything I got now—house in Aspen, apartment in Denver, clothes, jewelry, Porsche—I'd have it made."

"I know where you're coming from," Connie says. "Dunkin Donuts. Been there, done that. Don't care if I never see pink again."

"Don't get me wrong. I ain't gonna give it away." Lizzy goes on. "Hell, I was living in a rented room and driving a rusted-out Ford Pinto in G.J. Don't want to go back to that scene." They all nod. "It's what I did to get all this stuff and what I've got to put up with to keep it, that I don't like. I'm still not free to do what I want, would like to do. I'm wasting my life away in a pile of stuff and I'm not very proud of myself. I sure would like to figure some way to do something different. You know?"

"I know," Misty says.

"Looking back on it now, I think I was just stupid," Connie is slow in her response. "All I wanted was a horse and some place to keep it. I had dreams of maybe being a vet. But when Dad died, and I couldn't pay my tuition at State, this guy, he was on the Board of Trustees back then, believe it or not, almost 25 years older than me, looking for a trophy wife, pays it for me."

"Trophy wife, exactly," Lizzy says, "That's me too."

"Well, anyway, I finish school, he builds me a bunch of barns, buys more horses than I will ever ride," Connie says. "He was pretty rough at first when I wouldn't do everything he wanted when I was still naïve. But I got smart. I told him if he didn't lay off, I had guys working in my barn that could, and would love to, show him what being rough really is."

"Right on," from Misty.

"Our arrangement. He keeps away from me, I don't pay any attention to him. But I do want to be rid of him. I suppose I could just walk off and give up all this stuff it's got me. Maybe a horse and some place to keep it is all I really need."

"Wow." Misty takes a deep breath. "I guess my story's pretty much a variation on the same theme. Not sure I ever saw dear ol Daddy, he was gone for good by the time I could know what I was seeing. And Mom? Who was she? That all depended on where she was and who she was with and what she was smoking or sniffing at the time. Never knew from one day to the next who was going to show up. Early years were shit, one deadbeat's house after another, sleeping on couches, listening to the boyfriend beating up on mom, or mom beating up on the boyfriend, depending on who was the most stoned." Misty smiles. "Then I got to high school, and things started to change, for one big reason—I suddenly realized I was good-looking, no, I mean I was flat-assed, drop-dead GORGEOUS. Wasn't a boy in that school who wouldn't give me anything I wanted, or any man in town for that matter. So, I took my time, looked around for a way to cash in. My looks were the one thing I had to make sure I wasn't going to turn into my mom—and there he was. Hubert Wooten. The richest man in Wilson County. Hell, one of the top three or four in eastern N.C. Love? Shit. Not me." She smiles. "But him, he was so much in 'love' he couldn't see past his hard-on. And that's the way the whole thing's gone. He tried to knock me around once or twice. But I grabbed one of his priceless shotguns and told him I would blow his damn head off if he even thought of doing that again."

"You go, girl," Connie says.

"I just gotta figure out how I can get shed of that worm. I'm like both of you. I'd like to shake myself loose and see what else might be out there that I could do with the rest of my life."

They are serious for a moment. "Tell ya what girls." Misty changes the mood. "Let's fantasize. Best case scenario."

Another pause, less serious. Deep thoughts.

"Just hang out here for the next couple of years?"

"Get in a big convertible and drive it off a cliff. You know, like Susan Sarandon and, what's her name, Geena Davis did in *Thelma and Louise*? Naa, I guess that's going a little too far."

"Drain the bank accounts and move to Buenos Aires and tango ourselves into old age?"

"Margaritaville."

Sly grins. Then all three shout "Murrrderrr!" The laughter explodes louder than before.

Misty's forehead wrinkles. "Ya know, there's this hunk that I keep on call and let in my bed from time to time when I need him. Mmmmm," she chuckles, hand on her chin, "He'd knock all three of them off for one more night between the sheets."

"Mariano, my 'stable boy,'" Connie says, "Same payoff."

"I could get my 'ski instructor,'" finger quote marks from Lizzy, "to join them in a New York Minute. Well, maybe for a New York night. Wouldn't that be a happy hoot? Hey, let's call um up."

"Serial homicide," they all giggle, their laughter folding neatly into the purr of the surf.

Fists are pumped into the blue-black night and there is a unison shout of "Yeeeess." Guffaws, louder now, drowning the surf's murmur.

Connie sighs, "Yep, I got the life I thought wanted. Truth be told, it sucks." Dreaming. "But wouldn't it be awesome if it did happen."

Julio Sanchez, the night housekeeper, is cleaning the unit on the next floor. He almost pitches over the balcony railing trying to get a peek at the party in the hot tub. When he finally leans over far enough to see the bubbling water and what is floating there, he is flooded with vivid memories of bobbing for apples along with his eight siblings on the family porch in the countryside outside of Ciudad Juarez. Catching his balance, he tries to make sense of what the women are saying, thinking to himself, I gotta get down to the basement and tell my buddy Rasheed about what I just seen.

In her small apartment in south Des Moines, Amie Greene pops a chocolate chip muffin into her microwave, turns on her coffee maker, strips a banana from an overripe bunch on her kitchen counter, and thinks to herself, I need to stop eating like this. It's Monday morning, a little past six. Ignoring the ping from the microwave telling her that her 'breakfast' is ready, she folds her hide-a-bed into a sofa, turning her bedroom into a parlor, hangs her pj's in the closet, and spreads her lesson plans on her table. She is now well into her morning routine. She is always hurried and not a little frazzled before heading to her seven forty-five eighth-grade class in environmental science at Cohn Middle School. This morning, however, she is more than usually concerned. It's nothing at the school that's on her mind—she loves her students and colleagues and almost everything about her teaching. It's the four o'clock meeting of the Environmental Protection Committee that has been troubling her ever since the agenda was announced three days earlier.

The previous year, her second year of teaching had been anything but tranquil for Amie Greene. Cohn Middle School is located in an area of southeast Des Moines that Realtors don't post pictures of in the *Sunday Register*'s preferred real estate listings. It is not a middle school that parents all over the metropolitan area scheme to get their over-achieving darlings into. And yet, in the past year, the

27

school has received some very positive publicity and gained a bit of status, largely because of Amie Greene. First, there was the seventh and eighth-grade monarch garden that her classes had planted and maintained. They worked after school in a 200 by 50-yard strip of beer-can and broken-glass-strewn wasteland between the school's chain-link border fence and the railroad right-of-way. The project was a neighborhood joke in its first year. Amie and her students picked up the trash, recycled the beer cans, and pulled the plastic bags and old newspapers off the fence. Then they tilled the dirt and planted native flower seeds and tiny grass plants. For a year it was clean but unimpressive. According to the administration, it looked like a bunch of weeds. But by its second summer, when the little bluestem and Indian grass appeared, the coneflowers and black-eyed Susans began to bloom, and the butterflies came, it turned into something the school, kids, parents, and nearby residents began to brag about. Then there was the class project that she and her eighth-graders produced: *Imagine Des Moines as a Carbon-Negative City*, a dazzling array of posters, building designs, models, public transportation plans, solar and wind-power generating ideas, park and green space maps, and so on, that not only won city-wide notice but also impressive state awards and a National Green Ribbon Prize for Cohn Middle School. Shortly after this recognition, in mid-summer, Amie was appointed by the Guv to sit on the so-called Environmental Protection Committee (EPC) of the Department of Natural Resources (DNR).

Amie has no illusions about why she was appointed. The EPC is the last court of appeal for persons or groups with concerns about environmental degradation. Most of these appeals have to do with industrial agricultural operations' failures to abide by the few regulations against pollution the state has in place. The committee is stacked. Its membership consists of JJ Schittman, Jr, Chair, and his son Junior, Junior(JJ Schittman, III), Vice-Chair; an officer of the Central States Pork Producers Association and one from the Midwest Farmer's Coop; the CEO of a large fertilizer plant recently built with obscene state tax incentives; the state director of economic development; a DNR representative, ex officio; and Amie. Amie Greene, the token voting stakeholder who represents everyone who doesn't profit in one way or another from environmental wreckage. Amie Greene was not appointed to cause problems. Amie Greene, it was expected, would keep silent among these powerful men. And in the two meetings she has attended she has done just that. At the first, a let's let each other know how important we are, find out what this committee is all about, and establish our pecking order meeting, she spoke only to introduce herself. Then she listened to the older Schittman drone on about how Iowa agriculture has benefited the state and feeds the world and how stricter environmental rules would only slow the state's wonderful economic growth, and then watch him doze off when others had the floor. Amie knew quite well that a huge percentage of Iowa's farm produce goes to feeding animals and automobiles, not the world.

The second meeting was called to discuss penalties for a large hog lot manure spill into a small trout stream in the northeast corner of the state. The lot's manager decided it would be cheaper and easier to pump the shit from a leaky lagoon directly into the creek than to repair the leak. The violation was so egregious nobody could argue that a penalty should not be imposed. The cost of the clean-up was $80K. The fine was $1500, which did not even cover replacing the dead trout, Amie did quietly suggest that the fine was a bit low. JJ Farms owns the hog lot. Today's meeting, however, is going to be very different. Amie knows it and dreads it.

It seems that an outfit called Compassionate Family Farms, LLC, out of North Carolina has, in the previous year, built three medium-sized CAFOs packed with thousands of squealing little pink baby pigs about the size of rugby balls, feeding them on ground corn feed supplied by JJ Farms, until they reach a state that in a human

29

being would be called morbid obesity. Their accumulated manure is sprayed onto surrounding fields. At a predetermined weight, the corpulent piggies are shipped to Patriot Pork, a subsidiary of JJ Farms Inc., to be killed, cut up, shrink-wrapped, and sent to fast-food franchises across the Midwest. The buildings stretch from the northern to the southern border of Franklin Township in Nachawinga County. The noise and flies from these operations, and the stench from the animals, lagoons, and sprayed manure have made life from miserable to impossible for half the families in the Township. Children have developed asthma-like symptoms, and older residents are finding it difficult to breathe at all. Porch sitting and outdoor barbeques have ground to a halt. One of the buildings is fifty yards upwind of the Franklin Methodist Church, violating the separation limit mandated by state regulations, another too close to the local daycare center, but the CAFO owner has been granted a waiver by the DNR that allows the construction to go forward. Now, Compassionate Family Farms has applied for permits to build four additional buildings, forming a kind of Maginot line across the township, impossible to cross without encountering pigs, their poop, and their stink.

A citizens committee of township residents—*Franklinites Against Ruining our Township (FART)*—and the Nachawinga County Board of Supervisors have petitioned the EPC to deny construction permits for these additional buildings. Amie knows the meeting will be nasty. She knows she will take the side of Franklin Township. She knows that she will be alone in doing so.

That afternoon an ancient Jeep clatters slowly west on slush-covered Ivy Street in West Des Moines and makes a left turn into a nondescript strip mall. The parking lot is unexpectedly full as the driver starts toward a handicap space, thinks better of it, then pulls into a space marked "for deliveries only." The color of the vehicle is indeterminate, it has developed a patina from driving on dirt roads and an impressive collection of dings and scratches from timber two-tracks so it is hard to determine what its hue might have been, but it has evolved into a shade best described as algae green tempered with spots of rust, this mostly covered with a thin layer of chocolate mud. The driver turns off the ignition but the engine, apparently having enjoyed being alive for a while, continues to run, then it shivers, coughs, sighs, and dies, farting a small smoke ring out its exhaust. The jeep's tailgate and rear bumper are covered with stickers: *Stop Factory Farms, CAFOs Are Prisons, Know Your Farmer, Local Foods are the Best, Cows on Pasture Where They Belong,* along with those of conservation organizations: Pheasants Forever, Trout Unlimited, The Iowa Natural Heritage Foundation, and so on. Below all this, carefully hand-painted letters spell out *Together We Can Fix This Mess.* The fogged-up windows are difficult to see through, but the driver appears to be relaxing for a moment before exiting to whatever his destination might be.

At the east end of the mall, there is a Domino's Pizza, a real estate office, a State Farm agency, and two unoccupied units with For Rent signs in the windows. To the west, a check-cashing and payday loan emporium, Mei Thong's Asian Buffet, Gould's Clock and Watch Repair, *We buy gold, silver, jewelry,* and another rental space. These businesses are anchored in the middle by a long, low building, evidently constructed for small civic club gatherings, flea markets, and government agency meetings. Over the double-door entrance, a sign reads, The Iowa Department of Natural Resources West Annex. There is a receptionist's table inside the two doors that lead to a large room containing 40 or so beige folding chairs. A raised platform at one end supports a long ornate table (very much out of line with the rest of the room's décor), and eight leather-covered 'executive chairs.' There are fancy wooden name placards in front of each chair. The one at the far right reads, "JJ Schittman, Jr., Chairman."

The room is packed, all the chairs taken, a number of people are standing. A couple of latecomers are signing in at the reception desk.

31

Small clusters and pairs of folks are talking among themselves in low but intense voices, creating a rumble that sounds like a train rolling by in the distance. The crowd is diverse: seniors with walkers, college professors, high-school students, nurses in uniform, waitresses in little white caps with their aprons still on. Many of the attendees are farmers with their families, dressed in muddy boots, coveralls, camo hoodies, and jeans of all descriptions. The room is alive with a tension so thick it is hard to take a deep breath. Lining the back wall, a half-dozen men and women, dressed in what is best described as 'business casual,' from the legal division of Compassionate Family Farms here to argue their expansion case, are whispering to each other with expressions of arrogance and boredom. It is 4:35 PM; the meeting was to begin at 4:00.

The rumble immediately turns to silence as the door at the end of the platform opens and six dark-suited, frowning, late-middle-aged men and a young, clearly uncomfortable woman walk toward seven of the eight chairs. Three of the oldest of the dark-suits are leading/shoving a fourth, apparently the youngest, towards the Chairman's seat. After he reluctantly sits, there is a long pause, as all the other male committee members turn toward him and the lone woman looks in evident embarrassment toward the ceiling. Another awkward pause as the man next to the Chairman's seat whispers to its occupant, who seems not to understand but who finally nods his head, produces a small gavel, and raps it on the table. "OK, OK, Ummm...." He looks to his left and the men nod and smile, "Uh...the meeting of the Environmental...." he swallows, turns toward the others, one of whom growls, "Protection. Protection." "Uh...oh yeah. Protection, Protection Committee will now come to order."

Smiles and exaggerated nods all around the platform (except for the young woman who is trying to disappear into her chair.) Another pause, long enough for the audience to begin to rumble again. "I sure wouldn't mind being on a board with her," from one of the business casuals, sotto voce, but loud enough, along with the ensuing chuckles, to be heard in the back several rows.

After some hushed discussion on the dais the man in the Chairman's seat stands up shakily, "Uh…we will begin with introductions." This sounds more like a question than a statement. "Since Dad has been, I mean the …uh…Chairman of this Committee, Mr. JJ Schittman, Jr., has been called away somewhere on, uh…unavoidable, uh…something he has to do, so, I, the Vice-Chair JJ Schittman, III, will serve as, uh…run the…"

The sound of scuffling at the room's entrance interrupts the young Schittman, and the receptionist yelling "No…no, stay back. You can't come in here" silences the room. Again, every head turns as every eye focuses intently on the front entrance. The receptionist, flustered beyond words, scurries in, arms fluttering with palms up, stops for a brief moment in front of the platform, then, unable to utter any sound beyond a soft moan, continues her scurry and flattens herself against a sidewall. She points a shaky finger at the door as a pig, a huge six-foot four-inch pig, walks, erect on its hind feet, slowly through the door and stops at the front of the platform, standing far enough to the side for the audience to still see the committee members. It stands straight, looks slowly around the now completely silent room.

It clears its throat, and speaks, "Ladies and Gentlemen, good persons all. I would like to take the honor myself of introducing the esteemed members of this committee to you supplicants gathered here, thus saving our temporary chairman the possible embarrassment of forgetting their names."

There is a general uproar on the platform. Shouts from the dark-suits of "Out sir, or madam, I mean pig." "Leave this meeting at once." "We will not stand for this." "Get security in here right away."

Over the din, the receptionist can be heard yelling at the top of her voice, "The doors are jammed shut, sir."

JJ III is banging his gavel on the table to no effect as the other dark-suits shout, "This is an important government meeting, we will not tolerate such an outrage," and so forth.

As the noise reaches a crescendo, a small man in denim overalls, khaki work shirt, and a wicked smile stands and, over the uproar, slowly, in a deeply resonant bass voice heard by all, says, "Let the pig speak." The dark-suits slouch into their overstuffed chairs and the pig seems to smile.

"Thank you, Gus," the pig continues. "Ladies and Gentlemen, I thought it might be interesting if you could hear a brief biography of the distinguished members of this committee who will be deciding the fate of your beautiful township." Some of the audience nod but most are simply staring at the speaker with gaping mouths. The business casuals are anxiously whispering to each other, and the dark suits seem momentarily defeated. "I will begin with the acting chairman, let's call him JJ Jr. Jr. Junior, Junior is the son JJ Schittman, Jr, who is the son of JJ Schittman, Senior. Is that much clear?" Most nod. The dark suits have collapsed into their seats. The pig continues, "Years ago, JJ, Senior was a successful, fairly well-liked small farmer in Brown County. During the early eighties, just before the worst part of the farm crisis, when farmers all over the state were struggling with bankruptcy, he saw an opportunity. He realized he could make more money buying and selling these bankrupt farms than farming his own. He started by dividing and selling his farm near the suburbs for various non-agricultural uses and, with the profits, quadrupled the size of his holdings by buying out the bankrupt farmers at fire-sale prices. He then re-sold their land for so-called development: c-stores, storage buildings, fast food restaurants, and lots for house trailers."

Junior, Junior starts to rise in protest but the little man, apparently named Gus, points a finger at him and stares him down. Then he nods to the pig, who goes on.

"By doing so, he became one of the largest landowners and richest men in Central Iowa. He continued amassing his net worth by buying farms at estate auctions and bank sales until, in a particularly heated contest at a land auction in Fillmore County, he choked on a large bite of pork tenderloin he was trying to swallow quickly before making his next bid. Despite her best efforts, the local veterinarian, the only medical person at the auction, was unsuccessful in her attempts to revive him.

"The estate passed to JJ, Junior who, through his shrewd manipulation of the tangled web of government subsidies, economic development grants, tax evasion strategies, wealth managers, and contributions to political funds, has abandoned real farming altogether and turned these holdings into an empire of factory meat production, from the introduction of the boar to the sow to the introduction of the Whopper Burger to the fat kid. Unfortunately, JJ, Junior seems to have gone inconveniently missing, which is the reason Junior, Junior, appointed to the position of Vice-Chair by his father's friend, our esteemed Guv, is now seated in the Chair's chair.

"Not much need be said about Junior, Junior because up to this point in his forty-four years he has done little unless you count three marriages and divorces, six DUI convictions, a week of house confinement for leaving the scene of an accident (for which his license has yet to be suspended) and shooting the largest whitetail deer ever killed in Story County from the seat of his pickup truck out of season with an illegal rifle." Junior, Junior is slumped in his seat with nothing to say. "Shall I go on?"

There are murmurs of "Sure," "Let's hear it," and "Carry on" from those assembled. Gus's voice cuts through the room, "The floor is yours."

"Seated next to Junior, Junior is Mr. Cletus Rumley. It is difficult to ascertain Mr. Rumley's position with the Central States Pork Producers Association—a look at their web page does not list any officers or show any corporate structure—so let us just say he is the chief propaganda officer of the association. His job is to tell the public that the little piggies have fun growing up in those cubicles they live in, so much fun that they chew each other's tails off trying to give themselves a little more room to frolic around in. He also creates ads telling mothers how healthy bacon, pork chops, and ribs are for their young ones, how new technology is cleaning up streams and rivers, and how many good jobs are being created with each new CAFO. He belongs to the Texas Rumleys—oil, gas, and cattle—and his job was secured with a 100K donation to the aforementioned Pork organization (incidentally, non-profit)."

And so, the pig works his way down the line of dark-suits, pointing out the way each man inherited his money, how the Ag Bureau representative wields his influence to make sure no legislation whatsoever regulating agriculture makes its way through the State House and the rules that somehow slip through are inadequately enforced, and the amount of grant money from State coffers that has gone to the new fertilizer plant which, as it turns out, has created only thirteen minimum-wage jobs.

Having almost reached the end of the line, it pauses a moment, then adds, "On your far right is Kyle Czechowski. Kyle has no vote here and is not expected to speak. Kyle has been with the DNR for 18 years, starting as a wildlife field officer, a job that he loved, then moving to a management position, which he disliked but which he took because he needed the raise, which barely increased his compensation above the poverty level, to help his three kids through college. Most recently he has been designated an 'Inspection and Compliance Officer', one of 4 who cover 99 Counties, to make sure that all the several thousand CAFOs in the State are in compliance with what regulations there are. He is honest, funny, a great father, and a hard worker, trying hard to make a broken system work. He will retire next summer. He will be missed. He will not miss his current job. There seems to be no urgency to replace him."

"And finally…," the pig seems to be having some difficulty continuing as if it is losing its voice. It coughs and clears its throat. "And finally, the most wonderful…no, what I mean to say is the most positive, optimistic …well…I, uh. This is Miss Amie Greene, the only real hope for a better State among the voting members of this committee. Many of you know about her, have read in the papers about what she has done, is doing, at Cohn Middle School. Have seen her receive awards and talk about her dreams on the evening news. She is not happy on this platform. Believe me, she would rather be out there with you. Most of you know that. But wherever she is, she is going to push and shove to try her damned best to move this state in the right direction. She is …she is…" The pig is having trouble speaking. It is unable to continue.

It then pauses, looks slowly around the room, and pulls a large Bowie knife from a pouch, unnoticed until then, and holds it with both hands ceremoniously in the air, like a Japanese samurai. Then it points the blade point toward the dark suits as they dive in various directions for cover, some screaming, others groaning. With a flourish, it inserts the weapon into the lower part of its abdomen and pulling it up, accompanied by gasps from most of the onlookers, makes a long incision up to the middle part of its chest. It replaces the knife, reaches into the incision, and pulls out a clear plastic bag filled with what looks like about 40 pounds of bloody animal intestines, places the bag on the table in front of Junior, Junior, steps to the door, kicks it open, strolls into the parking lot, and climbs into its aging vehicle. No one makes a sound as the battered Jeep repeats its routine—shivers, coughs, sighs, burps its smoke ring, comes to life, and rattles through melting snow in the direction from which it came.

Pandemonium ensues. Junior, Junior whacks his gavel on the table, but no one hears it over the uproar. The business casuals are in a tight huddle, all talking at once. The largest of the dark-suits shouts, "This meeting is adjourned," as all but Kyle Czechowski disappear into the anteroom and through the slamming back door. Amid a cacophony of shouted questions, Kyle holds up his hands. "The meeting is postponed. It will be re-scheduled. Believe me, I will do all I can to make sure it is re-scheduled. You will be notified."

Amie Greene sprints out the main entrance and begins running after the Jeep screaming, "Shawn, stop. Please dammit, stop. This is not going to solve things. This is not going to help." For a half-block she seems to be gaining on the vehicle, but the driver shifts into second gear and disappears down Ivy Street. Amie walks slowly back to the parking lot, opens the door of her red Toyota Prius, and realizes that the left front tire is flat. She kicks the tire and sits without closing the door. It is not clear if the tears coming down her cheeks are the result of running into the cold wind or of something else.

The Jeep continues east on Ivy Street, north on Forty-second Street, and east on I-80. Interstate to state highway to county blacktop to gravel to level B to two-track. It finally pulls to a stop in front of the porch of a small but neat log cabin, wet snow on the roof and wisps of wood smoke rising from the chimney. The pig exits the truck, slowly ascends the porch steps, pulls the head of the pig costume off the head of the man inside, walks through the door, and looks at himself in a mirror hanging out of balance on the wall. "What the hell do you think you're doing?" Shawn Gallagher says to his reflection in the mirror. "What the hell are you thinking? What the fucking hell are you thinking?"

Back at her apartment, Amie Green looks at the night sky outside her window and takes off her wet shoes and socks. Perhaps it hadn't been the worst day Amie had ever lived through, but it was a close, the worst being the day she had to go to school with braces for the first time when she was twelve years old. But this day has been a total, absolute, complete disaster. She had gone back to the DNR room to find out if the meeting had been rescheduled, but the committee members had fled, scurried out the back to their Lincolns and Mercedes. Only Czechowski, the DNR guy, was still around and he didn't know anything. He offered to help with the tire, but she thanked him and called Triple A. By the time the flat was fixed, she had missed dinner at Zombie Burger with two of her teacher colleagues, and now she sits at her tiny desk nibbling on a frozen pizza she has undercooked, trying, with zero luck, to concentrate on her plans for the next day's classes. It is Shawn Gallagher that she can't get off her mind.

Amie first met Dr. Shawn Gallagher when she was twenty-one, at the beginning of her junior year. Her first two years at State had been brilliant, all A's except for a single B in Classical Greek Drama, so she was enthusiastically accepted by the biology faculty into the honors program in Environmental Studies. She was thrilled when she learned that her advisor was to be Professor Gallagher. She had heard much about this young professor, the rising star of the Animal Science Department. When she told her female friends who her advisor was going to be, they were beside themselves, using adjectives like dreamy, gorgeous, and hot, and offering to pay if they could go along on her advising sessions. 'The Shawn Gallagher' was going to be her faculty advisor.

So she knew why she was so nervous as she approached his office, Baker 137, a little disappointed when she saw a note attached to the door, but excited again when she read, *Those with appointments please come to my lab, 335 Baker Hall.* The long walk down the hall and climbing two flights of stairs didn't slow her heartbeat. She tapped on the door of 335. "Not locked." The voice was pleasant but obviously more interested in the work he was doing than in his new advisee—at least for the moment. Shawn Gallagher jotted a couple more notes on a yellow pad, turned around, and was motionless, speechless, as immobile as Lot's salt statue spouse. Something was happening on that warm autumn afternoon, sunlight struggling through dusty windows, reflecting off beakers, bouncing off Petri dishes. Her eyes, grey as a cloudy day, her smile letting enough sunshine through to make a mockery of the seriousness of any clouds, faded jeans, lightly tanned shoulders covered with delicate golden hairs, freckles spilling from her face into the dark V of her loose tank top. Completely guileless. Her look, one of unabashed enthusiasm. He had no idea how long he looked at her. A second, two, a minute, an hour—no idea.

And Amie. She knew she was gaping, that her mouth was open—but she couldn't close it. Her eyes as wide as they had ever been, and she was leaning toward him, almost beyond the angle of repose. The electric intensity of his expression tempered by warmth and vulnerability. Shortstop arms halfway into a gesture. She was going to fall into those arms, *Oh, Lord, don't let me fall, but please Lord, don't stop me.*

Then boom, red lights flashing in both their heads, like a highway patrol car in a rear-view mirror. This can't happen. This can't be. Crazy, dangerous, for some stupid reason or other it…screech, they slammed on the brakes, pulled over. Reality returned. Shawn cleared his throat. Amie took a deep breath…and extended her hand.

The advising session would have made a great SNL skit. Any concentration on what they were meeting for floated away each time they made eye contact. He looked for his files, then realized he wasn't in his office, then told her sheepishly they had to walk down the stairs to 137. When they got there and had the relative safety of a desk between them, she had completely forgotten the courses she wanted to register for, and any questions she wanted to ask popped like soap bubbles and evaporated as they lifted toward the office ceiling. He seemed to have forgotten where everything was. They spent a lot of time saying nothing, looking at each other but turning away quickly if eye contact was made.

Finally, they managed to finish the session. Amie stepped out of the office and into the hall. Shawn softly closed the door behind her and fought off an impulse to open it again so he could watch her disappear.

When Amie walked out the front door of Baker Hall, she was dizzy. She leaned against the wall and looked at the sky—crisp summer clouds, a squiggly V of geese—and wondered if she could make another appointment just to look at Shawn Gallagher. She walked back to her dorm to be swallowed up by a paparazzi covey of giggling dorm mates with a thousand questions. She said nothing. Dazed, she walked to her room, locked the door, and sighed herself on to her bed where she lay on her back until dark.

And that's how it went for the next two years of advisor/advisee meetings. Knock on the door, lab or office, eye contact, motionless, leaning in, defying gravity, almost giving into the power of the magnetic pull, then screech, red lights in their heads from that infuriating patrol car, handshake, perhaps a sigh from one or both, and retreat to opposite sides of that damned desk, as uncrossable as the mighty Mississippi River in a flood month. Somehow, they managed to get the advisor/advisee business done, but that was almost by accident.

Twenty-one months later Shawn watched Amie cross the stage on commencement day and receive her honors and medals and diploma. Watched as she walked toward him down the grassy lane lined on each side by solemn, brightly robed faculty, and stop where he was standing. What if I would just give her a farewell hug? That would be OK, wouldn't it? After all she has taken my advice for two years now. It could even be somewhat fatherly. But no. They just stood looking at each other until they realized they were holding up the line, and then, a handshake. A stupid handshake. Those red lights. Those fucking red lights.

Now Amie Greene sits in her small apartment staring through her tiny window at snow lit by street lamps falling on a slick sidewalk, unable to get Shawn Gallagher off her mind. Why is he doing that, just clowning his life away? He can do better than that, I know he can. He is better than that. God, I love that man.

There is a dense fog in Denver, Colorado, the morning after the EPC's chaotic meeting, when Donald Birdseed walks through the glass doors in the glass front wall of the corporate offices of Freebird Poultry, 'Happy Chickens for Happy Families,' located in the central business district. He wonders briefly what he will do for the next week with his trophy wife, Lizzy, gone, but he realizes that won't make much difference. They rarely cross paths in their lives of marital bliss and separate bedrooms. Anyway, a quick business trip he has to make later that morning to Des Moines might alleviate some of his persistent boredom. Birdseed waves to the receptionist as he exits. "Someone took my portrait down to dust it off, I suppose," he says as he makes some vaguely lascivious gesture toward her, which she ignores. Birdseed is short, overweight, dressed in an Under Armor running suit, and is leading a hyper-energetic Jack Russell terrier, also overweight, on a retractable leash. He enters the elevator, yanking the dog off its feet pulling it after him, and descends to the first floor. He steps hesitantly onto the fog-shrouded, slush-covered Bixby Street sidewalk, taking time to turn and look at the modern twenty-story office building, which he has just left, as if he owns it, which he does, and begins his dog-walking routine.

Two blocks west, a brand-new Denver Municipal Waste Authority truck is picking up the trash bins that are spaced along the street with its large mechanical arm and dumping them into the compacter in the rear of the vehicle. When the truck is even with Donald Birdseed, the mechanical arm extends and, with pincers that are designed like gigantic lobster claws, embraces the dog-walking man, who is about the same height and shape as one of the larger bins, lifts him and drops him into the compacter. The terrier's retractable leash extends to its full length as his master levitates, arms and legs flailing in the air, then, after lifting the dog two feet off the sidewalk, slips out of the man's hand as the dog falls onto the slush-covered pavement. Any sound the man or dog might have made is drowned out by the truck's engine. Inexplicably, the garbage truck turns up a side street. It is followed by what appears to be an antique pickup truck. The other bins remain on the curb unemptied. The dog sprints up Bixby Street, frightened but unharmed, looking as if it is being chased by its retractable leash.

In the office, one of the junior executives asks the receptionist, "Did Mr. Birdseed decide to have that stupid portrait of him moved? Ugliest thing I ever saw, him and that damn spoiled mutt."

"Don't know," she answers.

"He brought that artist all the way from Paris to paint it, but I guess there was no way he could make old man Birdseed look good. Probably figured it wasn't helping with customers, that being the first thing they'd see when they'd come in the door. It would sure put me off."

"Alls I know is it was gone when I came in this morning," she says.

Back on Bixby Street, two men watch the old pickup with interest as it follows the garbage truck up the side street. "You see that?" one of them says. "That's an International Harvester pickup, must be 50 years old, maybe more."

"Yeah, so what?" the other answers. "Just an old truck."

The first man says, "I ain't seen one of them in years. There was an old man where I used to live in Iowa had one of them back in the day. That one looks to be in pretty good shape. Just that rust spot on the door." He flips the cigarette he is smoking onto the wet road. "Wonder why that garbage truck didn't empty the rest of them bins."

It is the following morning, a long way from Denver. The Bubbling Springs Shooting Preserve is in the southern part of Nachawinga County, ten miles from Tripoli, the county seat. Two fairly large, stacked stone columns, each with a bronze pheasant in flight on top, mark the entrance off State Highway 57. On the other side of the columns, a grassy field of about a hundred and fifty acres, intercut with brushy draws but, for the most part, sorghum, neatly trimmed to knee height, extends to the north, surrounded by thousands of acres of harvested corn and soybeans. Footpaths meander through the field. At one end a large white farmhouse, which serves as a lodge and clubhouse, sits in a grove of cottonwoods and Chinese elms. Behind the house, discreetly hidden from the shooting area, are pheasant pens—long chicken wire enclosures with several hundred wet, worse-for-the-wear pheasants pecking at each other and running back and forth, looking for a hole in the wire through which they might escape. Expensive cars are lined up in the parking area facing the lodge. A black limousine sits apart from the other vehicles. Two large, dark-blue-suited men with buds in their ears lounge in the two front seats. The weather on this early November day can only be described as wretched: snow, sleet, freezing drizzle, and a 17 mph 'breeze.' Twelve men huddle under a wind-whipped canvas canopy, shivering in blaze orange hunting attire that appears, for the most part, to have come straight off the shelves of Bass Pro Shop—never before worn. A banner on the canopy reads, *The Guv's Eleventh Annual Pheasant Hunt*. A camera crew from the Des Moines NBC-TV affiliate stands in front of their van, blowing in their hands trying to keep warm and dry, with plastic garbage bags covering their cameras. A man and a woman with soggy notepads, press credentials hanging around their necks, are off to one side. In the middle of the huddle, a table holds a dozen undecorated shotguns, over-and-unders, and automatics, with one exception. Standing out from the other weapons is a classic English side-by-side double-barrel gun, beautifully engraved on the metal, with a fantastically figured wood stock and forend. Tastefully etched on the sidelocks is the word 'Purdey.' Conversation is sparse, with the exception of an exasperated Guv and his Chief-of-Staff standing apart from the others and speaking softly.

"Dammit, Tim, I told you to get everybody here by ten. It's past eleven and those pig and chicken guys still haven't shown. Have you heard anything? Where the hell are they? And what about my portrait? Has anybody come up with anything yet?"

"I told you, I don't know, sir. I've been trying for the last three hours to contact Wooten and Schittman—can't get in touch with them, their wives either. Birdseed was supposed to fly in yesterday, but his Denver office doesn't know if he took off or not. Talked to Wooten's lawyer and he says Wooten didn't show up for a meeting with JJ yesterday, and that's all he knows. And Schittman didn't show up for the EPC meeting yesterday afternoon—which was an A number one disaster. I'll tell you about that later, you've got other things to think about. Your picture is still a mystery but don't worry, I'm sure it'll appear somewhere."

The exasperated Governor peers through the drizzly mist toward the farm's entryway, "Well, we gotta get this thing underway. The Vice President says he's leaving at two." Then he growls, "Grab one of those shotguns and I'll tell Cline to line everybody up and turn the dogs loose."

Tim Taylor loses a bit of color from his chilled pink cheeks. "I don't shoot, sir. Never have. Don't know how. I'm scared of guns, hate the noise. I thought I'd just sit in the car and wait."

"We need you in the line, what with all the no-shows. Just pick out a gun, Taylor. If a bird gets up, point the gun at the sky and pull the trigger. Don't try to hit anything. In fact, try not to hit anything." Tim hesitantly touches the Purdey as if it might bite him, then picks it up as the Guv turns to the man who seems to be in charge, standing by a pickup truck. "Let's get going, Roger." And to the clutch of grim hunters, "This is what we came here for boys, isn't it? Damn, it's gonna be a great day. It don't get any better than this."

Roger Cline opens the doors and releases four handsome dogs—two German shorthaired pointers and two Labrador retrievers—from aluminum kennels in the back of his truck and attaches leashes to them once they hit the ground. Judging from the enthusiasm of the canines, it is clear that they are the only creatures anxious to get this day underway. Cline turns to the soggy hunters, "Gentlemen. You're going to form a line and stay in it, about 10 to 20 yards apart. Shoot only in your cone, not right or left, and shoot up. Nothing on the ground." He waits to see them all agree, then looks along the forming line, finding it difficult not to look at the sky and shake his head. The Guv and the Veep nod to each other, realize they have nothing to say, and take the spots in the middle. Cline releases the dogs, and the pointers bound with exuberant pleasure into the field as the retrievers obediently walk at heel, waiting for something to retrieve. The picket line moves forward through the manicured grass.

Fifty yards into the march, one of the dogs freezes, looking exactly like one of those fake bronze desk ornaments that are featured in the Wild Wings and Orvis catalogs. Cline steps in front of the seemingly frozen shorthair and kicks around in every spot in the grass that could possibly hide a bird. Finally, a bedraggled, soaking wet pheasant, trying courageously for take-off but unable to lift its water-logged body off the runway, flees the advancing orange line on foot, as the Veep lifts his gun and swings it far to the right, trying to locate his quarry. He seems to be having some trouble swinging to the left. Nevertheless, hunters on both sides hit the wet grass as if someone had yelled "Grenade." Finally, he fires three shots in the direction of the sprinting bird, coming closer to one of the dogs than his target, but missing both dog and bird. One of the retrievers, however, sensing that the small volley must have affected some contact between lead shot and intended pheasant, chases the bird down and proudly returns it to its handler. Congratulatory shouts echo up and down the line. "Great shot, sir." "Hell of a shot, Mister Vice President." "Musta been fifty yards." And so on.

"Give me that bird," the Veep barks. (Cline by now has discreetly broken its neck.) The ex-Vice President holds the soggy bird high, trying to get the attention of the camera crew who have retreated into the warmth of their van, as one of the secret service officers who has been shadowing his boss pulls out his iPhone and snaps a picture.

The party, snow on shoulders and rain dripping off hat brims, pushes on. More pheasants are pointed; most of them run onto the path and then scurry back into the safety of the tall grass. All of the ones that actually make it into the air are missed, and a miserable time is being had by all.

An hour and forty-five minutes into the hunt, the dogs begin to show almost frenzied excitement on the left flank. Suddenly both pointers freeze in classic poses that could grace a cover of Field and Stream. This time, there is no necessity for Cline to flush, as an outrageously colored, long-tailed wild bird catapults from a line of brush and cackles into the grey sky away from the firing line. Shots from almost every gun on the line sound like an artillery assault as the brave bird flies on unscathed. For a brief second all is silent. Then, as it seems certain that the quarry has escaped, a lone shot rings out, and, in a burst of feathers, the rooster summersaults to the ground. With the echoes of the gunshot fading in the distance, the assembled 'hunters' watch the Chocolate Lab make a TV-worthy retrieve and present the bird to Taylor.

"I got it. Hot damn, I hit it. Oh my God, did you see that Guv, guys? Perfect shot. Hot digitty damn, baby. I hit it. My bird. Gonna have that thing mounted. Myyyyy bird." Tim Taylor is holding the gaudy bird high, jumping up and down, and thrusting his fist into the air as if there is something up there to punch. The silence is long and irritated up and down the line.

The Guv, face crimson with cold and embarrassment and trembling with rage, pulls Tim roughly to the rear of the line and fixes him with an icy stare. "Goddammit, Tim, what did I tell you. I told you not to hit anything. You're not supposed to hit anything. I didn't want you to hit anything. That was the only good shot of the day, you little son-of-a-bitch." He jerks the pheasant away from Taylor.

The Guv's annual pheasant hunt cannot be described as anything but an absolutely miserable day for everyone but Tim Taylor. Although he would never shoot a gun again, he would dream of that shot for the rest of his life.

Later that day, Shawn Gallagher is again in front of his mirror speaking out loud to his reflection as he had been doing since the EPC meeting. "Is this going to do a damn bit of good, behaving like a clown, disrupting meetings, sending threats to politicians, corporate ag execs, living like a hermit out here in the woods? Am I making one huge mistake thinking I can just drop out, run around in a hog costume, make a lot of noise, be some kind of cornfield guerrilla, and turn things around?" He picks his costume up off the sofa where he flung it two days earlier. "And this thing is starting to smell like a real hog." He flings it into a corner, crosses the room, throws a couple of sticks of wood into the fireplace embers, flops onto a big, overstuffed couch sagging in the middle and losing its insides, sighs, and remembers.

He didn't use to ask himself questions like this. He believed he was going in the right direction. He believed he knew exactly what he was thinking, believed he and his science could lead the way to a better tomorrow. That was back when he was a star at State U in every way imaginable, cruising to a BS degree with high honors in Animal Science in three years while leading the baseball team to their best season ever, a shortstop with a three-sixty batting average. In five more years, he was the youngest member of the faculty in that same department, with a PhD from Texas A&M and two years of post-doc work at Cornell under his belt. His teaching was exemplary. Although he was not much older than his students, they loved him. His early research was in animal health—how healthy animals without additives or anti-biotics could yield more product in numerous small pasture operations than those treated with chemicals and drugs in mega con-finements. And as he worked, he became increasingly aware of the horrible conditions these chickens, swine, and cattle were in fact raised under, and the very real harm that was being done to the environment and human beings as a result. He also saw that the bottom line was the primary driving force in the business and that anything he suggested that didn't result in an immediate increase in profits was ignored. As his research pointed toward ways this harm might be ameliorated, he found little interest in amelioration. When his findings continued to point out the significant problems in the industry, financial support for his work, almost all of which had come from large agri-business and pharmaceutical companies, began to shrink. Colleagues hinted that the arc of his research was leading him in a direction that would make funding difficult for his experimental work, and perhaps for others in the department. Some of the University administration showed concern about his disappearing corporate support.

Finally, he remembers the day Dr. Morris Hamilton walked into his lab. "Are you busy? It's warming up out there. God, I love spring in this town."

Ham, as he was called, was a legend in the field of animal research. Shawn had first met him as his undergraduate advisor and still con-sidered him an indispensable mentor. Ham was his hero, but most of all, he was his friend.

"Yup," Shawn answered. "I'd like to get out of this lab before dark, just listen to the frogs down by the creek. Haven't even gone mush-room hunting and the season's almost gone. But I think I'm on to something, Ham."

"Yeah?" Hamilton said."

"You know those shelters I've been telling you about, the portable ones that can be put on sloping pastures for farrowing? The cost of using them is not much more per head than the cost of the giant confinement buildings, the well-being of the animals is exponentially higher, manure management…"

"Whoa, Shawn. That's what I want to talk to you about," Hamilton interrupted.

Shawn continued, "…and it's amazing how that cuts odor pollution and the risk of spills. About a quarter a head, twenty-five cents it's going to cost, and it can turn this whole…"

"Let's go get a beer, Shawn," Hamilton held up his hands. "You need a break. You've got some thinking to do, and we really need to talk."

Quarter till four and the Wild Turkey Pub was beginning to fill up. They found a quiet booth in the back and ordered two draws of a local IPA.

Hamilton spoke, "Ya know, Shawn, we've known each other ever since you walked into my lab straight out of the boonies, a red-nosed freshman eager as a setter pup on his first day in a pheasant field. You knew what you wanted, and you had the energy and the drive to get it. It got you all the way to a faculty position at a fine University. You are making discoveries, and in your papers, you are exposing problems and dangers that everyone in this department should have been working on years ago. But they haven't been, and the problem is the corporations, big ag, the people who approve the grants that fund your research don't want to hear about these problems and don't want anyone else to hear about them, either. They are not at all interested in anything that doesn't put more money in their pockets—right away."

"But they need to," Shawn said. "And so does everyone else."

"Just listen to me," Hamilton continued. "If you keep going in the direction you're going, that money is going to dry up like a prairie pothole in a midwestern heatwave. You're not going to get another dime looking at the super germs that result from overloading antibiotics in animal feed, or the harm to communities, the land, and the people, from toxic gases and runoffs. You know I'm retiring at the end of next semester. I'm not even going to keep my lab. I'm tired of doing what other folks want just to keep them giving money to me and the U and keeping the Administration happy. I'm going to spend my time in my place up northeast, fly fishing and chasing turkeys. I've tried, but I'm worn out. But you, with your energy and skill and youth, might be able to make some changes if you go at it the right way. Do what they want you to, for a while at least, make them and the department happy, get your grants. Things might…" He pauses here, feeling he has gone on too long. "You have said that I'm your hero—well I can tell you, you're mine too, and I don't want to see you hurt or busted."

They both took long swallows of their beer before Shawn answered, "I know what you're saying, Ham. I've gone over all that with myself a hundred times. But people are being hurt, the environment of my state is going to hell in a bucket, and these big money people are torturing animals to produce millions of tons of cheap unhealthy meat and not even covering their real costs of production." He smiled at his mentor. "It just feels like we're running out of time, Ham, and I don't want to waste any of that time on those causing the harm. I think I can find a way that will work better for everyone."

Hamilton smiled. "Got time for a couple of more beers."

The next day Shawn Gallagher resigned his faculty position.

The sun is just coming up on Thursday morning, fifteen miles north of the little town of Tripoli. Lucus Pickle and Travis Van Gorp are trying to maneuver a rendering plant dumpster truck east on the county blacktop, only the road is covered with two inches of new wet snow, and they can't tell if it's black or not. Travis, with a cigarette hanging in his mouth, is driving, and Luke, with his head out the window, is squinting to see as best he can through the mixed precip, trying to keep Travis on the road.

"See that bean field over there?" Luke pulls his head inside and looks over at Travis. "Used ta have a brushy draw right down the middle of it, kinda seepy. I could start at the west end with Moby, you remember, that big ol Lab I had, and have my limit o pheasants by the time I got to the east fence. Hell, when it was wet, they was ducks in the potholes. Them fence rows had birds too. Sometimes quail even. Look at it now, a fuckin desert. Fuckin Roundup soy-bean desert. Ain't enough cover fer a sumbitchen cockroach to hide in, let alone a cock pheasant. Big tractors an combines an Roundup. No fence rows, not a single sprig a brush." He sticks his head back out of the window. "Damn, that was one pretty draw. In the Spring they was …"

Travis pokes him, "Just shut up and keep yer eyes on the damn road before we end up in the fuckin ditch. You go on about that shit every time we pass here."

"Well, it was one damn pretty draw."

Both are now thinking of the two miles of mud and gravel they're going to have to navigate before they get to their first collection at Holmgren's hog lot, one of Compassionate Family Farmers' lots in Franklin Township. Neither one is happy that they'll be driving these sloppy roads for the next ten hours while a late Iowa winter weather event is turning every gravel road in their three counties into gumbo the consistency and color of old chocolate pudding.

Travis keeps squinting through the one piece of windshield the defroster is able to keep clear in its losing battle with the ice and sleet. He is forty-one, divorced, and two years behind on child support. He lives in a wheel-less travel trailer, to which, in an attempt at insulation, he has hot glued Tyvek on the north and west sides. The trailer sits on the edge of the nearly abandoned town of Jersey City, Iowa (no one knows how it got that name) which boasts a good bar, The Thirsty Buffalo, a co-op grain elevator, a hairstylist, and the Church of the Holy Flame located in the building that used to be the Shell station before it went out of business. His Carhartts are so frayed at the limb exits they look like they might be decorated with fringe. He takes off his grease-stained John Deere cap and turns it backwards so he can get closer to the windshield and tucks his long ponytail under his collar. His black hair is having a hard time fending off the encroaching grey. *Van Gorp Animal Rendering—You find 'em, We grind 'em* is stenciled on the truck door. Van Gorp Rendering is run by two of his cousins out of Onkalumpa. He's been working there for twelve years, off and on.

Luke's coveralls are a carbon copy of Travis's, but he has a hoodie under his, the hood over his head, with a blaze orange wool stocking cap pulled down over that. He is tall, at least six-five, and couldn't weigh over 150 pounds, a perfect Abbott to Travis's five-foot-ten, 298-pound Costello, who can barely squeeze behind the steering wheel of the truck even when he sucks in his gut. Luke wipes his snow-soaked blonde hair plastered over his forehead away from his eyes. He is twenty-eight, a vet, married for two years to his third wife, Malinda, and lives on the east side of Onky, just past Hardees and a KFC. He picks up the dumpster truck every morning at five-fifteen and stops at Travis's trailer at five-forty. This morning, as usual, he was late. Travis then takes over driving so he won't have to get in and out of the truck. Luke has worked at Van Gorp's for thirteen months, still on minimum wage, still no benefits. Every two weeks he swears he's going to quit.

Travis steers the truck onto the gravel and heads east. There is no way now to make sure they are on the road, except to straddle the center crown and hope nothing is coming the other way. Twenty minutes later, they are backing into Holmgren's.

The confinement is a large, low metal building sitting on about four acres of bare ground with a half-acre parking area in front. The building is almost 50 yards long; three-foot-high openings run along the length of both sides. Dirty canvas curtains hang over these primitive windows. There are several round, 15-foot-high feed bins spaced along the outside. A large exhaust fan has been built into each end of the building, but both are dust-and snow-covered, and look like they haven't been used for a while. Off to one end, the ground slants and there is a big pond or lagoon at the bottom of the descent, about the size of an Olympic swimming pool, greenish liquid in the middle, and dirt-grey ice around the edges. There seems to be a leak at the lower end, as a brown sludge is visible seeping out from under a dirt dam. Fifty or sixty little brown sticks line the gravel road in front of the operation, a half-hearted attempt at a border of shrubs now dying a slow death, the result of total neglect. A din of grunts and squeals can be heard over the growl of the truck's struggling diesel.

At one end of the lot sit two green dumpsters, full to overflowing with the bodies of pigs, almost all the same size, 60 to 80 pounds. What immediately attracts the attention of someone coming in the entrance are all the little legs sticking up in the air like another failed tree planting, and the dead pigs that have overflowed. A small sign next to the driveway says *Compassionate Family Farms, a Division of Wooten Plantation, LLC, Wilson, N.C. In case of emergency call Lyle Holmgren, 319 262 9978.*

"Look at all of um laying there… Yuck," Luke groans. "They're half-rotten and froze to the ground. Looks like the coyotes woulda ate um. We ain't gonna have to clean um up, are we? It'll put us an hour behind."

"Well, you were half-hour late with the truck, dickhead. Anyways, we got to." Travis is as disgusted as his partner. "Lyle's already pissed at us for not cleaning the place up last month."

"Don't know why Lyle keeps running this place anyways," Luke says. "He told me he ain't making the money them people down south promised him. Had to pay for the building and now he has to buy their feed and their pigs at their price and sell um back for whatever they'll pay. He's just a hired hand feeding their pigs out. Don't sound like much of a deal to me."

Luke opens his door and steps into the mud. He guides Travis as he slowly backs the truck so the lift hooks make contact with the first dumpster.

"Yer on." Luke yells and Travis pulls the hydraulic lever. The dumpster rises over the truck, tips, and unloads its contents into the bed. Luke picks up the two carcasses that have missed and heaves them in after the others. The compacter is engaged and the whole load is pushed toward the front. Luke manages to get some of the other corpses off the frozen ground and into the truck. He motions to Travis, this time with exaggerated gestures as if he was directing a giant airliner, as he backs the truck to the second dumpster. He starts to lift another frozen corpse off the ground, decides to leave it, and climbs into the cab filled with Travis' cigarette smoke. He lights one of his own in self-defense and squints through the back window.

As the load is tipping into the truck, Luke leans closer to the window, "Whoa, whoa, whoooa. Sumbitch. Put it back down. You see that?"

"What?"

"A foot."

"I see lots a feet back there."

"No, a FOOT."

"Yeah, feet. I seen um. Lots of um."

"No. Toes. One with toes."

"They don't call them things toes. They're hoofs. Pigs ain't got no toes. Trotters. They call them things trotters, don't they? Ain't that what they call um, trotters?"

"I seen a foot. A foot on a leg. With toes. Not hoofs. Toes dammit. I know the difference between a foot and a damn—wha'd you say—trotter."

"C'mon man. It's too early to start that shit. You're crazyrn a damn hoot owl."

"I seen it."

"Yeah, and I seen Miranda Lambert sitting side you at the bar last night. You been smoking dope already?"

"I'm telling yuh."

"Well, I ain't gonna go back there digging through that crap to see if there's no damn leg with no damn foot on it because some crazy-ass moron thinks he seen it through a fogged-up window ya can't even get the ice scraped off of. You go back there yerself if yer so damn sure."

"But I'm telling ya."

"No. N. O. No."

"But… Ah, forget it. Pack it in an let's get the fuck out o here."

Six o'clock, long after sundown, Lucas and Travis turn the dumpster truck into Cyril Duffus' hog lot, the last of the day. They are creeping, hoping to keep the wheels from spinning as they ease up a slow rise. The lot looks the same as all the others, but this one is longer by 150 feet or so. The building sits on the very edge of a deep ravine, at the bottom of which is a small creek, partially frozen on both sides, but somewhat open in the middle. Old cottonwoods and American elms line the upstream and downstream banks, but the trees closest to the hog lot are all dead. The building seems to be leaking on the stream-side and brown streaks stain the snow, going down the high banks of the gorge into the creek. It is clear the builders of this pork factory are taking advantage of a sewage disposal system that nature has made available to them. The two dumpsters are older and rustier than those at Holmgren's—only one full of little pink corpses. One dead pig is on the gravel, but temps have dropped ten degrees since morning and Luke rips it in half trying to get it off the freezing ground.

"Shit," he growls, "There's gotta be a better way to make a living. Maybe cleaning rest-stop toilets on the interstate," he laughs. "Any damn thing."

"Just guide my ass back so I can hook up and dump this mess and we can get the hell home," Travis growls back at him.

Luke clears a circle in the frost on his window and peers through it. "I don't like the way they let that shit run into the crick. I used to trap that crick, from the Durr farm near bout to the county line. Clear Crick, they call it. That's a laugh now. It was full of mushrats and mink—even got me a coupla beavers. Now they ain't nothing alive down there but leeches and worms. Coons won't even wash their food in that water. Damn shit hole, all the way to the Wolfe River. Under 500 and you can do any fuckin thing ya' want."

"Under 500 what?" Travis is puzzled.

"500. I told ya about that a dozen times. Under 500 animal units and there ain't no rules according to that damn matrix thing." Luke frowns. "Theys thousands a pigs in there and there ain't no rules. Nothing nobody can do."

"Ya know that deep hole down to the bridge?" Luke goes on, "Bet I caught at least 50 ten-pound catfish outta that hole when I was a teenager before they put this lot up. Used to lay out a school and fish from the bank. If it didn't rain for a coupla days, you could see plum to the bottom, five or six of them big cats, movin just enough to keep up with the current. Sit there under that big cottonwood with a cold six-pack. God, it was beautiful in the springtime, peepers chirping all along the banks, all kinda birds in them big trees. Now it's gone. Ain't even seen a chub or a shiner in that crick since they built this shit house."

"You eat them fish?"

"Hell, yes. You could almost drink from the crick back then. Put them fish in a washtub a well water fer a couple a days. Fry up them filets. By God, they was some kinda good." He trails off, a smile on his face as if he can smell them.

"Yeah, well, that's over with in this county," Travis says as he shifts into reverse, "so forget about it. Let's roll."

Luke looks through his 'porthole' one last time. "Whoa, whoa, hold up. What the fuck's that? Look inside the hog house. You ain't gonna believe this."

"C'mon, Luke. Goddammit, it's late an the roads ur freezing. Just cut that shit out."

"No. Look in there. Just look. They's a big ol picture in there, hanging on that post."

"Alls I know is you're crazy'rn hell. I can't believe a thing you say anymore. Jeezamighty, Luke. Let's just get our asses outa here."

Luke rolls down his window, "See fer yerself."

"Son of a bitch." Travis leans over Luke, shoving him against the door. "What ya reckon Cyril's got that up there for. Ugly ain't it?

"Fancy ass frame though," Luke says. "Bet that's worth some money—pretty damn fancy."

"Looks like Cyril's losing it," Travis says, "hanging a picture in his pigpen. Reckon he thinks it'll make them pigs get fat sooner—it'd make me quit eating if I had to look at that stupid thing all the time."

The portrait, in an ornate gold leaf frame, hangs from one of the 8 x 8 posts that support the steel roof of the confinement building. A man in typical golfing garb stands by a golf cart leaning on what appears to be a two-iron. A tree-lined fairway provides a backdrop and a green with an 18th hole flag is visible in the distance. The painting, obviously an oil, is in an ornate frame. A gold plate at the bottom is engraved James 'JJ' Schittman II.

They both turn at the sound of a huge Ram extended-cab diesel pulling into the parking lot. The driver's door opens and Cyril Duffus, a very large man in jeans and a padded camo jacket, gets out.

"Ain't you clowns done yet? Roads gonna be slicker'n bat snot by the time you get to Onky."

"Hey, Cyril, what'n hell you got that picture in there for? Frame must be worth a thousand bucks."

'What d'ya mean, Luke? They ain't no pic…" Cyril looks into his building, "What th'…"

Luke gets out of the truck and walks into the confinement with Cyril. Travis, after struggling to slide from under the wheel and out the door, follows them in. They walk down the fenced runway surrounded on both sides by manure-stained pink piglets fighting each other to get to food troughs extending along both sides of the building, looking like hundreds of huge pink maggots. The three bewildered men stand in front of the portrait.

Cyril takes off his Kent seed cap and scratches his buzz-cut head. "That's a picture a that Schittman feller. I know that guy—runs the company that sells me pigs to feed with his feed, then I got to sell them back to him at his offer. Asshole. They made me think I was going to make a fortune, and I ain't made shit. Reckon he put that thing in here?"

The stench in the building is so thick it makes their eyes water. Travis moves a few feet further into the building and suddenly covers his mouth and begins to retch. Luke and Cyril look at him, thinking it's the stink. He shakes his head, red-faced, eyes watering, mouth open, and points to the middle of the swarming swine. There, soaked in manure and pig urine, is the body of a human being, probably male judging by badly ripped clothing—leather coat, khaki trousers, a yellow shirt. The face and hair are gone, as are all but the ring finger on the left hand, and the pigs are beginning to feed on the right leg, starting at the ankle.

Cyril sprints out of the building and climbs into his truck, "Git in, boys. We gotta get a holt o Patrick."

Halfway across the county, Sheriff Patrick Kavanaugh scowls at his two deputies, "Put that damn thing out Phil, you know you ain't supposed to be smoking in here."

Bill and Phil Dill, twins, but not identical, are both sitting in metal folding chairs, leaning against the dingy inner wall of a thirty-by-thirty-foot room with a suspended ceiling and a cement floor, under a sign that reads, This Is A Smoke-Free Environment. It's 7:15 PM.

"I'm Bill," Bill says. "Bout done." He takes two more deep drags, holds the smoke in for as long as he can, then exhales and carefully stubs the cigarette out on the side of a green metal trash can. He rips the butt open, drops the remaining tobacco into the can, rolls the paper into a little ball, and flips it at Patrick Kavanaugh, who is seated in a swivel chair with his feet propped on a large army-style desk covered with loose papers, an old computer, and various other office paraphernalia.

"Fuck you think you're doing?" Patrick flips the paper wad back with a little more force and accuracy and it hits Bill smack between the eyes.

Bill jumps. "If you'da hit me in the eye I coulda sued you big time and had me one hell of a big spree on your money."

"You could sue me for all I got, and it would still be a long way from a big time." The three men laugh.

Patrick Kavanaugh and the two Dills are, respectively, Sheriff and Deputies of Nachawinga County. The building they occupy, built of locally quarried stone, has been in use, with little improvement, for over a century. Chiseled into a stone slab over the entrance is Nachawinga County Jail and Sheriff's Department, 1908. The jail and Sheriff's office sit on the south edge of Tripoli, population 1,236, the county seat.

Patrick continues, "I guess things are pretty pitiful around here if all we can think of to do is flip paper wads at each other. The way this weather has gone to hell—looks like it's turned to snow out there—everybody has crawled into their little hidey holes and we ain't gonna have a fight or a car wreck or any damn thing till it clears next week. When was the last time we had any excitement around here?"

"Well," Phil drawls, "we pulled Miz Kerley and her six grandchildren out of Vacation Lake when she forgot to put her car in park, and it rolled down the hill into the water. That was about a week and a half ago. None of um drowned."

"Yeah, that was big fun," Bill says.

They all chuckle.

"How bout we put in for a flat-screen TV?" Phil goes on. "Tell the supervisors we need cable to watch NYPD. Professional development."

Patrick looks around the room. "That board of supervisors we got won't even give us the budget to upgrade our Walmart walkie-talkies. They'll be icicles in hell before they'd spring for a TV." He yawns and stretches. "We can wrap it up and get outta here in another ten minutes. Nelda'll keep things running."

Phil points to the pack of Camels in his brother's shirt pocket and crooks two fingers in his direction as Bill shakes one out and hands it to him. Phil snaps his Bic a couple of times before it fires and lights his cigarette.

"Godammit, Phil," Patrick looks at the sign above the two brothers, "you're a deputy and you're supposed to act like…" He is interrupted by the sound of a truck pulling onto the gravel parking lot—unmistakably a diesel. "Who just pulled in, Nelda?" he calls to the dispatcher/office manager, who is sipping on a Diet Coke in front of a switchboard in a small front room, looking out the front window.

"That'd be Cyril Duffus. He's the only one around here with a pickup that big. Must be making megabucks at that stinking hog lot of his."

Three doors slam and Cyril, Lucus, and Travis stamp their feet on the front steps trying, with little effect, to get the snow and manure off their boots.

"Get the mud off, too, before you come in here," the Sheriff yells toward the door. "What you boys got on your mind at this time a night—lost a cat or something?"

The three walk into the office, dripping a trail of melting snow. Cyril speaks. "We got us a big problem here, Sheriff." He pauses, "they's a, I mean they's a, well, they's a dead body in my hog lot."

Patrick takes off his decorated officer's ball cap, squints at Cyril, then puts it back on. "I expect there's a bunch a dead bodies in that damn lot of yours. I thought Travis and Luke here were supposed to clean um up and put um in their dump truck."

"Don't give me a hard time, Pat. I ain't kidding around. It ain't my pigs I'm talking about. They's a person's body, a human body, in my hog lot. A dead man."

Luke adds, "And it's damn near eat up by the pigs."

And Travis, "They's a fancy-ass picture hanging on a post that Cyril don't know nothing about. And, well, I guess I better tell ya, this morning Luke said he seen a leg sticking out a dumpster a dead pigs over to Holmgren's. I told him he was crazyr'n hell, still stoned from last night or something, but he swore it was a human leg. I didn't believe him, but now, well, I dunno. He mighta been right. Maybe we ought to take a look in our truck too."

"Whoa. Slow down." Patrick looks over at the three men, then at his two deputies, pauses, then says slowly, "Well boys, we were hoping for a little excitement—looks like maybe we got some. We better get our butts over there and see what this is all about. We'll keep you posted, Nelda," he shouts to the dispatcher, unnecessarily. She has heard every word.

The six put on coats, coveralls, and hats and head out the front entrance. The lawmen get into the squad car, an ancient Crown Victoria bought used from the State Patrol, the others get back into the Ram diesel, and the convoy heads west. The Ram handles the snow and mud with no problems, the Crown Vic fishtails most of the way, barely making it over each little rise on the grease-slick road. In twenty minutes, they are parked outside Duffus' lot.

Cyril leads the group into his building, and they all gape and gag at what they see. Not much has changed since Luke and Travis made their discovery except perhaps a bit more of the leg is gone. A number of the pigs are sitting or lying around looking as if they have had enough. The men look into the pen for a good while with various expressions of disgust, holding handkerchiefs or hands over their faces.

"This is a genuine fucking mess," the Sheriff scratches his head as he removes a handkerchief from his pocket and holds it over his nose. "And this picture, you've never seen it before, Cyril?"

"I ain't. But I know who that Schittman feller is. He's the one who got me into this hog feeding business and I'm still losing my ass. Best I can see, he's also the only one that's making any money out of it. I know I sure as hell ain't. I'm telling ya, Pat..."

"Okay, okay." Patrick looks at the body. "I know we ain't supposed to move a body from where we find it, but if we don't get this one out of here there's not gonna be any body left, what do you call it, any corpus, left." Patrick looks around at the others. No one moves.

He clears his throat. No one moves.

He clears his throat again. Still, no one moves.

Finally. "OK. Cyril, get me a tarp and lay it by the front door there. Travis, Luke, you boys got a manure fork or a scoop, or something like that in that dump truck you're driving?"

Tools are assembled, and with due care but also as much haste as can be managed, the workers clearly wishing to be finished as soon as possible, the human remains are scraped onto a blue tarp. The six walk over to the Van Gorp rendering truck and the Sheriff climbs onto the bumper so he can see into the bed full of dead pigs.

"We're not gonna go digging through that stuff now looking for a damn leg. You boys take it over to the garage at the county shop so it can thaw out a little bit. Wrap that tarp around that body good and put it on top. Don't go dumping anything out of the truck until somebody tells you to. Let's get on over to Holmgren's and see what we can find over there."

A worried Cyril Duffus looks at his building full of grunting, squealing pigs that have just fed on a dead man's body. He takes his hat off and rubs his forehead. "They ain't gonna dock me on the price o my pigs are they, just cause they ate part o that guy?"

At about the same time, Alejandro Gutierrez is winding up his shift at the Freebird Poultry's egg and chicken fingers facility, a quarter-mile north of the dying village of MacDuff. The last thing he has to do is check the sewage lagoon for trash and any dead animals or birds, or workers for that matter, that might have fallen into the sludge over the past twenty-four hours. A brisk north wind is blowing snow and stench straight into MacDuff, whose 98 or so remaining citizens are grateful it is winter so they can keep their windows sealed shut. Gutierrez hurries his inspection on the south side, squinting into the snowy wind and stink. He knows that even if he runs, and even though he is wearing a yellow rubber rain suit, he is going to smell so bad when he gets to his trailer in town where he lives with his family, his wife is going to make him undress outside, then take a shower as soon as he steps through the door. And his two daughters probably won't come near him for the rest of the day. As he rounds the southwest corner of the lagoon, he stops short. A huge bale of something is floating in the waste, pushed up against the shore like some river barge by the lapping waves of manure. Squinting into the wind and snow, Alejandro is having a hard time making it out. At first, he thinks it is one of those big square hay bales that farmers all around are making, those that can afford the expensive equipment needed. As he looks more closely, he sees it is trash, and there seems to be some kind of ornately framed picture strapped onto the bale's top side. He leans in, moving around to get upwind, and sees that the picture is of a short, overweight man holding an arrogant Jack Russell terrier. Engraved on the bottom of the ornate but tastelessly decorated frame is, as best he can make out, the word, Birdseed. Alejandro runs toward a low long building, about the size of a small airport, that holds more chickens than the human populations of Iowa, Nebraska, and South Dakota combined and shouts at the top of his voice, "Morales. Get out here." Morales, pulling on his yellow slicker, comes out to the lagoon bank. Alejandro motions to him, "Ain't the dude who owns this place named Birdseed?" Morales nods, "Si, I think so."

"Come on," Gutierrez says.

The two of them, this time going around the north side of the lagoon to keep the stinking snow from blowing into their faces, arrive at the corner where the bale is still bobbing up against the bank of the lagoon. Alejandro looks at the bale, "We need to get it out. Get a couple of rakes."

When Morales returns with the tools, they manage to get the bale on dry land, turning it over in the process. "Hijo de puta!" Morales and Gutierrez cross themselves as they look at the flattened body of a fat man in an expensive running suit with a look of horror on his face, tightly tied with baling twine to a square bale of trash.

Almost a week has passed since the ill-fated Annual Pheasant Hunt. The Guv is seated at his oversized desk in his office at the State Capital. His face is the color of gray potter's clay as he listens to Tim Taylor read a top-secret report from the State Division of Criminal Investigation: "It is the conclusion of the Division that there is a clear connection between the disappearance of the portraits and the murders of the three corporate executives. In addition, it is possible that other officers of businesses connected with the large-scale production of pork and poultry may have, up to this point, been targeted, and may be at risk. There is, of course, no guarantee that even others more remotely connected, such as support organizations and supportive politicians, might not be targeted in the future. At present no suspects have been definitely identified, but the Division is beginning to compile a list from which suspects might emerge. The Nachawinga County Sheriff's office is cooperating on the investigation, but the DCI does not expect them to be of much help."

The Guv's eyes widen, his voice is shaky, "All three dead? Birdseed, too? How? When? But they haven't found Wooten's portrait yet, have they?"

"I'm afraid they have." Tim tries to match the Guv's grimness. "Lyle Holmgren, the operator of the lot where they discovered Wooten's remains, found it. It was hanging in the pen; hogs had chewed the bottom off it. Brought it into Sheriff Kavanaugh yesterday."

"Can't be." The remaining color drains from the Guv's face. "Half my goddamn campaign contributions came from them last election. And where the hell is my picture? I want that thing found and then I want it burned, don't ever want to see it again. We can't have another murder connected to that picture." He is visibly shaken. "You get that damned DCI chief in here and tell him to put the whole bureau on it—every last one of um. Right now. If they don't find it soon you tell Chief Hinman he'll be looking for a job in another state, maybe another country."

"Sir, they're all tied up with the murder investigations—working over in Nachawinga County. You can't pull them off that just to look for a picture. They're understaffed as it is, you know, because of those budget cuts last year."

"I can and I will. You tell that son-of-a-bitching chief to stop whatever he's doing and get over here. You see what happened to those other poor bastards when they got their picture stolen. I want them to find my picture and shred it."

"Not so sure that will take care of it," Taylor says.

"Just do what I said. Oh, and get the state patrol deployed around the capital and the mansion. Then they should follow me wherever I go. Every one of them. I don't want to be out of their sight."

He gestures to Taylor, "The hot line's on my desk there. You tell Chief Hinman what I just told you." Taylor hesitates. "Pick it up!" the Guv says.

By now the Guv's ashen face has turned to a radish red and he is yelling, "Go, dammit, GO!"

Taylor reaches for the official hotline phone on the Guv's desk, upsetting a picture of the Governor's family and knocking an auto-graphed picture of the presumptive Republican presidential candidate to the floor, shattering its glass. The Guv throws his hands into the air.

Taylor, picks up the phone, "Yes, that's right, he says pull them out of Nachawinga County and get them over here."

Pause. "Correct, all of them."

Pause. "He says the County can run the investigation until you find the picture and destroy it."

Pause. "That's right, the picture, the portrait."

Pause. "No I'm not putting you on, he's standing right here beside me. You are to stay in Des Moines until…"

Pause. "Well, I'm just not going to say that to him. I said he's right here."

He turns to the Guv, "All of um? Now?"

A badly shaken Governor turns to his Chief-of-Staff, who is trying to hide the fact that he is not a little amused by what he is hearing. "Every last one of um as soon as they can get their asses over here. And don't forget the patrol."

Later, less than two blocks from the Governor's office, on the third floor of the DCI building, Charles Hinman, Chief of the State Department of Criminal Investigation, is beside himself. No, he has completely surrounded himself. He slams his iPhone onto his desk, then picks it up and checks it for damage, slams it down again, and begins pacing. He feels like an alpha lion who has just been chased off his kill by a pack of hyenas. Following him is a small covey of DCI officers who have been pulled off the investigation of what has quickly come to be called the 'pig-pen murders,' all of whom are hoping their Chief will stop moving long enough to give them a briefing or some indication of what is going on.

Charles Hinman is an impressive-looking man. A six-foot four-inch African American with a perpetual scowl, he is the epitome of "all business." He is called "Charles" by all who don't call him "Chief Hinman." God help the person who calls him "Charlie," and anyone who makes the mistake of calling him "Chuck" might fear the 9mm Glock in the concealed holster strapped under his left arm. He is straightforward, honest, fair, humorless, and extremely good at what he does. He has no tolerance for incompetence. Unfortunately, he views the man for whom he is working, his boss, as one of the most incompetent individuals he has ever encountered. Hinman is immaculately dressed in a midnight blue pin-striped suit so perfectly tailored that his sidearm in its slim holster creates no bulge at all. His shirt is white and pressed, and the half-Windsor knot of his yellow tie is without a wrinkle. A native of Los Angeles, Hinman began his career as a street cop in the LA Police Department and rose to the position of deputy chief with unprecedented speed. But he would go no higher. The current LA Chief was very good and very popular, and three years younger than Hinman. He was not likely to die or retire soon enough for Hinman to take his place, and Charles Hinman did not want to spend his career being deputy anything. So, he applied for and accepted the job as head of the Iowa Department of Criminal Investigation. And now he has been ordered to turn over the biggest investigation his department has seen since he arrived in the state, barely a year ago, to one of the smallest, most ill-equipped, and in his estimation, most ill-prepared county sheriff's offices in the Midwest. He finally stops circling the room and his men line up in an orderly group in front of him.

"Officers." There is a long pause. "I'm not exactly sure where to begin," he begins. His voice is deep, resonant, and so full of rage as to be almost visible as it cuts across the room. However, aside from the cell phone abuse, he is completely under control. "I'm sure you wonder why we are all being pulled out of Nachawinga County, off a murder case, and back to our headquarters building in Des Moines. The work you have done up to this point has been exemplary. We have positive ID of the three victims, autopsy reports—although it's difficult to call them autopsies with no more of the bodies than we had to work with—lab work, a list of suspects, particularly that ex-professor fellow Gallagher, the pigman. Probably ought to be at the top. I'm sure we could find enough on him to convict in a week. In other words, we are underway with a well-ordered, completely professional investigation. And yet we have been yanked."

Hinman walks to the window behind his desk and looks out, as his puzzled officers follow him.

"Of course, you would like to know why? Well, it seems our esteemed Guv, our boss, has lost a picture. His portrait that was hanging in his mansion alongside all the other governors that have governed this State has gone missing. And we, all of us, members of Iowa's top criminal investigating body have been ordered home. Ordered to abandon our work." The furious Hinman pauses and looks toward the ceiling.

Elizabeth Orchincross, his second in command, reluctantly breaks the silence. "To do what, sir?"

"To look for the god damn picture. We are aware, of course, that the three murder victims had portraits stolen before or after they were murdered, and the Guv might have reason to be somewhat nervous about any connection his portrait might have to these disappearances—and murders. He might even worry that he is in some danger. But he is ordering the whole highway patrol to follow him everywhere he goes. They are more than capable of protecting him. Doesn't seem to me like he is in any danger, although I do worry about those who need a patrolman or two somewhere else in the state. So, we are supposed to look behind all the furniture in the Capital and the mansion, check the trash bins, peek under the beds—jobs the custodial staff could easily take care of until the damn thing is found."

He covers his eyes with his hand and breathes out a long sigh.

"But so be it. You people in the lab, send what you've found over to Nachawinga County. And the rest of you get suspects' names and everything else we have over to the Sheriff—Kavanaugh I think his name is. After all, they discovered the bodies. They're nice enough folks over there, but I don't think they're going to have a clue what the hell to do with this case."

The next morning at the Sheriff's office, Nelda Womble, the only one who seems to have herself under control, clears the various items tacked, taped, or otherwise attached to the wall between the office and the jail cells: A pin-up-girl calendar from a local tractor repair garage, a couple of wanted posters, the 'Smoke-Free' notice, and a copy of the Miranda rights. The taped items pull chunks of paint with them as she rips them off. She tears the pin-up calendar in half, one month at a time with dramatic flair, making sure the males in the room notice before she chucks it in the trash. A framed photograph of the Guv and his lieutenant hanging on nails, she ceremoniously puts on the floor and kicks under Kavanaugh's desk.

"God, I hate looking at those jerks every time I come in here. Ain't it wonderful we need all this space to put up the victims' pictures and the suspects' and draw lines and arrows on a map and make notes? Just like I seen on Miami Vice."

Nelda is in her fifties, not tall, a couple of pounds short of plump. Hair piled on top of her head, she wears jeans and a purple Polar Tech hoodie. She doesn't quite make it to 'good looking,' but she has wonderful green eyes and a smile that gets her close. She takes care of everything in the office that the guys can't or don't know how to do. Her excitement level has broken the meter. She is talking at warp speed.

"The DCI has sent pictures, suspect lists, lab reports, that kind of stuff. Chief Hinman himself spoke to me on the phone. He was real nice. Said to just take it slow and not make no mistakes. Said they might be able to get back over here to help out before too long. We'll need to put all their stuff on the wall, and anything we come up with. Pat, where's that old bulletin board you bought about five years ago and never hung up. It should go over there by the coat rack—we'll need that. One of you get a county map in here." She looks at Bill, "Phil, you put the chairs in some kind of order." She looks at Phil, "Bill, get a broom and sweep this place up. I swear I don't know how you guys get anything done in this mess. Come to think of it, maybe you don't."

"I'm Bill," Bill says.

"I'm Phil," Phil says.

Patrick takes off his cap, looks into it, and puts it back on. "Tell me what Chief Hinman said."

"I just did," Nelda says.

"It just doesn't make any sense," he says. "Last time I saw him was when we were working on that bank robbery over to Newland. He was nice enough to us back then, but I could tell he didn't think any of us were going to make it as top-of-the-line criminal investigators. He thanked me and said, 'good job,' but he sure didn't invite me to come join his elite forces up to Des Moines. I repeat, it doesn't make any sense at all, him turning the biggest murder case of the century over to an underfunded, understaffed county sheriff's office."

He looks at his deputies. "To tell the truth, we fucked that Newland deal up pretty good until he got it straightened out.

"Don't use that word around me, Patrick. If I've told you once, I've told you a hundred …"

"OK, OK." He blows out a long breath, "Now, tell us once more what the Chief said. Bill, Phil, put out them cigarettes and get over here. You need to hear this."

Nelda sits in the Sheriff's chair and begins throwing out-of-date papers, directives, and flyers into the trash. She looks over the three men and leans back, enjoying the attention. "There are the three identified bodies."

"Well hell, we know that. We found the damn corpses, what was left of them. Just get on with it. What else? Who were they?" Kavanaugh is beginning to get a bit agitated.

"Simmer down, Pat. I'll get to it. They were Hubert Wooten, J.J. Schittman, and Donald Birdseed. All were owners of big livestock corporations that have to do with pigs and chickens—raising um, killing um, packing um, and selling um. All the bodies were found in facilities that one of their corporations owned. Hinman said he was under special orders from the Guv to suspend all his operations and put his personnel on an investigation into some missing portrait of the Guv. He said he was turning the case of the murders over to our department. What do you think about that, boys? The Nachawinga County Sheriff's Department is in complete charge of the biggest murder mystery in the state in the last hundred years. Maybe more. They might make a TV series about us." She indicates quotation marks with her fingers as she says, "Nachawinga County Vice."

By this time Phil and Bill, wide-eyed and open-mouthed, are leaning over the desk. Patrick goes on, "OK. Autopsy reports, suspects, what about forensics, lab work?"

She looks at some of the papers. "We got blood work. Schittman, no alcohol, no drugs, no poison. But he had enough animal growth hormones to turn him into Godzilla. Wooten, pretty much everything, alcohol, coke, weed, pain meds, and a higher concentration of swine antibiotics than you'd find even in a sick hog. Birdseed, an unbelievable amount of sildenafil." The three officers look puzzled. "That's Viagra.

You boys ought to know about that. They feed that to the roosters to make um frisky. I guess that gets the hens all worked up and they lay more eggs." Nelda grins at the men. "As you know, all three bodies were beat up pretty bad, but none showed wounds that would have been fatal—no bullet holes, stabs, blows to the head, or anything like that. Schittman and Wooten had just been chewed up by the pigs, Birdseed strapped in a bale of trash and soaked in chicken manure."

"Suspects?" Phil and Bill speak simultaneously.

"Almost everybody in Franklin Township," she says. "There's Marylin Jacobson, who wrote up the petition to the EPC and has threatened to lie down in front of any tractors that try to start working on those new buildings. She's the president of FART, you know. She will be happy to hear that those three got what they got. And proud to be a suspect."

"Hell," Bill says. "That sweet old woman can't hardly walk from her porch to her car, no matter how mad she is. Ain't no way could she drag them three men to their CAFOs."

"Those people in Des Moines are desperate," Nelda goes on, "They're trying to nail anybody they can who might be happy to see those three gone. Of course, that would include most of the citizens of this county."

"Who else?" Pat asks.

"Our own Shawn Gallagher. I know, he's criticized enough politicians and executives to fill a warehouse. He's sent letters to every paper in the State with pretty harsh words. I know they'd like to pin something on him. They found letters from him in the papers mentioning all three of the dead men. He called them criminals, saying they should be locked up, but no mention of killing or anything like that."

"Well that ain't enough to arrest him for murder," Bill says.

"Still," she says, "they sent down that Hinman has him down as one of the prime suspects."

"Hell, we know him," Kavanaugh says. "He's home folk, an old friend. Went to school at Tripoli before he went off to college. Turned into a big deal at State—Ph.D., professor, and all that. Then he quit his job and started making a fool of himself. He's mad as hell about what big ag is doing to the county and the whole State for that matter. Still, he's turning into a dumb joke with all those costumes and protests, and that's a damn shame. But there ain't no way he's a killer. They're desperate for suspects over there. I don't think he should even be on the list, let alone at the top. Any more?"

"It gets interesting here. There's the three wives of the dead men. A night janitor at a fancy beach condo somewhere in Florida said he read about the murders in a newspaper, the Pensacola News Journal. He said when he saw the names of the dead men, he realized that they were the same as those of three women that were staying at the condo where he was working. He claims he heard them talking about how they'd like to see their husbands snuffed out, said each one of them talked about knowing someone who would do the killing for them in return for, umm, don't know exactly how to say this." She pauses. "For, uh, you know, a little frolic in the hay. You figure it out. That was not exactly the words he used. Anyhow, these three gals are on the list. But as far as I can tell, their husbands were already dead when the janitor heard them. Anyhow, these are the suspects we need to get on the wall, and I guess get in here for questioning."

"OK. I think it was Marthy Durr and Hiram Walker who found the vehicles the victims were last seen driving," Pat says. "I guess we ought to get them in here to hear about them finding the Escalade in the crick and that Lexus in the road ditch."

"I've taken care of that," she says. "I think I see Marthy getting out of her truck right now. Hiram ought to be along directly."

Marthy Durr's age could be anywhere between sixty and ninety. She looks to be about eighty-five pounds in her bib overalls and padded Dickies jacket, and her neck appears to have been made of lengths of hemp rope. She kicks off her rubber chore boots as she enters but leaves on her black wool watch cap fringed around the bottom and sides with her steel-grey hair.

"Morning Miz Durr. Cold enough for ya?" Bill and Phil speak together.

"Got no time to talk weather. It's as bad as it gets out there and you know it. Let me do my bit and get outta here."

"Let's wait for Hiram," Patrick looks into his hat and replaces it. "It'll be good to hear what both of you saw at the same time."

"Can't do that. Ain't got no time to sit around talking. Hiram'll rattle on till sundown—ain't got nothing else to do. I got work — twenty pigs to slop, a hen house to clean out, and dinner to get ready. Ya know George don't get around so good these days, don't do much a nothing, but he can still eat. That ol man sure can put it down."

She points at Bill and pats her coat pocket in the location where she can see his cigarette pack. He shakes one out and extends it to her. She lights it with a wooden match that she has managed to find after going through five of her pockets just as Patrick begins to protest, pointing to the spot on the wall where the Smoke-Free sign was. He says nothing when he sees it's no longer there, just throws his hands in the air and shakes his head. He looks into the parking lot. "I think I see Hiram now." He takes a deep breath and blows it out as the room slowly fills with smoke. "Dammit Bill, gimme one of them cigarettes."

Hiram Walker enters the room, leaving perfect black mud footprints behind him. He stops as he notices that everyone is silent, and he is the center of attention. It's Nelda who points to his tracks. "Wouldn't nobody have trouble trailing you if by any chance anybody wanted to find you." Sheepishly, Hiram bends over, unbuckles his galoshes, and steps out of them. His heavy wool socks are mismatched—one red and one grey.

"All right, let's all get comfortable and find out what you two saw, and Phil, tape that county map up on the wall so we can start putting tacks into it." The Sheriff steps toward his desk, but Nelda is firmly planted in his seat so, after taking his hat off, scratching his head, and putting it back on again, he pulls a chair into the semi-circle the others have formed, facing his office manager. "Marthy, you start since you've got stuff to do and you want to get to it. We just need to know about that black Cadillac you found in the crick. Then you can go."

Marthy Durr, who spends most of her time alone, or with a husband who neither talks nor listens, looks around and cocks her head to one side, relishing the presence of an audience. "Well, it wasn't hardly daylight and I was going to check my traps—most of you know I still do a little trapping. Me 'n George used to trap together. Made us pretty good money back in the day when prices was good. Nowadays, hides ain't worth what the traps cost. I could make more money knitting potholders. Just wasting my damn time. But ya know—old habits. And George wakes me up every morning wanting to know if I've checked the traps. I was a little later than usual cause I had me two cups of coffee. Knew it was going to be cold and that extra cup helps sometimes. So, anyways, I started down to where there's that little dip north of the house, ya know, where the crick makes that bend to the south. It's pretty marshy down there but if I'm going to catch mink anywheres, it'll be there. That was such a pretty spot before Duffus had that manure spill. Flowers all over the place in the summer. More'n I can name. Now it's all growed over canary grass and wild parsnip. I could catch a mink near bout every day or two down there. Sometimes more. Up-stream, they ain't nothing but coon and they ain't worth what a bushel a corn is worth nowadays. Damn crick ain't nothing but a sewer anymore, anyhow. I had my waders on. I'm always glad I got my waders on down there where it's boggy. I near bout always wear um, them chore boots ain't no good if it's wet and I step in a hole or slip on the crick bank. I was out there one morning last spring in near about the same place and I stepped in a hole, musta been a badger or sumpin dug it, went in plumb to my crotch, cold as a January blizzard I can tell ya, and me with nothing but them damn chore boots on. No sir, I don't want to do that again."

Patrick looks around the room, then at Marthy, "And the black Cadillac?"

"Oh, yeah. So, I was walking, mostly wading through that mess, half-inch a ice, snow on top a that, a foot a water underneath, bout half froze. Foggy as hell. I get to my first trap and would ya believe it, I done caught me the fattest, prettiest mink ya ever seen. She was drowned, half in the water, half out, not messed up though, shiny as a brand-new dime. I was real careful getting her out. I wiped her off and put her in my coat. I was plum excited I can tell ya. I figured it was my lucky day 'n I mighta caught another cause I had a coupla more traps along that same bank. But when I got to um, they wasn't nothing. One was sprung and the bait was gone from both. So, I started on up, I'm headed west now, and all I got is one coon for the next half mile or so. He was big though, felt like he weighed forty pound. I throwed him up on the bank. I wasn't gonna carry him. I figured to come back and get him when the ground was froze hard and I could come down with my four-wheeler."

Kavanaugh breathes in deeply. "The Cadillac, Marthy?"

"I'm getting to that, Pat, just hold your mules. Anyhow, I was near to the end of my line, just a coupla more sprung traps to bait and set. One nice mink and a worthless old coon. It was foggy, it sure was. I'm sure glad I'm not trying to make a living off trapping. I bet I got fifteen coon and 'rats in my shed stretched out and scraped clean, all of um, and I won't get twenty-five dollars for the lot. I think I'll just keep the mink for myself."

"Marthy." Pat snuffs his cigarette on the side of the trash can.

"OK. OK. So, I'm ready to head back up to the house and I look over to that big pasture, up by the county timber to the west. It was foggy. Did I tell you that? Damn foggy. But I could see good enough. So, I was looking around and out there right in the middle of the

77

field, fifty yards from the crick, I seen Craven Snuggs's old green International pickup. I did. I seen it sure as I'm settin here. I couldn't believe my eyes. I seen it sure as I'm born."

"No, Marthy. Can't be," Pat says. "That truck's been gone for fifteen years or more. Burned up in Craven's shed with the house and barn and his machinery and everything else that night they burned him out. You know that."

"I know that. I do. But I know that pickup and I seen it. Green International Harvester pickup, tire on the side, boards above the bed sides so's he could haul livestock in it. Rust spot on the door, looks just like a big old wild turkey. Must be fifty, no, I'm thinking sixty years old by now and there it was biggern life. It was Craven's all right. They ain't never been another truck like that around here. I bet I seen that truck a thousand times before we lost Craven. Even rode in it a time or two. Bless his cranky old soul."

Kavanaugh starts to speak.

"You just hold on Pat—I ain't done yet. So, I starts walking towards the truck to look at it up close and make sure I wasn't just seeing things. I knew it hadn't been there the day before when I checked my traps. I do that every day. Don't want no half-caught critter to suffer no more'n it has to. I'm looking straight at that truck, didn't want to take my eyes off it, as I got closern closer. You know, the way you don't want to take your eyes off a quail or a duck when you knock it down, cause you know you'll never find it if you do. I could read the model IH L110 on the side, see where the running board was sagging a little, and I swear I seen that wild turkey on the driver's door. Not many of them trucks left. Craven was peculiar about that truck, and he kept it in good shape. Probably would'a took care of them spots come spring. Then I tripped over a damn stob or something under the snow, couldn't see it cause it was covered over, and when I looked back up the truck was gone. Plum gone. Fog was still there but the truck was gone. I looked around at the snow and they wasn't no

78

tracks, nothing but clean snow. That snow that come down a coupla days ago hadn't been touched. Crusted over a little, but not even a deer track. That's when I looked down towards the crick, thinking I might see the truck again, and I seen that Cadillac. I walked down to it, thinking somebody might be hurt or something. The door was open but there weren't nobody in it. Nobody anywheres near it. And this is what I couldn't figure out. The snow all around it was just as clean as that pasture, not a track anywheres. I was sure it musta slid off the road and down the bank to the crick, but they wasn't no skid marks nor nair a single track anywheres. That's when I figured I better call you."

Hiram Walker has been on his feet from the time Marthy started talking about the truck, unsteady, seemingly disturbed. He points a shaky finger at the woman, who seems to have finally finished talking, "I seen it too, Marthy Durr, I seen Craven's pickup. I swear to goodness, I seen it. I drove by it twice and seen that turkey rust spot too. Then I parked right behind it. I figured I was losing my mind and I wasn't going to tell nobody about it. I didn't want people to think I was old and crazy too. But I'd know that truck anywheres. Craven and me used to fill in down to the sale barn. Used to swap off driving to go over there. I bet I rode in that old truck a hundred times. I ain't gonna make a mistake about Craven's truck. Neither one of us is crazy, Marthy Durr. I seen that truck."

"Go on, Hiram." The Sheriff doesn't know if he is amused or puzzled. "Tell us about the truck, and then tell us about finding the Lexus. Far as we know you were the first one to see it, just like Marthy and the Caddy." Patrick looks at the deputies as if he is going to wink, then thinks better of it.

Hiram looks around the room. "Anybody got a smoke? I left mine at home."

They all look at Bill. He pulls the almost-flat pack out of his pocket, takes the last cigarette out, and hands it to Hiram. Bill crumples the empty package and makes a high arcing Hail Mary shot at the trash can—and misses. He hands his Bic to Hiram. Nelda scowls at him as she picks up the empty package and slam-dunks it into the trash can.

Hiram lights his cigarette. "Ya see, I'd been over to Walmart in Newland and I thought I would go on over to Onkalumpa for some lunch at that new Subway place they just opened up. You know, over to the south side a town. It looked like Sharon Church Road was pretty clear. So, I decided to take it for a shortcut. It was near about noon. They wasn't no tracks in the snow on the road so's I just took it slow. 'Bout half-way between here and there I seen a truck parked on the side of the road. My window was pretty fogged up so I couldn't see real good. I drove on by, but right after I passed I thought that looked like Craven Snuggs' old International Harvester. It took me half a mile to find a place to turn around, but when I passed by again, real slow this time, I was sure it was his truck. Nobody in it. I could see the seat covers. I seen that knob he had on the steering wheel. It was his truck all right. I had to go plumb to the blacktop to turn around again but it was still there when I got back, shure's the world. I pulled up behind it real slow. It was kinda spooky seeing that old truck. I got out of my car. Couldn't see into the bed on account of them planks all around it, so's I walked around on the ditch side to get to the front. Then I seen that white car laying in the ditch. I could tell right away it was a fancy car, and it was clean as it could be, and a door open. I figured I oughta look and see if they was anybody down there hurt. So, I walked real careful down the ditch bank, fell on my ass if you want to know the truth, but they wasn't nobody in the car. And they wasn't a single track around that car. No marks how it slid down the bank. No tracks o' nobody getting out. Snow was clean as it was the minute it come down. Then I commenced to climb out of the ditch and when I got near to the top I took one more look at the white car to see if there were any tire tracks or anything I might have missed. When I turned back around Craven's truck was gone. Didn't hear it start up or nothing. Just disappeared into the fog. I couldn't see no tracks from his truck neither. Clean as a bedsheet where it was parked. I looked up and down the road and they wasn't nothing I could see. Only tracks on that gravel road was mine. Then I called you about the car in the ditch. I wasn't going to say nothing bout Craven's truck, thought I was seeing things, but when I heard what Marthy just said I figured I wasn't plum crazy. That's all I know."

Marthy, agitated during Hiram's telling, jumps up, "Ya see Sheriff, ain't neither one of us crazy. I know old Craven's gone, but his truck's around here somewheres. They's sumpin strange going on in Nachawinga County, I'm telling you, real strange."

There is a long silence in the room, finally broken by the Sheriff. "Well, I guess that's what we needed from the two of you. Thanks for coming in," Patrick has taken his hat off again and is scratching his head. He puts it back on. "We might be in touch. I'm sure we'll have some more questions about that truck."

Marthy starts to pull her boots on. "Wish you could have seen that little marsh back then. Them little wild blue irises was thick around the edge and black-eyed-Susans all over the place. And them tall pink flowers, I forget what they called um. I'd go down and pick a bunch every morning when they was blooming. Every now and then George would bring me a little bouquet. It sure was a purty place. Then they had that damn manure spill. I tell you if I had my way I'd …."

"Thank you Marthy. You two drive real careful now." Kavanaugh gets up and moves toward the door. "Those roads are a mess. Don't want any more vehicles in the ditches. Give my best to George."

By now Marthy and Hiram have their footwear on and are walking together onto the snowy parking lot.

Patrick watches them leave. "That's sure interesting but it's not gonna help us find who killed those three."

"Well, what're we waiting for?" Nelda gets up. "Let's get this wall decorated."

Shawn Gallagher's log cabin sits in the middle of 60 acres of second-growth hardwood timber in the far southwest corner of Nachawinga County, on the northern edge of a part of Iowa where the vast, flat, boring monocultural fields of corn and beans give way to small rolling hills dotted with oak savannahs, plum thickets, and cedar groves. Shawn's timber is fronted by 12 acres of restored prairie. At one end of the property is a pristine half-acre native plant remnant which Shawn reckons hasn't changed much since pre-settlement time. It is Friday afternoon. A light snow is falling.

No other habitations are visible from the cabin or the porch, and at night only a few lights can be seen in winter; none in summer when the leaves are on the trees. If there is an area in the county, or the state for that matter, where a person can almost feel they are in a wilderness, it is here. His land can only be reached from the south by a mile-and-a-quarter of poorly maintained level-B road that is barely navigable in dry, snow-free weather only, and from the north by a farm lane between two fields. The best winter access is the lane. It is along this lane that Shawn can hear a vehicle struggling to make some headway through a couple of inches of half-frozen snow. When he sees it is a Chevrolet Volt, he mutters to himself, "Who the hell is dumb enough to try to navigate a farm lane in the snow with that thing?"

Shawn is in no mood for visitors, particularly since it is likely that the car will get stuck, and he will have to tow it back to the county road. He has spent most of the afternoon walking around his cabin asking himself, "What the hell are you thinking?" At least at State, he had a platform—a pulpit. People listened to him. What he said carried some weight. The problem was that when he spoke about what he was learning in his research about the harm that was being done to the people and the land of his State by giant meat production operations, only the choir was listening. The students and some of the faculty, particularly the younger ones, agreed with him—cheered him on. What he really wanted was for his message to reach into the corporate board rooms, the offices of the top administrators of his own university, the State House. But in those places, there was a barrier that he couldn't penetrate. Although most of the corporate executives lived out of state, with their money they kept their politicians in office and funded the research they wanted in the University labs. They didn't want to hear anything negative. Threats to rural health, destruction of property values, creeks becoming sewers, Iowa hog shit in the Gulf of Mexico—no problem. As long as the profits were there—full speed ahead. Shawn couldn't stop thinking of a line from a Guy Clark song, 'I'm OK, you're OK if the check's OK.' It was driving him nuts.

He thought he would just drop out like his friend, mentor, and hero Morris Hamilton had done. To hell with it. He could tend his prairie, his timber. God knows there was plenty to be done there—plenty to occupy his time. He could eat off the land: wild asparagus and morels in the spring, wild mushrooms all summer long. He could hunt turkeys, pheasants, deer in the winter and pay them back by improving their habitat. Just lay back and let the world go by. But no, he couldn't do that. He had to continue to protest what he saw going on, to shout out, to scream. But he was beginning to have real doubts about the way he was going about it. The pigman? This wasn't getting him anywhere. He was just making a fool of himself—a laughingstock. He couldn't get the image of Amie Green out of his mind, running after him in the snow after he broke up the EPC meeting. What was she shouting? Probably, "You idiot!" Amie Green. She had become a good friend since she graduated, and he quit. "Friend" is not exactly what he would wish to call Amie, but so be it. It is what it is. At least she still seems to believe in him—to believe in his message. But he's pretty sure she also thinks he is going about it the wrong way; thinks he is doing himself more harm than good.

The small blue sedan has made it to the side of Shawn's Jeep and stops. The driver slogs through the snow to the front door. He knocks. Shawn opens the door. Tim Taylor, dress shoes soaking wet and snow on the shoulders of his suit coat, looks him in the eye and says, "What the hell are you thinking?"

"Jeez, Tim, what're you doing in the boondocks? I haven't seen you in months and you drive all the way out here in that little toy vehicle of yours just to speak to me that way." Shawn moves away from the door and motions Tim in. "Oh well, come on out of the weather. You can stand by the fire and dry out that upwardly-mobile-grooming-yourself-for-Attorney-General suit you got on. And give me a better greeting. Like maybe 'Good to see you, Bud, or, you've lost a little weight, you look better than you did when we were room-mates at State.' Or something like that. Anyhow, aren't you afraid some of those not-so-grand-old-party cronies of yours will see you talking to the big troublemaker and put you on a black-list or whatever it is they do."

"Bug off, Shawn. You know as well as I that I'm just doing what I think I need to do to be a viable AG candidate so that someday, maybe, I can accomplish some of the things that you just go around yelling and screaming about."

"Point taken," Shawn says.

"But I didn't come here to talk about me or argue about different paths to the mountain top. I came here to tell you that you might finally be in serious trouble. Maybe better wording would be deep shit."

"For what, going to an open public meeting in a pig suit?"

"Sit down, Shawn." Tim sits in a straight chair, Shawn flops onto his broken-down sofa. Tim continues, "I could get my ass kicked out of my job for telling you this. What do you know about the murders?"

"What murders?"

"What d'ya mean, 'what murders?' Don't play dumb. You know what I'm talking about."

"Haven't a clue."

"Good Lord, you really have dropped out, haven't you?" Tim looks around the room. "No TV. No newspapers. Don't you even listen to NPR anymore?"

"Where are we going with this, Tim?"

The conversation is interrupted by the sound, the quiet sound, of a red Prius trying to stay in the Volt's snow tracks toward the cabin.

Shawn, watching out the window as the driver manages to maneuver the car so that it is pointing in the direction from which it came says, "Well, what do you know, looks like we're having a meeting of the eco-car owners club. I don't suppose that old Jeep of mine will pass muster."

When Shawn sees Amie Green step out of the Toyota, his knees get a little wobbly, as they always have since that first day in his lab. He has seen her since, they have met for coffee, gone on hikes, always with other people around, but she's never come to his cabin—except in his dreams. He feels like he is going to have to sit down again. He suddenly wishes he could make Tim disappear. "Amie Green. What in the world is she doing out here? How did she even know how to get here?"

"I told her how to get here and I asked her to meet me. She's here for the same reason I am, Shawn."

Amie slogs up the porch steps. Shawn opens the door, and she looks him in the eye. "What the hell are you thinking?"

Shawn, regaining his composure, somewhat, sighs. "You guys need to get a new playwright, somebody who can add a little variety to your script. Anyway, you stole that line from me."

Tim looks over at Amie who has taken a seat at the table and begins, "OK, Professor Gallagher, late star of the State University

Department of Animal Studies, or whatever they call it, who no longer pays any attention to what's going on in the world around him. Who from time to time appears and puts on solo guerrilla theatre performances. Let us fill you in. It seems that the chief executive officers of the three biggest animal factory corporations operating in the Midwest have turned up dead—not, I repeat not, from natural causes. It seems that these three big shots have met a bloody, stinking end by some kind of foul means. That means they appear to have been murdered." He glances at Amie. "Am I being too dramatic?" She shakes her head. "To be specific, we are talking Hubert Wooten of North Carolina's Compassionate Family Farms, Donald Birdseed of Freebird Poultry, and your old friend J.J. Schittman of…"

"No kidding," Shawn interrupts. "Him, too? Awesome."

"Let him finish," Amie says.

"Their bodies have been found in facilities owned by their companies in Nachawinga County—all of them having suffered various forms of abuse—Wooten and Schittman half-eaten by swine, and Birdseed floating in a pool of chicken manure. To add to the mystery, portraits of all three men have gone missing from their palatial homes and offices in Colorado, Carolina, and Ames, and they have turned up alongside the gruesome corpses. Also, for some reason, a portrait of my esteemed boss, the Guv of our state, has disappeared from his mansion. This has gotten him freaked out to a level that has almost blasted the roof off the Capitol."

"Wow!" Shawn is excited. "It gets better and better."

"Get serious, Shawn." Amie's concern is showing. "You've written open letters to all three of these men, for god's sake, and the Guv, too, and sent them to newspapers all over the State. These might not have been specifically threatening, but they've been close. Maybe you didn't say straight out that you were going to murder them, but you implied it wouldn't be a bad idea if they, and their enterprises, were no longer with us. We would have been here yesterday, but we thought you knew about it and would come in to see us."

"Of course," Tim takes over, "as soon as they got word of the bodies, the DCI was all over Nachawinga County like ants on a picnic donut, and then it really gets strange. When the business of the missing portraits comes out, the Guv, as you might imagine, goes all weird. He is now totally paranoid and has called the DCI agents off the case. He wants them, every one of them, to spend all their time looking for his missing portrait and has ordered Charles Hinman—he's the Department chief—to turn the investigation over to the County Sheriff's office. Of course, Chief Hinman has gone bonkers as well. Oh, and by the way, the Guv has also ordered the State Patrol to protect him day and night, wherever he might be. I think this leaves exactly two officers in the whole state actually on patrol duty."

"Tim told me yesterday that you were on the suspect list," Amie says. "I told him we ought to get out here and talk to you. It was in the papers this morning about the case now being in the Sheriff's hands."

"I know the Sheriff," Shawn butts in. "Pat Kavanaugh. We went to school together. He was a couple of years ahead of me, but he showed me how to play shortstop. He's a good sheriff but he's underfunded, underequipped, and understaffed. He doesn't have nearly what he needs to handle a situation like this."

Tim holds up his hand, "OK, but shut up and let me go on. So, Chief Hinman, and make no mistake, he's a tough SOB, wants to find someone quick to hang this on so he can calm the Guv down and get his department and his life back to normal. Who do you think he has decided to go after?"

"I'm sure you're going to tell me," Shawn grins.

Tim speaks slowly for effect. "At the top of his list is someone who dresses up like a giant pig and goes around disrupting meetings and who writes threatening letters to corporate executives and politicians. The DCI has been hoping to pin something on you ever since you left State and they think this might just be their chance, although they are seriously frustrated that it's a county sheriff's department they have to depend on to do the dirty work. They think Professor Gallagher has finally stepped over the line and they're chomping at the bit to nail him."

Tim pauses to make sure Shawn is now taking him seriously. Amie continues, "This is no joke, Shawn. Have you stepped over the line? Please tell me you haven't."

"C'mon, you two. You don't really, you don't think—I haven't been out of these woods for weeks, except for that stupid stunt I pulled at the EPC meeting. Colorado and North Carolina? I can't even afford a bus ticket to those places, let alone a plane ride. How in the world could I pull that off? Sounds more like some big conspiracy—maybe an eco-terrorist group or some rival corporations."

"Do you know anything, anything at all about it? Any clue?" Amie asks.

"I didn't even know it had happened until you guys told me. So that's why Schittfink wasn't at the meeting. I sure did want to put that bag of guts in his lap."

"I believe you, Shawn." Amie is partly relieved. "I never thought you were involved, but I had to come here with Tim to hear you say it."

"I believe you, too," Tim says, "but we have to make sure you're covered. I think we need to go to Tripoli and see where Sheriff Kavanaugh is with this and make sure you don't have to go hide in your woods. I don't think they've got anything on you that they can use for a warrant. But if they can find something they will get one in a minute."

Tim gets up from his chair.

"By the way, where'd you get that old pickup that's parked outside? Looks like it has "International" on the back and a big rust spot or something on the door that looks like a big bird. Never heard of an International pickup. Looks like it's older than your Jeep. You opening up a retirement home for old vehicles?"

Shawn looks out the window, "Where? I didn't see anything when you drove up."

"Right out there where we parked our cars." They are all by the window now, staring into the falling snow. "What the—it was there when I got out…"

"I saw it, too. I saw it when I drove in," Amie breaks in.

"Old International pickup?" Shawn rubs his eyes and peers through the frosted window. "There hasn't been one of those around here for—gosh, I'm not sure how long. They don't even make them anymore."

He looks out the window with the others.

"Well, it's not there now. I think I better make us some coffee before I pull you two out of the slush. Maybe then you won't be seeing old trucks or anything else through the snow."

Coffee finished, the three, two pushing and one at the wheel, work at maneuvering Tim's Volt so it is turned toward the county road.

Tim sticks his head out the window. "I'll text you guys tonight when I check my schedule. We should get over to Tripoli as soon as we can." Amie and Shawn lean into the Volt and begin to push, as Tim accelerates much too quickly and sprays them both from head to foot with cold, half-melted slush. Their loud laughter follows Tim down the lane as he fishtails toward the gravel road.

Back in the cabin, they are still laughing, two wet, mud-spattered people in the almost dark. Shawn hands Amie a towel and turns on a lamp. Drying off, they are having a hard time looking away from each other—Amie, trying not to breathe too hard, and Shawn, almost unable to breathe at all—both remembering that day, almost five years earlier, in a lab on the third floor of Baker Hall. As it did then, time stands still, until Shawn finally breaks the silence.

"I can fix us some supper. I think I can come up with something worth eating."

"Oh, hell." Amie is deeply disappointed, not to say devastated. "I've got to get back. One of my colleagues is bringing salad to my apartment and we're going over lesson plans. Doesn't that sound like big fun?"

Amie's mind is running in overdrive. *Maybe I should just not go back. Maybe I should not show up at school tomorrow. Maybe I should just move in here and stay in this cabin in these woods with this man I'm looking at from now on. Maybe I should just tell him that's what I want more than anything and there is nothing he can do to get rid of me.*

Shawn, as disappointed as Amie, "Maybe another time?"

"I'd like that," Amie says.

Silence, again, until Shawn breaks it. "You're still muddy. I'll get you something dry." He goes into his bedroom.

"Don't bother, I'm OK." She speaks so softly that Shawn doesn't hear her, or he doesn't want to.

Shawn comes out with a red and black flannel lumberjack shirt and hands it to her. "You can put it on in there."

In the bedroom, she looks at Shawn's unmade bed. She has a strong inclination to climb into it, but instead, she spreads the wrinkles out of the sheets. She holds the shirt, buries her face in it, and breathes deeply. It smells like smoke. She takes off her wet blouse and puts the shirt on. Then she pauses, takes the shirt off, takes her bra off, and puts the shirt back on so it can touch as much of her skin as possible. She wraps it around her body and hugs herself with it. It's old and soft. Then she buttons the shirt, hides her bra in her wet blouse, and joins Shawn by the fire. The shirt looks like a nightgown on her. Amie takes her puffy down jacket off the hook by the door. Her voice sounds a little sad when she says, "Thanks for the shirt. I'll bring it along tomorrow." Then, almost an afterthought, "And, by the way, we need to get you off the suspect list."

"I'll come out to your car in case you need a shove," Shawn says. "I'm not going to get any wetter. You look better than I ever did in that old shirt"

The temperature has dropped at least five degrees and the slush crunches as they walk toward the Prius. Amie opens the door and Shawn holds out his hand. She takes it, and after a few seconds, says, "Thanks again," trying not to give in to her desire not to let his hand loose. She skillfully gets her car moving toward the county road. Shawn watches the two-track long after the taillights' red eyes are closed in the twilight by falling snow.

The cabin has never seemed so empty as Shawn walks into his bedroom. *She was here*, he thinks. *Maybe she touched my bed. God, did it have to be such a mess? She took off her shirt—in my bedroom. I wish I was that shirt I gave her.* He blows out a long sigh and shakes his head to clear it. He will sleep well, or not at all. His bed will never feel the same again.

Saturday morning and the Nachawinga County Sheriff's department remains at a high level of excitement, the likes of which have probably not been seen since the old building was opened. Although there are only four people in the office, the impression they create is of a litter of puppies that have just discovered a cat in the room. Nelda, who at the moment is trying to impose some kind of order, is still tacking and retacking pictures, autopsy reports, notes, and all sorts of other stuff to the wall. She has also replaced the Smoke-Free Environment notice but immediately asked Bill for a cigarette, which is now lit and hanging from her lips. She snaps at Phil, "No, Bill. I said bring me the red tacks. The yellow ones are for the lots that ain't been built yet."

"I'm Phil," Phil says.

"OK. Phil." She answers. She looks at Bill. "Phil, you get that magic marker and connect the tacks where people think they saw that truck."

"I'm Bill," Bill says.

"OK, OK. Whatever! You just gonna sit there, Pat? You are Pat, ain't ya? Get that red marker and put names under the suspects' pictures. You shoulda done that yesterday. Get the names under the dead body pictures, too."

Pat finds the marker in the desk drawer.

"I guess I should say remains. God, they look awful. Worse than them corpses in pictures after a big gunfight out West." She squints at the pictures. "Ain't much left of that first one, not much more of the next."

"We did the best we could with Wooten," Pat starts writing names and details under the corpses' photos. "Had to dig through that dump truck of Van Gorp's for two hours to come up with all his pieces, well—most of um anyway. Laid um out on a tarp and put um together like a jigsaw puzzle to get those pictures. That was a lot of fun." He finishes with Wooten and moves to Schittman's picture. "This one was just chewed on pretty bad." He points to Birdseed. "He was all there, but he looked like one of those rubber punching clowns, blown up and then mashed flat."

Finally, Nelda appears to be pleased with their progress on the wall. "OK, boys, look up." She picks up a ruler and points at the large county map that takes up much of the wall. "This is the way it's supposed to be done, the way they do it on every cop show I've ever seen on TV. We got the map up, pictures posted, coupla newspaper articles, everything we need." She nods towards the map. "Here's Holmgren's, where we found most of that North Carolina guy and his portrait. That's the red tack. The other lots he controlled in Franklin Township are red, too. The yellow ones are where he's got permits to build more, although they're under protest with the Environmental Protection Committee. The black tacks are where the folks up in Franklin live, and their school, and the church. You can see quite a few folks are getting stunk out of their comfort zone and might like to see that Wooten fellow dead."

"You're right about them wanting him dead," Phil speaks up, "but I know them folks. They ain't the kind that'd go around killing people. Anyways, how could they get all over the country stealing them pictures? Most of um couldn't afford the gas it would take to get to Omaha."

"I know there ain't anybody up there who's murdered anybody," Pat says, "but we got to get it all on the wall. That's the way it's done. If those DCI fellows ever do come here and see we've left some of the suspects off the map, they'll think we're a bunch of Minnesotans."

Chuckles around the room. Nelda goes on to show that she has pinned other tacks for the confinements, where the other two bodies were found. She has tacks for the people and businesses that might be hurt by the confinements and might want to see those responsible come to harm. She has also has tacks for all the other CAFOs in the county.

Bill, looking at the concentration of tacks, blows a smoke ring toward the ceiling. "It's a wonder they's room for any other thing in this county except them damn hog lots."

Kavanaugh looks at the pictures fastened beside the map. "These are the three wives, huh? Where'd you get their pictures, Nelda?"

"You ever heard of the internet, Pat?" She cocks her head toward him with a snide smile. "They'll be in Des Moines tomorrow to give the final ID on the bodies, although there's not much for um to ID. Then they'll come over here for us to question um."

Bill looks at the three women. "They look like they got a few miles on um, but they still look pretty hot." He elbows his brother in the ribs.

"Yeah, I wouldn't mind kicking their tires." Phil answers.

They both break into silly giggles until Nelda stares them down. She looks at Kavanaugh. "Where the hell did you ever pick up these dumb nuts, Pat?"

Without answering, he looks at the picture of a man in a pig suit. "There's Shawn in that stupid costume. Don't any of us think he had anything to do with these murders."

"God, no," Nelda says, "But we gotta have his picture on the wall just the same. He's the DCI's primo suspect. They're scraping the bottom of the barrel if ya ask me, but I think that guy Hinman has it in for Shawn, wants us to pin anything he can come up with on him. Shawn has just been a flat-out nuisance to those boys ever since he quit up at State, writing letters, breaking up meetings, and all. There's nothing they'd like better than to nail him to the jailhouse floor." She points to the last picture. "And finally, that's Marylyn Jacobson. Sweet old Marylyn. I know she organized that Franklin Township committee that's been raising a ruckus about those new CAFOs, and she's threatened to lie down in front of the next dozer that comes into the community and bury some land mines if she has to, to keep the new confinements from being built. We all know she's eighty years old if she's a day. Having her on the wall is a joke, but they sent her name and picture, so it's got to go up, too."

"That's not much to go on, is it?" Pat takes off his cap and scratches his head, then puts it on again. "I don't think we are anywhere close to having an idea of who might have done this or how it was done. This thing keeps getting curiouser and curiouser. It's possible somebody around here killed those three sons a…I mean those three big shots. But how in the hell could they get all those portraits from all over the country and put them in hog and chicken houses in our county all on the same night, and get the one of the Governor out of his mansion without being seen? They've got security cameras all over that place. It just don't make sense." He looks back at the wall. "Are those purple tacks what I think they are, Nelda?"

"They are," Nelda says as she points her yardstick at one of the purple pins. "That's where people saw, or at least think they saw Craven Snuggs's old International pickup. They've all come in here since yesterday. Now I don't know how there could be any connection, but you know when he was alive, Craven hated those big CAFOs more than anybody else in the county. He was doing anything he could to stop um from coming to Nachawinga when nobody else was paying any mind, and that's why folks say he got burned out. But nobody ever proved anything. You remember, Pat, how Sheriff Townsend was in the pocket of the big ag guys? He wouldn't even investigate, said it was an accident, cold case. I sure am glad you beat out that son-of-a-bitch." Nelda walks to the desk and looks into a box filled with purple tacks. She shakes it. "Now they're a bunch more people say they've seen Craven's truck. Of course, there was Marthy and Hiram. But Roy Voght said he saw it pulling out of Duffas' parking lot, Greg Johnson said he saw it at Holmgren's, and Janet Carl said she saw it parked in front of the Birdseed chicken factory. Oren Van Zee said he saw it out there where they burned Craven's homestead down. That old truck's showing up all over the place and each time it's some place that has something to do with Craven or the dead men. I guess you could put that down to people just seeing things. Power of suggestion isn't that what they call it? But all those folks swore they seen that truck."

"And it don't leave any tracks or anything," Patrick adds, "Just disappears into the fog. I don't know what you call it, but if you want my opinion, I think those people who claim they've seen that truck have just gone flat crazy. Course everybody in the county's talking about it now. Maybe it's just that nobody wants to get left out."

The phone on Kavanaugh's desk rings. Both Pat and Nelda go for it—Patrick wins. He picks up the receiver. "Sheriff Kavanaugh. What—who? Twenty minutes?" There is a pause as Patrick listens. Then he speaks. "We do want to talk to you. You bet. We'll be waiting for you."

They all look at Patrick. He takes his hat off. He looks into it for a long moment, smooths his hair back, and puts his hat back on, enjoying the suspense. Finally, he says, "I reckon that call's gonna save us a little trouble. Shawn Gallagher is on his way over here—be here in twenty minutes. In the meantime, we got Cletus Grundler and Dora Belle Doty waiting in the front room swearing they saw Craven's pickup, too. Before long, there'll be a line all the way around the building of folks claiming they've seen that truck. We better get those two in here and see what they've got to say. Maybe we can get it done before Shawn comes.

Twenty minutes later Shawn's Jeep pulls into the gravel parking lot in front of the Sheriff's Department and does its little shaking and burping routine before it farts its smoke ring and dies. Amie, Shawn, and Tim pile out of the front and only seat and walk through the front room into the office. The Sheriff smiles and extends his hand. "Been a spell, Shawn. You ought to get over here and see your old buddies every once and a while. It's not like your shack's that far away." He turns to his cohorts. "I believe you all know Shawn Gallagher."

"Never met you, Shawn," Bill says, "But I've heard of you and seen you around. Bill Dill. This is my brother, Phil."

Nelda beams a big smile at Shawn, "Don't think I've seen you since you was in high school." Her eyes sparkle. "I used to love to watch you play ball."

Shawn, slightly embarrassed, turns to his friends. "This is Amie Greene. She was a student of mine at State. You may have read about her work at Cohn Middle School in Des Moines. And Tim Taylor. Believe it or not, he's the Chief of Staff of our esteemed Guv. In spite of that, he's not such a bad guy. These two seem to think I need some help getting myself out of a bad spot." Amie smiles and nods at everyone, Tim shakes hands all around.

Pat goes on, "Shawn Gallagher, pride of Nachawinga County. First graduate of Tripoli High to get a Ph.D. Star shortstop at State—of course, I taught him everything he knows about baseball. Brilliant professor and researcher in the University's Animal Studies Department, who gave it all up to go live in the woods in the most deserted part of our county and come out from time to time to get himself into trouble. What the hell are you thinking?"

"With all due respect to you, Sheriff Kavanaugh," Shawn replies with not a little irony, "I'm getting a bit tired of hearing that question to which, quite frankly, I have no answer."

Pat takes his hat off and puts it right back on. He looks at each of the newcomers in turn, then back at Shawn. "We were going to have to call you in here for questioning. Looks like you've saved us the trouble. You may or may not know you are a huge suspect in these murders, at least up there in Des Moines." He pauses. His expression is sterner. "I'm gonna put it to you straight, Shawn, because those people at the DCI sure would like to lay it all on you, wrap this case up, and go back to their normal routines. Did you have anything to do with the murder of those big-shot executives and dumping them in the shit that they've been spreading all over our county? Or do you know anything about it? We both know I got no evidence to use to issue a warrant for your arrest but if I come up with a shred…"

"You're the second person that's asked me that in the last twenty-four hours," Shawn interrupts, "and the answer is the same as before. Much as I would have liked to, no, I did not. I didn't even know anyone was murdered until Tim told me about it yesterday. I must say, however, that I approve of the murderer's choice of victims. Hell, the only time I've been away from my woods in the last two weeks was my stupid little trip to the EPC meeting."

Patrick takes a deep breath. "OK, we're going to hold it at that for now. I sure hope that takes care of it. Don't think any of us suspect you did anything wrong. We may still have trouble with Hinman, but up to this point, I don't think we have anything we can legally hold you on. I don't believe you'd a walked in here this morning if we did. And after all, we are in charge of this investigation, at least for now." He looks around at the rest of his department to make sure they agree, then smiles, and breathes a sigh of relief. He looks up at the wall. "I don't think a good Irishman would be involved in such terrible deeds. Nelda, we can cross his picture out, at least for now. He looks stupid in that silly outfit anyway. Of course, Shawn, it wouldn't be a bad thing for you if you would hang around the county until we can find out who the guilty party, or parties, is."

The three newcomers turn their attention to the wall. "Looks like there are not many suspects left," Amie says.

"They're getting pretty scarce," Patrick agrees. "Tell the truth, if you look at those four faces we got left up there, there ain't a real suspect among um." He then begins to explain the other stuff tacked to the wall.

Amie looks closely at the map, "What are those purple tacks?

Nelda has been quiet as long as she can stand it. "That's the weird thing that's been happening. That's where people claim they saw an old pickup truck, belonged to a man named Craven Snuggs. But Mr. Snuggs has been dead for over 15 years. Every place they've seen it has something to do with finding the bodies or something to do with the murders—or with Craven. He had this old green International pickup. Wasn't any other like it in the county as far as anybody can remember. And people keep coming in here saying they've seen it. We need to put two more tacks in, boys, for those last two that we talked to."

"Wait a minute." Tim looks at Amie. "Amie and I saw an old green truck yesterday afternoon at Shawn's cabin. It had International on the back and a big rust spot on the door, but when I tried to show it to Shawn, it was gone. Disappeared. Without a trace—or a track in the snow either. We both are sure we saw it, though. Shawn said he thought we were seeing things in the snowmelt."

"I did think that," Shawn says. "The strange thing is, neither one of them has ever heard of Craven Snuggs or his pickup as far as I know. But they described it perfectly, just as I remembered it. I didn't even make a connection with Craven, but now that I think of it, their description was spot on."

"Whoa here," Patrick interrupts Shawn. "You two saw a green pickup, International on the tailgate, with a big ol' rust spot on the driver's door?" Tim and Amie nod. Pat continues, "Did that rust look kind of like a wild turkey gobbler?"

"I'm not sure what a wild turkey gobbler looks like," Tim says, "but it did look like some kind of big bird."

"A wild turkey, just like the whiskey bottle label," Amie fills in for him, "that's what it looked like."

Pat, at a loss for words, takes his hat off and scratches his head for a long time before he puts it back on. He looks at Shawn. "What the hell was that truck doing at your place? And why the hell did they see it? There ain't no power of suggestion suggesting anything to them."

"I didn't see it, Pat." Shawn answers. "Does this mean you believe they saw the truck? Because I'm not sure. Sounds like you're getting just as goofy as all those other people, including Tim and Amie."

"We don't know what the fuck to think," Bill says, and Phil nods in agreement.

Nelda shakes her ruler at him. "Watch your language, Phil."

"I'm Bill," Bill says.

Nelda grimaces, "Whatever."

There is a long pause in the conversation. Amie looks at Shawn and breaks the silence. "Who was this Craven Snuggs everybody's talking about? The name is familiar. Seems like you mentioned him to me before all this happened. As I remember, you liked him a lot, didn't you?

Shawn narrows his eyes, thinks for a moment. "Craven? Yes, I did, a lot. He was kind of a legend around the county and was a big influence on me. Everyone knew of him when he was alive, but I don't think anyone really knew him. He was a throwback. If he needed something from the feed store or at Dad's hardware store downtown, he would trade for it. He said he didn't want to keep any money around. Yeah, there used to be a real hardware store in Tripoli,

Gallagher's Hardware, 'Locally Owned' up over the door. There was a wonderful little grocery, too, and two cafes. Anyhow, we usually had three or four of his chickens all cut up and wrapped in our freezer. I can remember once he brought a whole lamb he had butchered to exchange for something from the store. Not sure what it was, but it must have been pretty expensive."

"His great grandparents built the big house they lived in, back further than anybody can remember," Pat cuts in, "Was one of the oldest in the county. Word is they traded their homestead in North Dakota for eighty acres in north Nachawinga. They always said that the land around here was so rich and black, eighty was all they needed. Craven worked on the farm till he got drafted and did a spell in the service. Korea maybe. He stayed away for a while after he got discharged, nobody knew where. People thought maybe some city, maybe went to school, maybe got married, but nobody knew for sure. People kinda forgot him, didn't think he'd come back. Then one day he drove back here in that International pickup towing a big saddle horse in a homemade horse trailer. Told people he'd been around the world and never seen anyplace he loved like the Snuggs' eighty acres in Nachawinga.

"He didn't have any brothers or sisters and his Mom and Dad were getting too old to keep the place up so he just took up where they'd left off and kept the farm going. Said that eighty was more than enough for them, and it was. Course those 5000-acre farmers wouldn't call what they did farming. He hadn't been back more than a coupla years when that bad flu came through Tripoli. Took out a lot of people, and Craven's parents were among um, but he stayed and kept on farming those eighty acres by himself. It wasn't too long after that Craven started getting riled up."

"He sure was a nice man." Nelda picks up the story. "Always willing to help out anyone who needed it. I remember when we had that big ice storm back in—I never can remember dates. Maybe twenty years ago? Anyway, he came into town with that old bow saw of his and started cutting up big limbs so people could get them off their roofs. Didn't wait to be asked. If he saw a limb that needed to come down, he would just start cutting. Everyone else had chain saws, but he was about as fast with that bow saw as they were with their chains. Said he didn't have anything fallen at his place and he wanted to help out. Next morning, somebody drove by that ol house and he was up on his roof cutting up a big box-elder limb that had come down on it. He just had to help other people first."

Bill says, "He raised sweet corn he'd sell, or give away, out of that pickup. Best sweet corn in the state, I'm thinking. All kinds of other stuff: tomatoes, squash, strawberries. Park that pickup in front of the courthouse full of vegetables on Saturday morning and sell um to them that had money and give um away to them that didn't. It'd be gone in two hours."

"Had all kinds of livestock," Phil puts in. "Raised his hogs in them little A-frame shelters. In the spring they'd be about twenty of um on that hillside east of his house, and they'd be a sow an a litter in each one. It was like a neighborhood. Each house would have a bunch of littluns bouncing around in the front yard an the fat ol momma layin there watching um."

"Remember them big ol longhorn cows he had?" Pat asks around. "Looked mean as hell, but Craven would just walk up and put his arm around their necks and feed um a ear of corn out of his hand."

"And those beautiful horses," Shawn goes on. "Two Clydesdales his mom and dad had farmed with for years, looked like they should be pulling the Budweiser wagon. He'd use them for all kinds of work, said they'd pull more than his tractor would. Then there was that tall, gaited horse. The one he brought with him when he came back from the army. He would ride it around the back roads and in the woods. But things changed with him when big ag started taking over everything."

"You bet," Pat says. "He was a nice, kind, and generous man, but you wouldn't have wanted to get on his bad side."

"You're right there, Pat," Shawn says. He hated those changes as much as I do now. He would go to auctions and watch the big guys swallow up all the little farms. He'd talk to anyone who would listen about what he saw happening. That's where I got to know him. I would go out to his farm just to see those longhorns and his draft horses, and he would talk to me. 'Look over there,' he'd say. 'See them fields? A whole section, half beans, and half corn, and nothing else. Farmed by one man, owned by somebody lives out of state. And them damn tractors and combines they use, hell, they ain't room enough to turn one of them around on my farm and they are tearing up our gravel roads. They're taking out the waterways and fence rows and filling the fields with poison. And mark my word, them corporations are going to ruin the livestock business and all of farming for the small farmer.' He'd go on and on if he could find anybody who would pay attention. But no matter how much he talked against it, the machinery kept getting bigger, and more marginal land kept going under the plow. 'No matter about tomorrow if a dollar can be made today,' he would say. Then came the CAFOs and that was the last straw for Craven. That was about the time I went away to State. You were in town then, Pat."

"Yup," Pat says. "Nobody here paid much attention when the first CAFOs went up. They were pretty small, not much bigger than the old hog houses. Pretty isolated. There weren't any buyers around anymore, so farmers were happy to raise hogs on contract. They didn't mind so much that the control and most of the money was going over to the big guys, out of the county, out of the state. At least it was helping them keep their heads above water. But Craven saw what was going on and what was coming, and he started getting rough. He disrupted supervisors' meetings, petitioned against the building permits, stopped big machinery on county roads, and demanded that it should be weighed before they could move on. Rumor had it that he sugared the gas tanks on some of them big rigs. Then one day all the hogs in two of the lots got out. They were running all over the countryside—free pork for anybody with a good rifle. It was a shooting gallery for a couple of weeks. That first day Craven was watching and laughing his head off. 'Get yourself a real hog,' he yelled at the shooters, 'them things ain't fit to eat.' Of course, they blamed all that on Craven."

"And was that when the fire happened?" Amie asks.

"That's right. I was a volunteer fireman back then. It was in the fall, dry as a box o' matches. We got a call about dark there was a fire out to Craven's place. We got there soon as we could, but it was too late. Whole farm was lit up like a football field on homecoming night. I remember when we got out of the fire truck, it was so damn hot we couldn't get anywhere near that house. No way we could get water on it. But there was Craven standing right out in front of the house, yelling. The crowd was real big and him shouting at um, like some tent preacher up on his pulpit, telling them they was gonna lose their farms, their homes, their whole county. Bout then the flames jumped to the sheds and then the barn. I don't know how he wasn't burnt to a cinder already, close as he was. It looked like he was gonna say something else, but them horses started screeching and that stopped him. It was awful. I ain't heard such a horrid sound in my life, except in my nightmares. Sounded like there were twenty of um in there. He shook his fist at the crowd one more time and held his hands up like he was praying for everyone. Then he ran into the barn. In a few seconds, a bunch of goats ran out and then the two Clydesdales tore out the front. They ran on into Durr's hayfield about a quarter-mile away, stopped, and started grazing. Finally, that big, gaited horse busted out tall and proud as a prince and trotted toward the timber like nothing was happening. Just about the time that horse was clear, the whole barn roof caved in." He clears his throat. "That was the last time anybody saw Craven Snuggs."

No one speaks for a minute. Finally, Amie almost whispers, "What did they find when the fire was out? Did they find his remains?"

"It was hot for a long time," Patrick responds. "Hottest fire I've ever seen, almost like it had tapped into hell. Nobody could go near it for three, four days. When we did get to it, there wasn't much left. Melted tools and appliances. What little farm equipment he used was all burnt up too. Couldn't hardly make out what any of it was. Folks started going around with their metal detectors, thinking there might be something in there that was worth digging out. Didn't find much. Bunch a nuts and bolts was about all."

"Nothing left of Craven?" Amie persists.

"It was as hot in there as one of them cremating places. There wasn't nothing left but ashes. Ashes blowing all over the county. Some claimed they saw his horse from time to time, but nobody got close to it or could catch it."

"And his truck," she says.

They all look at each other. "Nope," Patrick says. "I don't think anybody ever found a sign of it." He pauses. "Folks had an idea who started that fire, but Sheriff Townsend said it was an accident. Those two boys, the two we're pretty sure did it, are dead now, too. They died rough. One of um went through the ice with a ice fishing shed on Emerald Lake."

"I think he was one a them Snook boys," Phil says.

"Yep." Pat Says. "The other one broke his neck when he fell out of a deer stand,"

"That's right. That'n was Jake Crawford," Bill says.

"Both on the same day," Pat says. "Those deaths were weird, too. The one who went through the ice didn't like fishing. And the one that broke his neck, Jake, nobody had ever heard of him ever hunting."

Nelda looks at the wall. "And that was about when Sheriff Townsend disappeared, wasn't it? " Nobody knew where he went or what happened to him either. Nobody much cared."

Finally, Pat clears his throat and blows a sigh through his lips. "Now what we need to do is get this thing figured out."

"Any way I can help?" Shawn asks. "As the current prime suspect, I sure would like to dig up another suspect who's a little more prime. Maybe Amie and Tim would be interested."

"Well, I don't know about that," Patrick replies. "Don't think the big boys in Des Moines would look kindly on having a suspect involved in the investigation."

"C'mon, Pat. It's your call. The big boys turned it over to you."

"Well." Pat scratches his head. "Look around you. What you see is the entire Nachawinga Sheriff's Department, four of us. Nelda wants us to look like the LAPD special investigation unit, but at present, we look more like Mayberry. Looks like we could use a little help, some beefing up on this big case. Maybe I'll just deputize the three of you. Is that legal, Nelda?"

She hesitates, "Hell, Patrick, you're the Sheriff. I reckon you can do what you please—but I tell you right now there's nothing to pay um with."

"Pro bono." Shawn notices the puzzled looks. "For free." He looks at his two comrades. "How about it, in for a little adventure?" Four thumbs extend skyward.

Pat looks again at Nelda, then at the Dills. They all nod. "OK then, raise your right hands." They do so. Sheriff Kavanaugh swears in his new deputies.

"Hot damn," Bill almost shouts. "We just doubled the size of our county's law force. That Hinman feller'd shit a brick if he knowd what Pat just done."

"Watch the language, Phil," Nelda snaps at him.

"Bill," Bill says.

Nelda throws her hands in the air, "What fucking ever."

"Awright, Nelda!" Bill and Phil shout together and bump fists.

"Watch that language, Nelda," Patrick tries to look serious. "If I've told you once I've..."

"That will be enough from you Sheriff Kavanaugh," Nelda looks at Amie. "I can't believe I said that. Aw, forget it, it's time for lunch."

At Yolanda's Tacos 'n' Tequila, the seven members of the newly expanded Nachawinga County law enforcement establishment pull two tables together and look at the specials chalked on a blackboard behind the bar. Several people stop by their table to say hello to Shawn and, of course, Pat, the Dill brothers, and Nelda.

After they dig into their orders of, as it turns out, really good Mexican food, Pat leans toward the others. "I guess we need to talk strategy," he says as he takes one more bite of taco. "There's at least three folks gonna come in this afternoon to tell us about Craven truck sightings. The way they keep showing up, it's likely there'll be more before the day's over. I'd like the new 'deputies' to hear what they got to say today. Tomorrow's Sunday. I reckon you three'll have some time to do some investigating. I think we ought to take a look at all the places those folks saw that truck. I might be crazy as a June bug thinking there's anything to it, what'd we call it, power of suggestion, but we ain't got a thing else to go on. I don't want those people in Des Moines to know that we're chasing some old truck all over the county, but I sure would like to get this thing solved before they come back around. Might help out our ruined reputation. So, we better finish up here and get back to the office and see bout those truck sightings."

"They also call it mass hysteria," Shawn grins. "That means everybody's crazy."

And, indeed, there are more sighting reports. When they get back to the department parking lot, they find eight vehicles with their motors running and their windows fogged up. There are the three who were scheduled to come in, Geraldine Nothnagel and two of the Luttman boys—and five more who have showed up without appointments. It is well after dark when they have finished with all the stories, Patrick pretty much in charge, the others listening and taking notes, and Nelda putting tacks in the map. When they have finally heard them all, the Sheriff turns to his new deputies. "OK, troopers, let's meet here tomorrow morning and we'll see if you bran new lawmen, I mean law people, were worth signing on."

Six-thirty Sunday morning. It is still dark. Shawn's Jeep chugs into the department parking lot, headlights cutting through the last of the night's snow, and shivers to a stop. The fact that the heater hasn't been doing its job is evidenced by the speed with which Shawn manages his way through the now-frozen slush and lingering snowflakes to the front steps and into the Sheriff's office, leaving his down coat on and blowing on his hands. Amie and Tim follow almost immediately, parking and exiting her red car. Pat, Phil, and Bill are busy organizing pictures and tacks on the wall under Nelda's direction.

Pat turns to the arrivals. "Welcome to the world of law enforcement. Get your coats off, and let's take a look at what we got on this wall." He picks up a yardstick from the desk and points. "We got our so-called suspects, but so far there ain't much hope that they'll help us. If Nelda didn't think we needed at least some pictures up there to make it look right, we would have already taken um down. All the reports and stuff from the labs at Des Moines we already know about. What we know is that none of the dead guys was shot, stabbed, poisoned, or beat to death. There's no evidence of a human-caused wound or trauma on any of them. They were just eaten by hogs and soaked in manure. None of that gets us any closer to an individual or individuals we might be looking for."

"How about PETA and the other radical groups that have been lobbying and putting out information about the harm this kind of livestock agriculture is doing?" Amie asks.

"They just go around raising hell and getting in everybody's hair, just like Shawn's been doing," Nelda says. "They might sugar some trucks or damage buildings or let pigs out, but they don't kill people."

"This thing is damn complicated." Pat removes and replaces his hat. "How'n hell can somebody kill three people, dump um in three different confinements, steal three big money pictures that are a coupla thousand miles apart, and get another that's ten feet up on the wall of a locked and guarded Governor's house so full of security cameras it looks like a photographer's studio, all in about a day an a half? It just doesn't seem possible." They all look at the wall for a long moment before the Sheriff continues, "I reckon all we got to go on are those purple tacks."

Tim, too excited about his new role to remain silent any longer, steps up to the map. "So we've got," he stops to count, "fourteen sightings—where the two cars were found, where the three bodies were found, where Craven Snuggs' house was burned, and eight more. What's the significance of these other eight?"

"Confinements, or planned ones, the dead men were involved with all over the county," Pat says.

"Most of um up to Franklin Township," Phil adds.

"There is one more," Amie says. "Remember? Tim and I saw that truck at Shawn's cabin. We didn't know what it was at the time, but we saw it."

"Can't leave that one out," Nelda says, "But Craven didn't have much connection with that part of the county, and there's no hog lots out there. I've got no idea why that truck would be out at your place." Surprised at herself, she continues, "What am I saying? I'm talking like I think people really did see that truck."

They are interrupted by the sound of the Van Gorp rendering truck crunching onto the parking lot gravel. Nelda looks out the window. "It's just Luke and Travis. Probably wanting to check out your new deputies. They're not gonna miss anything they can gossip about. They've got a bag with them to make it look like they came over here for some reason other than to gawk." The two of them clump through the front door, snow prints trailing them on the office floor.

Nelda yells, "Won't you boys ever learn how to stomp the snow off yer boots before you walk into a place somebody's gotta keep clean?"

"We got sumpin the Sheriff's gonna want," Travis hands Pat a dirty Casey's plastic bag. "Found this stuff when we cleaned the truck. Two fingers, a beat-up college ring, pair of shoes, an' a credit card."

"Figured if we didn't turn um in, you folks mighta thought we was stealing from the dead," Luke says.

"Thanks, boys." Pat takes the bag. "This'll help confirm the ID but it ain't gonna tell us anything we don't know."

Travis takes a long moment looking around, "See our Sheriff's department's done got bigger in the last day ur so. If'n ya need any more depties, ya could sign me an Luke on. Always wanted to be a lawman, like them Texas rangers."

Pat introduces Travis and Luke to the new deputies, "Thanks for the offer, Luke. I believe we're OK for now. I'll let you know if we need you. And thanks for bringing in the evidence."

"Jus let us know," Luke says. "An we'll keep on the lookout fer Craven's truck. Sure would like to see it again. It was one cool fuckin truck. Scuse the language. An now I remember you from before, Shawn. We used to play you boys in ball. I played fer Onky. I think you boys wuz the only ones we never beat. Good to see ya again."

"Likewise," Shawn answers.

Luke and Travis make their way toward the door, slowing to cast admiring glances toward Amie and doubling their tracks, now muddy water instead of snow. Travis turns toward Pat, "How much you paying? This ain't gonna make my taxes go up is it?"

Nelda says, "It's pro bono." In response to their puzzled looks, she snaps, "They're doing it for free." She's very proud to have used the two words she just learned.

Travis and Luke exit the door scratching their heads.

"OK," Pat says, over the labored sound of the rendering truck engine trying to turn over and finally coming to life, "We're wasting daylight. We need to check out all the places Craven's truck's been seen before this day's over." He looks at Tim and Amie. "Here's a county map. We'll mark half the sightings on it, and you two can see if you turn up anything that might help us. Shawn an' me'll take the other half. Go over each site real carefully, we don't want to be missing anything. Nelda, you an' Phil an Bill stay here an' talk to anybody else who claims they've seen the truck. There'll be some, I'm sure."

As much as they try to hide it, it is clear from their body language that Shawn and Amie are disappointed with the pairings that the Sheriff has set up. Tim, perceptive enough to notice, speaks up, with a sly grin, "You better let Amie go with Shawn. Neither she nor I know the county as well as you and Shawn. It would slow us down if we had to spend all day with our faces in a map."

"That's good thinking, Tim. You an me'll go up to Franklin Township. Shawn an Amie, start with the two places where those cars were found in the ditch, then check the places in the southern part of the county. Here's a list of what you two can cover." Then Pat barks his Rawhide imitation, "OK, troops, head um up, move um out. We'll meet back here at sundown."

It's one of those midwestern winter mornings carried in by a high-pressure blast from the west. The temp has dropped fifteen degrees overnight, and the air is so clear you might expect to see all the way to the Rocky Mountains. The last remaining moisture being squeezed out of the twenty-degree air falls as miniature ice crystals made gold by an impossibly bright sunrise, or clings to bare tree limbs, making them appear to be wrapped in silver wool from tiny lambs. It is into this dawn that Shawn aims his ancient Jeep along the now-crunchy gravel road, pressing against his door as Amie, at the other end of the bench seat, presses against hers, each afraid to destroy the decorum they have maintained for so long. But each is so intensely aware of the other that they can hardly breathe, and their heartbeats are out of control. Amie shivers slightly as the old heater fan, its worn bearings chattering away, tries valiantly to raise the cabin temperature at least above the freezing mark.

I've got to say something, Shawn thinks. *I can't just spend the whole day trying to catch my breath in stupid silence. But what? I can't say what I would like to, but anything else I can think of seems dumb. Small talk, like talking about the weather or something. It's like I am still her advisor. I'm not that anymore—I'm free to make some kind of move, aren't I? After all, she did run after me when I walked out of that stupid meeting, and I was too embarrassed to stop and talk to her. And she came out with Tim to warn me about the murders and now she's gonna help us try to solve them. She's a grown woman now. I think she feels something like I... Oh, hell.*

And Amie, *Do I have to wait forever for him to say something about us? I can be the first? I feel like that stupid undergraduate who just worshipped at the brilliant professor's feet. That's over. I'm a grown woman— at least I think I am. Yes, I am. We women are supposed to be able to pick up the ball, lead the charge, take the floor. I don't think he's indifferent to me, I don't. Yet here I sit, feeling stupid. Damn it, damn it, damn it.*

Finally, Shawn screws his courage to the sticking place, or whatever, and breaks the silence with an incredibly romantic question: "What's the first place on that list Pat gave you, the list we're supposed to follow?" And then he thinks, *Shit, is that the best I can do?*

And Amie thinks, *damn, is this the best we can do?*

But she says, "It looks like the first stop is where Marthy Durr saw the Escalade."

Another five minutes in silence and Shawn slows the Jeep to a crawl, looks to the left. He says "I think this is where they found Wooten's rental Cadillac. We'll have to go out into the field to find the spot." He turns the Jeep into the primitive field entrance and hits an anthill that jolts them both into the low spot in the middle of the bench-seat, almost smack against each other. The current between the two of them is crazy. With a little less light, it is certain that sparks would have been visible. Their impulses are completely confusing to both of them—lean in? Pull apart? Finally, Shawn says, "Sorry."

Sorry? Amie, to herself. *Sorry? What in the world does that mean, sorry?*

Shawn slows when he sees a solitary figure standing in the crusted snow. Looking into the sun glancing off the ice, it's impossible to make out much about it, but he touches Amie's shoulder and points. "I see it," she says as she squints into the glare. "This is where Craven's truck was spotted the first time, isn't it?"

He nods. They slowly exit the Jeep and walk tentatively forward. "Who're you?" comes from the person that Shawn and Amie can now clearly see is an old woman.

"We're working with Sheriff Kavanaugh. We've come to see where Craven Snuggs's truck was spotted."

"Ya come to the right place. Marthy Durr here. I be the one who seen it. I come back to check my traps an see if I can find anything peculiar around. Anything that mighta made me see that truck. Jus want to prove to myself I wont crazy. But I don't think I wuz. Folks seeing that damn truck all over the county now."

"Marthy Durr. I believe you were friends with my mother. I'm Shawn Gallagher. My folks owned the hardware store. This is Amie Green."

"Be damned, Shawn. I knowed you from when you wasn't knee-high to a toad frog. An Amie Green. I read about you in the paper. Folks don't have no idea how much I read, but I read. Just finished a book by one o' them Rooshians. I'm working my way through the Rooshians. They's a sad bunch. Ain't a laugh in a carload a them damn books. That Do-sto-yev-sky. Ain't never said his name out loud before. But they sure knew how to write a sad book. The papers? I read um every day. Kind of a waste a time, if you ask me. Ain't much in um that's any count. Most a the time they's as sad as them Rooshians. But I read about you, Amie Green. In the papers. I like you, Amie

Green. I sure am glad to lay eyes on you. If all our younguns was like they say you are, my crick would still be running clear. Yup, we'd be in a damn sight better shape nowadays."

"That's nice of you to say, Ms. Durr," Amie says. "We're trying to help the sheriff make some sense of all that's been happening in your county. Have you seen anything else unusual out here since you saw the truck?"

"You two just follow me." Marthy leads them along the tracks she has made earlier. She points. "That's where I seen that black Cadillac. You can see over yonder with that yellow tape all around it. They's tracks all over the place now, but they wasn't no marks there when I seen it. None. And look there." She points to an area where the snow has partially melted and re-frozen. That's where I seen Craven's truck." The three of them walk over to the spot Marthy has indicated. "Now look real careful down there." She points to the words KEEP AT IT, written in the snow, easily missed by a casual passerby, but very clear to a careful observer.

They both lean closer as Shawn begins taking cell phone pictures of the words. "Any tracks leading up to this when you first came out? I guess the ones we see are yours."

"They are," Marthy says.

"I've got no idea who would tell us to keep at it—or who even knew we would be here for that matter," Shawn says. "Have you seen anything else? Anything at all?"

"That's it. They never was nothing else that I could see. Not even no tracks the day I seen the truck. But I know I seen it, and today I found them words."

"And you've got no idea who might have written them," Amie says.

"No idea," Marthy says.

The three of them spend the next fifteen minutes looking for anything more that is unusual. Then Shawn says, "Well, Marthy, it's good to see you again, and thanks for the help. We got a lot more to look at and you got traps to check, so we best head out. If you find anything else, let us or the Sheriff know."

Shawn and Amie walk back to the Jeep, which by now has lost the little heat it had gained. On the way out the Jeep hits the same anthill with the same result, throwing the passengers together in the middle of the seat, generating the same electricity as before. Only this time the pulling-apart part is a little slower. They begin to work their way down the list: the ditch where Schittman's Lexus was found, and Duffus's CAFOs, searching each place but finding nothing.

By the time they get to the entrance to Craven's eighty acres, it seems that whatever energy has been keeping the two bench seat riders apart has begun to give way to an energy pulling them toward each other. Or is it simply an unthought-out realization that two bodies in somewhat close proximity can keep warm more efficiently than those same two bodies some distance apart? Perhaps it is yet something else.

When they reach the burnt-out home place, they can see where the house and the barn and other outbuildings once stood. Thick, rich, dormant prairie grass surrounds the old foundations, but within the walls, nothing seems to have grown. Some withered velvetleaf and a few dead Jimson weed plants droop along the outer edges, but nothing else. Four or five crows are hopping around the bare ground as if they might be able to find something buried that the human scavengers had missed. Shawn gets a little choked up as he tells Amie more about his visits to the place when Craven was still around, their long talks about farming and conservation, and Craven's deep misgivings about modern agriculture. He remembers how Craven loved the land and how beautiful his house was, always seeming to be freshly painted, never a hanging gutter or missing shingle. He points out where the huge Clydesdales were stalled and remembers how elegant Craven looked astride his tall, gaited saddle horse. They walk carefully back and forth across the ruined foundations. Then they start back toward the Jeep, careful to follow the tracks they made coming in. As they reach the edge of what was the front yard they see, clearly melted into the snow, the words, DON'T STOP. YOU'RE ON THE RIGHT TRACK.

Amie looks at Shawn, astonished and a little unnerved. "Oh my god. Did you see this when we came in?"

"I did not. This is a little spooky. Here are our tracks—we came in side by side. This is actually on top of our tracks."

Amy moves a bit closer to Shawn, "I don't know whether to be intrigued or terrified. Do you see any sign of other tracks—or anything else? Did you hear anything?"

"Not a thing."

They retrace their tracks and walk the perimeter of the Snuggs home place, looking for any sign of disturbance in the snow other than what they made. After about fifteen minutes of searching, Shawn says with a sigh, "Nothing." Then after one last look around, "I'm going to take pictures, then we better drive on to where you and Tim saw the truck if we're going to make it back to Tripoli when we said we would."

As they turn for one last look, the crows lift off the foundation and are joined by twelve or fifteen others corkscrewing straight up. As they climb, they look like a plume of black smoke rising from the burned-out ruin.

"Where did they come from?" Shawn turns to Amie.

"Don't know." She pauses for a long moment as she watches them disappear. "Do you know what a bunch of crows is called?"

"No idea."

Amie stops and looks where the crows vanished. Then at the crumbled foundation.

"A murder." She looks straight at Shawn. "They're called a murder."

They are silent when they climb back into the cold Jeep, but a new kind of current is growing between them, replacing the electric uneasiness of their earlier moments of closeness. Maybe it's the temperature, which continues to drop, or the fact that they have at least eight inches of down jackets between them fending off any real danger of intimate contact. At any rate, there is little hesitation on Amie's part when she slides across the seat to be closer to Shawn, and there is easy laughter as sparks, this time static electricity, really do fly when they touch the metal of the dashboard.

By the time they reach the two-track leading to Shawn's cabin, their conversation is easy and comfortable. They have mostly talked about the wonder of the rural Iowa countryside: the small woodlots still sparkling with the early morning rime that the winter sun has been unable to completely erase, the reds and purples of the fields of bluestem and Indian grass peppered with the black seed heads of coneflowers and mountain mint, fields that some farmers have allowed to rest from frenzied year-after-year production. Even the nudity of the harvested bean fields, desert-like weeks before, has gained a kind of serenity under their quilt of ice crystals and crusted snow.

They pull up to the end of the 'driveway' and Shawn cuts the engine that shakes the whole Jeep before it gives up. They sit for a moment, reluctant to leave what little warm air is left. Amie stares into the timber. "It's beautiful. It is so beautiful."

As the ticking of the metal signals the exit of the last bit of heat, they step into the snow and look around. Shawn says, "Show me the exact spot where you and Tim saw the truck."

The latest snow has erased any signs of previous human movement, leaving only the heart-shaped prints of deer hooves and the small hand-like tracks of raccoons.

"I think that is pretty much where we saw it," Amie says as they step a few yards toward the cabin, "It's hard to tell. There's nothing there now, that's sure. No disturbance or anything. Not even a message in the snow."

"I don't think we're going to find anything else here, but I've got the makings for hot chocolate in the kitchen and there should be a few embers in the fireplace. Let's go warm up a little before we go back to Pat's office."

Walking to the cabin and up the porch steps, Shawn feels some of the tension and frustration he felt earlier that morning, and even in their advising sessions back at State. Maybe the red light in the rear-view mirror is a little dimmer and it doesn't exactly say 'Stop,' but it still says, 'Slow down.'

Amie's mind, on the other hand, is reeling. *God, I love the smell of that fireplace, And there's his bed. I'll bet it hasn't been made up in days. I'd love to go in there and fix it for him, or better yet, climb in it and drag him in with me. I could stay here for…*

The sound of Shawn putting wood on the remnants of the fire and pouring water into the teapot snaps her out of it. "Can I help?"

"Nah. I'm pretty good at boiling water." Then he laughs, "I don't do too bad with frozen pizza either."

They shed their down jackets and, with steaming cups of hot chocolate in hand, sit on the threadbare sofa, the sag in the middle making it impossible not to be at least as close to each other as they were in the jeep.

Shawn takes a deep breath and looks upward, "I guess I made pretty much of a fool out of myself with that pig business at your meeting the other day, didn't I?"

Amie closes one eye, "Wellll, it was pretty dramatic. But you sure made your point. And broke up the meeting. They weren't going to vote to stop the new CAFOs. Now, at least they can't start construction until the committee convenes again. And the committee chair is dead." They both almost giggle.

"I wonder if Professor Hamilton would be ashamed of me." Shawn looks into his cup. "He thought I should stay at State and fight it out. Thought I could do more good sticking it out at State than just raising hell in general, writing letters to editors, sending almost criminal messages to big ag executives and their toadies. But it drove me up a wall—all the hypocrisy—doing research on how to make raising animals safer for people and for the animals and burying the results to keep the big corporation money from disappearing. It's just wrong, all the power politics driving out common sense, ruining people's lives, our land, and our state. Maybe I should be like Tim. He's comfortable working his way through the system. I thought for a while he'd gone over to the dark side, but I can see what he's doing. He'll get his power. He'll make a difference. Probably more than me. But I just can't do it that way."

"You're good, Shawn. You were good before you got to State. I know that from the way your Tripoli friends talk. And I know you were good at State. You will be good when you work it all out for yourself." Amie feels the strangeness of advising her advisor. "You're even a damn good pig impersonator."

"Who knows?" Shawn laughs. "If I make it on this deputy sheriff gig, I might graduate to US Marshall. Move over, Mr. Dillon."

Amie gets up, stretches to feel the warmth, and walks toward the front of the room. Suddenly she stops. She leans toward the window. She whispers. "Shawn."

He turns. She points.

Standing next to an old, gnarled burr oak at the timber's edge, is a majestic sorrel saddle horse. It stands under an old cavalry saddle, reins draped over the pommel, head high, muscles rippling on its neck, its ears forward, eyes wide, and nostrils flared. The beams from the descending sun reflect off it as if it were cast bronze.

Shawn gasps, unable to speak.

The horse snorts and shakes out its mane.

Finally, Shawn, whispers, "Holy Christ. That's Craven's horse."

He moves toward the door, motioning for Amie to follow, signaling quietly and slowly. They get the door open without a sound and step gently onto the porch. The horse shakes its mane once again, paws the snow, and quietly nickers. They can scarcely breathe.

Then, from Amie, "It's gone."

"Into the woods?"

"No. I think it's gone. Just …gone."

Quickly, now, they run to where the animal stood. Nothing. No horse. No tracks. No disturbance. Nothing. Only the rattle of the breeze in the dry oak leaves and the distant calling of a crow.

They spend the next few minutes looking around the spot where the horse stood until the fading sun's rays make searching impossible. Finally, with both their cell phone's lights on, they return to where they started, and there, clearly melted into the snow, are the words, I'LL BE IN TOUCH.

They look at the words for a long time, then at each other. Finally, Shawn breaks the silence. "Something is happening and we don't know what it is, do we, Amie Greene?" Then, with a bit of a smile, "that's Dylan, not me."

Amie punches him in the arm. "I know that."

Shawn takes pictures and holds his phone up. "We better get back to Tripoli. Nelda'll want to put these on the wall."

The trip back is slightly warmer, much less tense, and a little more intimate.

Sunday afternoon at the Des Moines International Airport, a Gulfstream 550 corporate jet drops out of the clouds, looking like an attacking shark in the murky waters off a stormy Atlantic coast. Taxiing to its designated parking space, it makes the surrounding aircraft look like vehicles in a used car lot. On the tail of this magnificent flying machine is a picture of a large bird that appears to be a cross between a fighting cock and a California condor; however, a closer look confirms that it is just a chicken. On the fuselage, in large letters, are the words, FREEBIRD FAMILY FARMS, LLC, HAPPY CHICKENS FOR

HAPPY FAMILIES. Standing in the mixed precip, which has resumed with a vengeance, are half-dozen men and one woman, all muttering to each other, clearly irritated, except for Tim Taylor in his Burberry overcoat, who is by now used to wet snow and cold weather. He seems to be trying to hide his amusement. Alongside Tim are the Guv and two more aids; Charles Hinman, DCI chief; his deputy chief, Captain Elizabeth Orchincross; and a uniformed DCI officer. Scattered around the airport runways are 25 or 30 Iowa State patrolmen, shivering and looking bored. It is 6:26 in the evening. The Gulfstream was scheduled to land at 10 am. The crowd of curiosity seekers that had gathered that morning to get a look at the 'murder suspects' are long gone.

The aircraft stairway descends, and three beautiful thirty-some-thing male flight attendants in gray exercise suits walk through the door, open umbrellas, and assume their positions on the tarmac, as impervious to the weather as Green Bay Packers linemen in a December playoff game. After enough moments to heighten antic-ipation, the three widows make their entrance and walk down the stairs like models on a fashion show runway. Misty and Lizzy come first, wearing almost, but not quite, identical ankle-length down coats with fur lining the hoods and around the bottoms, and tailored slacks. Their boots, also with fur spilling out the tops, are incredibly high-heeled. Finally, Connie appears, wearing what might be called a working cowboy's duster, although this duster, with its fleece lining and its soft leather collar, never had any intention of working. Stetson hat, designer jeans, and custom-fitted western boots complete her couture. Everything the women are wearing is jet black, except for Connie's boots, which are inlaid with pink flamingos and flowers of every color imaginable. The Guv steps forward to greet them, but they are quickly led by their attendants past the welcoming party through the gate into the terminal building, with the Guv and his entourage tagging behind. Finally, Hinman is able to take enough charge to herd the group into a secure conference room, where he introduces himself. The Guv and the three widows take seats at the table.

"I can't tell you how deeply sorry we all are," the Guv begins, "about the horribly tragic events that have brought the three of you here this evening. We will try to keep things as brief as possible. You must all be terribly tired. I assume you had aircraft trouble or airport hold-ups that delayed your arrival for so long."

"Oh, my heavens no," Misty purrs. "When we got on Lizzy's little ol jet, we realized we had absolutely no proper mourning clothes— widah's weeds, I think you call um. So, we decided to stop into Nieman Marcus, that's in Dallas you know, and pick up something so we wouldn't look like a bunch of hayseeds."

"By then we were pretty hungry," Lizzy adds, "and there is not a single decent restaurant in Dallas, so we made a tiny detour to 'N'awleans', that's the way Misty says it. I think that's so cute. We had a late lunch at the Bywater Bistro. Misty suggested it. I have my favorite New Orleans eateries, but this little place was fabulous. Tucked away in an out-of-the-way alley. The curried rabbit was unreal. If you get a chance, it's worth the trip just for a late lunch. Now we've got a chance to see what the city of Des Moines has got to offer us while we make use of our new outfits."

"I hope we didn't hold y'all up." Misty smiles.

Tim Taylor can hardly disguise his mirth.

The Guv can hardly disguise his confusion.

Charles Hinman can hardly disguise his frustration. Through clenched teeth, he speaks, "We are sensitive to your losses, and we will try to make things as easy as possible, but we will need you all here tomorrow to make some positive identifications for us. We have arranged suites for you at the Savery Hotel, and a car is waiting to take you and your luggage there."

"Thank you, sir, but we'll spend the night at my farm," Connie answers. "I want my friends to see my house and my horses. And we've already arranged for a rental car. Our boys will see to our luggage. We don't want to be any trouble. What time should we plan on?"

"I'd like to get underway a little after eight," Hinman croaks.

"Oh, no, no, no, no," Misty says. "I'm hardly asleep by eight o'clock. Let's make it after lunch. Say three?"

The Guv, anxious to avoid what he sees as a looming confrontation says, "Anything you say, ladies. Whatever makes you comfortable in these trying times. Around three, then." He goes on, "Oh, and I know we could talk about this later, but maybe, just for the record," his voice squeaks a little, "I'm sure the commitments your late husbands made to my continuing campaign fund remain intact. You never know what an election will bring." He goes for a casual chuckle, but it sounds more like a croak.

"We have been discussing that matter among ourselves and agree that we should take a close look at the distribution of our late hus-bands', now our, assets," Connie says, "and see how maybe a lot of that money can be spent in a better way. So, none of our late husbands' commitments necessarily remain intact." The Guv blanches as she continues, "As far as your campaign fund is concerned, you might talk to my stepson and see if he wants to continue to support you. Although he was cut out of the estate by JJ Jr. several years ago and probably will not be able to match my deceased husband's level of largesse, my late husband's will leaves him a modest trust fund that provides enough money to maintain his pickup truck, buy beer, and pay fines for shooting animals out of season. He might have a little left over." She stands. "Gentlemen, we will expect you to pick us up at the JJ—no, the Connie Schittman— farm at three tomorrow af-ternoon." She turns to the attendants, "You know where to bring the luggage? You boys will be staying in the guest apartments above the barn."

The three widows walk out of the conference room and stride to the Avis counter, where they are handed the keys to a bright yellow

Volkswagen Beetle ragtop. When they get to the car, Misty and Lizzy have a friendly argument over who will sit in the rear, both trying to give the other the best seat. Finally, Connie says, "Both of you sit in the back. It'll be warm and cozy back there. I'll be the chauffeur."

The members of the welcoming party watch in bewilderment as the three women squeeze into the little bug and head onto Fleur Drive north, toward I-35 and the Connie Schittman farm, followed by their 'attendants' and luggage in a bright red Hummer.

It's three-twenty the following afternoon and a white stretch Lincoln limo has been parked in the circular drive in front of the huge 'farmhouse' for fifty minutes, motor running and wipers ticking at the wet snow falling on the windshield. The driver is holding a paper coffee cup and playing a game on his cell phone. In the game, he is a SWAT sniper looking through the 20X telescopic sight of his specially designed long-range sniper rifle. What he sees through the scope is a comely maiden in the arms of a horrible-looking terrorist who is holding a knife to her throat. Just as the driver settles the crosshairs on the ugly man's temple, the three widows exit the front door and stride down the semi-circular stairs. In his haste to open the passenger doors before the women reach the limo, he manages to spill his coffee and slip on the icy drive. He is too late. Connie Schittman has beaten him to it. He retreats to his seat behind the steering wheel and starts the engine. Presumably, the comely maiden got her throat slit.

Cars and overturned semis are stranded in the median and the ditches as the limo, at a little above safe speed, moves onto the snowy Interstate toward Des Moines and the City Mortuary. After some fishtailing and close calls with other cars, which seem to amuse the passengers, the driver stops at the curb in front of a gray single-story stone building with no windows, a plain flat porch, and ten-foot-high metal doors. The welcoming party is waiting on the porch next to the Metro Police station. Uniformed state patrolmen scattered around the snowy grounds are blowing into their hands and hugging themselves to keep warm.

This time, the chauffeur is able to reach the doors and open them for the three women to step out of the limo, still looking like high fashion models. Their new outfits are dark but with subtle variations on their apparel from the day before. Lizzie is in a House of Versace vicuna trench coat in a subdued window pattern, black with dark wine frame edges. She carries a maroon Bottega Veneta handbag that matches her crocodile shoes. Misty's outfit is all Hermes—very deep gray baby cashmere jacket and gray slacks. Connie wears an outfit much the same as Sunday's, but her duster is Johnny Cash black suede and her ostrich boots, breaking from widow's norm, bright red. Hinman, immaculate as always in his dark suit, yellow tie, and black overcoat, opens one of the big doors. The women and the rest of the party enter a large stone-walled room with old wooden benches that look like church pews. A surprisingly glamorous and disarmingly cheerful young woman in green scrubs stands by another immense door, this one stainless steel.

Hinman turns to the widows, "I know this will be difficult, but believe me it is necessary. Would you prefer to do this together or one at a time?"

Misty answers, "In this trying time we are going to need each other's comfort and support. We'll go in together." Her sarcasm hovers like a puff of smoke.

Hinman turns to the Guv, "Guv?"

"Uh, I, uh, no, no." He blushes a little. "I, uh, I'll stay out here." Then, trying to find a reason for his reluctance, "It's such a personal, uh, matter, I, uh, I'm sure the ladies would prefer to be alone."

"Suit yourself, Guv." Lizzy chuckles, along with the others.

Charles Hinman nods to the attendant. She opens the door and the four walk through. The walls of this room are stainless steel-lined, with large cabinets, two deep. There is a locking handle on each door.

There are no chairs. Three gurneys are in the center of the room, each covered with a green canvas sheet.

The attendant walks to the first one, removes the sheet, unzips a long, heavy plastic body bag, and announces, "Mr. Wooten," almost as if she were presenting a dessert tray at a fancy restaurant. There's not a whole lot there: a lower midsection with the left leg attached, fairly intact; the right leg, unattached; and a partial skull.

Hinman looks for a sign that might show how Misty is affected. "I'm sorry Mrs. Wooten. We made every attempt to recover as much of your husband as possible."

She studies the remains, "For heaven's sake, Hubert, why did you have to wear those awful shoes. They might have knocked um dead when you were a freshman at Dook, but that was 50 years ago. They look terrible on you now. Aren't they a scandal, girls?"

The other two nod, attempting to look serious.

Misty turns to Hinman. "That's him. I don't know of anyone else in the world who would wear those stupid shoes to die in. Worse than having holes in your underwear." Then to the attendant, "You can put him in the fridge."

After zipping up Hubert and sliding him into one of the cabinets, the attendant moves to the second gurney, removes the covering, and unzips the bag. "Mr. Schittman."

Most of JJ's pieces seem to be present, his clothing draped in shreds around his chewed body. But he looks like a hunk of bait that's been in a crab trap for a week.

Connie takes a moment, her face completely expressionless, then, "Yup, that's him. I would recognize that self-satisfied smirk a mile away." She motions the attendant, "Put him back in the cooler."

The body in the third bag is in better shape than the other two although it looks as if it has been run through the roller of an old-fashioned Maytag. Again, the attendant, this time lifting the sheet like a bullfighter trying to provoke a charge, and with a wicked smile, makes the announcement. "Mr. Birdseed."

Lizzy moves in to have a closer look. "Why, Donnie, you seem to have finally lost a little weight, you are so nice and flat. Still a little too wide though—you better work on that." And to the waiting attendant, "Zip him up."

The other two can hardly contain their laughter.

It's apparent to Hinman that the widows have no desire to linger with what is left of their late husbands, so, without asking, he opens the door and leads them into the waiting room.

"Now, there is the matter of the portraits of your husbands," he says. "They are presently being held as evidence, but when investigators are finished with them, would you like to pick them up yourselves or take delivery at your residences? I imagine they are of some value."

Lizzy walks to the window and looks out, then points, "You see that big green dumpster over there, Hon? You can deliver them to that address. Right, girls?" They answer with thumbs pointing straight up.

Hinman, somewhat taken aback, looks at the three women to make sure they are serious. Then he proceeds, "We need to talk about your remaining schedule. Tomorrow you will all go to Tripoli, that's a little town about sixty miles from here, and meet with the Nachawinga County Sheriff, Patrick Kavanaugh." He takes a short breath through his nose and the muscles in his clenched jaw quiver. "The procedure is a little unusual, but because of extenuating circumstances, they have jurisdiction in the case at this point...." He is having a little trouble choosing words as he glares at the Guv. "They will doubtless have a few questions for you. It shouldn't take long. We have checked out the time when Mr. Sanchez, the witness to your, uh, discussion about, uh, about your wishes for your husbands. It appears the three men were dead when he heard your conversation. So, I think you have all been pretty much cleared as viable suspects, but we should extend the Sheriff the courtesy of a brief interrogation. In all likelihood, the investigation will be back in the hands of the DCI very soon."

"Let's put that off for a short while, Chief," Connie says. "What's today, Monday? How about we go to Nachawinga County on Thursday. We want to spend a couple of days looking over our enterprises. We now own a lot of business and property in your state, you know, and I think we should do an inventory as soon as we can. Now that we are owners and executives of these corporations, we need to investigate the details of their operation. We might want to make a few changes—maybe more than a few. So, just give us a couple of days, and then we can go see this Sheriff—Kavanaugh is it?"

"I believe the investigation should take top priority," Hinman barks.

Before he can go on, the Guv interrupts him, "You ladies take all the time you want. These times have been terribly trying for us all and there's no need to hurry."

Hinman blows out a long breath underneath his scowl and takes a step toward the exit.

"Nachawinga," Misty says almost dreamily. "That's such a beautiful name, Nachawinga. Sounds like something Mister William Faulknah might a thought up. You know that county of his in Mississippi he wrote about. What did he call it? 'Yoknapatawpha' I believe. That's it. An Iowa version of Yoknapatawpha. I do love Mister William Faulknah. I think I've read most of what he wrote. I might just go back to school one of these days so I can study some more of that wonderful Southern literature."

The three widows walk toward the limo. "Well, that was fun, wasn't it?" Lizzy says. "Now we know for sure they're dead and I don't have one single regret."

"Kind of a dream come true," Misty says.

"We might have been a little crass in there, but I couldn't agree more," Connie says.

The driver scrambles to open the doors, but Connie holds up her hand, "Just keep your seat. We'll get um." As they climb into the Lincoln, she says, "Now girls, get ready for a treat. We're going to the best smokehouse in the lower forty-eight to pick up enough take-out ribs to feed a large army—enough for us, our flight attendants, and our driver if he wants to join us. We'll take um to the farmhouse. We're going to see what the late JJ has in his liquor cabinet and his wine cellar. We're going to put Lyle Lovett and Levon Helm on the box, and we're goin to have a lickin good time. I sure hope those boys can dance. Driver, take us to Smokey D's." She yells, "Bar-bee-que!!!"

An hour later they are in the farmhouse bar and have just broken the seal on a bottle of 25-year-old McCallan single malt. Connie is about to pour for Misty when she puts her hand over her glass and stares into the enormous liquor cabinet, "What is that I see a way in the back? Could that be Pappy, Mr. Pappy Van Winkle? I think I'll just have a couple or three big thimbles-full of that. I am so very fond of my Pappy. I'll just have one or two tiny ice cubes in it."

"JJ used to drink that to impress people," Connie says. "He drank it with ginger ale." They all laugh.

"Donnie used to put big ice cubes in his vintage red wine," Lizzy says. Laughter again.

"Speaking of wine," Connie moves to one of the many wine racks and removes several bottles, "This is JJ Zinfandel. Comes from a special little half-acre vineyard on a Sonoma hillside. It's seven years old. It peaks at seven so it should be perfect with the ribs." She hesitates for a moment, "OMG, I just realized, I own that vineyard now. I'll have to change that stupid name. And while I'm at it, I might want to change some other stupid things."

They finish their drinks and move to the dining room, where the 'boys' have laid out ribs, cole-slaw, corn chowder, curly fries, and a tub of sauce. The seven of them dig in like a pack of wolves over a freshly killed moose. Robert Earl Keen singing, *The Road Goes on Forever and the Party Never Ends*, floods the house-wide speakers.

This party does end, but not until well after midnight.

It's eight AM, Tuesday morning in Tripoli, and most of the Nachawinga County law enforcement establishment are in Sheriff Patrick Kavanaugh's office. Bill, Phil, Shawn, and Nelda are seated. Two of the new deputies are not present—Amie is teaching her eighth graders and Tim is babysitting the Guv.

The Sheriff, pissed off, is pacing the floor. "What d'ya mean they're not coming 'till Thursday? They were supposed to be here at ten this morning. Here it is Tuesday. Our whole investigation has boiled down to looking for messages in the snow, and we didn't find a damn thing yesterday. What're we supposed to do for two more days waiting for um? Twiddle our thumbs?"

"Hinman called just before you came in," Nelda is trying to keep the Sheriff calm. "Said the bereaved have some business to attend to and they need a coupla days before they can come over here. Surely you understand—poor ladies, husbands murdered like that."

Kavanaugh, irritation growing, "What we hear from Florida, the poor ladies are most likely happy ladies, but probably not serious suspects. Still, Hinman's been calling here every damn day asking when are we going to get this thing wrapped up and telling us to get our asses on the move—acting like we're not doing our damndest to make some progress here. Now he tells us the people we still need to question who might give us a clue as to where we might go from here have got a little business to tend to. You should've told that pompous SOB to take the case and stick…"

"OK, Pat." Nelda holds her hands palms out in front of her. "It's OK. Let's just look and see what we've got up to this point."

"Them widders ain't gonna be much good to us anyways," Bill says. "Alls we got on um is they hated their husbands. Hell, half the wives in Tripoli hate their husbands."

"Yeah," Phil continues. "We jes got what some janitor or somebody says he heard um say that when them gals was drunk an floating around in a hot tub."

"You're right, Bill," Nelda adds, "They were in Florida till they came to Des Moines Sunday. No evidence that they could have hired anyone here or in Carolina or Denver."

"I'm Phil," Phil says.

"I'm Bill," Bill says.

"Whatever!!!! Jeez." She glares at them before she goes on. "Besides, there wouldn't have been time for them to organize the whole thing, get the pictures stolen and the husbands done in between when that janitor heard um and they were killed. And we do know when they were killed. Those murders had taken place before that janitor heard the wives."

"So," Shawn looks up at the wall. "We've got three dead men. And an old pickup truck showing up all over the county that seems to have belonged to Craven Snuggs, himself a dead man. And three messages that don't make any sense melted in the snow." He looks at the photos: KEEP AT IT; DON'T STOP, YOU'RE ON THE RIGHT TRACK; and I'LL BE IN TOUCH. "And no human suspects. I repeat, that's not much to go on."

The phone on Patrick's desk rings. He goes for it, but Nelda snatches it from him. "Nachawinga County Sheriff's office."

Pause. "Yes, yes, we're working on that case."

Long pause. "Yes. Yes. That's right."

Pause, "Well, thanks. Thanks a lot for the call."

Pause. "Yes, yes, that's a big help. Where can we reach you if we need to?"

Pause. "Yes, we'll let you know."

She slowly writes down an address on a yellow pad, relishing the fact that she has an audience. "That was Jamey Meekins, Janie Meekins' boy, calling from Denver. He lives there now. Says he was talking to his mom the other day and she told him about Craven's pickup being seen all over the place. He says he could swear he seen that truck last week in Denver. Says his buddy seen it, too. On Bixby Street."

"In Denver? Where on Bixby Street?" Pat says.

After a long pause, Nelda says, "In front of the Freebird Family Farms corporate headquarters."

No one moves or speaks. Finally, Patrick says, "What in the hell are we chasing after here, a fuckin' ghost?"

They look at each other for a long time in silence, which Nelda finally breaks, "Language, Patrick, language."

Eighty miles west on the same morning, the bright yellow VW adds a splash of color to the late autumn countryside as it stairsteps its way northeast (north, then east, then north, then east—no diagonals) over county blacktop roads toward the small town of Rockville. None of the three passengers is used to being up this early, but as Connie said at their almost-daybreak breakfast, "We're business gals now so we better get out there and see what the hell our businesses are." Brilliant sunshine piercing the clear blue sky is beginning to melt some of the snow on the asphalt and raise the mid-November temps both inside and outside the now-cozy little auto. Misty and Lizzy, having shed their bright down jackets, are comfy in their roll-neck sweaters. Connie keeps her denim jacket on. They all wear designer jeans.

Misty gazes out the window, "It is kinda pretty out there. I never thought of Iowa as being pretty. Don't get me wrong, Connie, I like your farm an all, but I always thought you were just s'posed to fly over Iowa."

"That's what people say, and it really pisses me off, you excluded, Misty," Connie replies. "There are places I ride my horses in the western hills or the northeast that will make you cry. They don't jump out at you, like those mountains in Lizzy's country, but they're there. You just need to pay attention. We'll be driving by some of them so keep your eyes open." Her mood changes. "I have a feeling, though, where we're going to end up is not going to be one of those pretty places."

Lizzy picks up on Connie's seriousness. "I'm afraid none of what we're going to see will be very pretty. I think we might be close to getting our faces rubbed in what has paid for our luxury lives all these years. What I have avoided looking at since I started living in the world of the rich and famous. Thinking all that was Donnie's business, not mine."

"Guess we might have a hard time blaming everything on our hubbies now," Misty says. "We've been talking about our feelings, about wasting our lives ever since we met, looking for something worthwhile to do. You think maybe we're headed toward our chance?"

"Well," Connie says, "the rubber's on the road."

They talk little for the next two and a half hours, unusual for these three. Just watch the red and yellow autumn leaves that remain on the trees and tweed fields pass as they listen to Bob Seger's memory songs on XM Radio. Connie announces they are near their destination as they pass a modest sign announcing, *Rockville, Iowa, Population 2,262. Home of the Fighting Boulders and Boulderettes. Little Town—Big People.* As they turn onto Center Street, they see a couple leaving Hardee's who together would easily tip the scales above five hundred pounds plus. Lizzy Chuckles, "They got that slogan right."

Continuing past a couple of bars, a Dollar General, and several empty storefronts, they pull up in front of a huge compound enclosed by chain link fencing. Over what appears to be the main entrance, a sign proclaims *Patriot Pork, Packing and Production, Premium Pork from Perfect Pigs.* Inside the fence, there is an array of dingy greenish metal buildings that look like military surplus, mostly single-story, with the exception of several towers and a three-story office building. The overall impression is that of a prison. There are two unloading docks with four livestock-hauling semis lined up in front, waiting to unload their writhing, squealing, tail-less, pink pigs to join others in three very large covered pens. The smell is uniformly awful. "Well," Connie observes, "this sure is something to be proud of, huh? Hold your breath, girls, we're going in." She takes her iPhone from her purse, snaps a few pictures, drives up to the closed gate, and honks the beetle's diminutive horn until the gatekeeper, a dark, heavy man who has pretended not to hear, finally marches to the car. "You can come een here."

"OK then, open the gate," Connie answers.

"No, no, no, you can no come een here. Only beeznis," the man answers back.

"We have business," she responds.

"No, no, no, something happening to beeg boss. Nobody come een. Beeg mess inside. No come een."

Connie removes her sunglasses, puts them astraddle her black hair, and looks hard at the gatekeeper, "I know all about what happened to the big boss. You see, my name is Connie Schittman, and I am the grieving widow of your big boss. I am your new big boss. These are my partners. You can either let us in or you can find someone who will. Either way, be quick about it. Make sure you don't waste a lot of our time."

The gatekeeper's eyes widen. He starts to say something but thinks better of it. He opens the gate.

"Good move," Connie waves to him. "You'll do well working for this new big boss." She drives through as the gatekeeper dives for the phone to call the office and issue a tornado warning.

By the time they reach the building with *Corporate Offices* over the entrance, three nearly identical, very nervous men in white coats with name tags over left pockets holding plastic pocket protectors and ballpoints, and 'Patriot Pork' and a grinning pig embroidered on the right side stumble out the door to meet them.

The one who seems to be the leader steps forward. "Mrs. Schittman, we are so very sorry about Mr. Schittman. Let us assure you, however, that this division of Patriot Pork is fully operational, and will continue to operate smoothly."

"Thank you, Mr. …," she looks at his name tag, "Mr. Perlmutter. We are going to look around the place and will likely have some instructions for you when we get back. Just wait for us in the office."

"I'll be more than happy to show you around." Perlmutter answers.

But by this time the women are walking toward the pens, out of hearing, leaving the three flustered Patriot Pork execs muttering to each other.

Connie, Lizzy, and Misty follow the pigs from the trucks, to their slaughter, to their dismemberment, to the final shrink-wrapped product at the end of their journey. The three women are thoroughly put off by what the pigs go through but are appalled by the condition of the workers. Literally shoulder to shoulder, these workers sit in front of a moving line of carcasses on which each person performs a part of the butchering process, barely managing to do their bit before the next carcass comes by. Thrust into a world from which they had been completely isolated for so long a time, Connie, Lizzy, and Misty are suddenly confronted by an emotion that had almost atrophied in them: empathy.

Connie gets the attention of one of the workers over the din of the assembly line. "Who controls the line?" A young Hispanic woman who looks to be about nineteen points to a glass booth at one end of the room. Connie walks over and gives a time-out signal to the man inside, who vigorously shakes his head. She walks into the booth. The other two can't hear what she is saying, but there is no mistaking its force.

After more headshaking, the operator finally stops the line. The huge room goes absolutely silent, puzzled workers up and down looking at each other. Connie comes out of the booth and walks to the butchering line, the flustered operator following. She approaches another young woman. "How old are you?" she asks.

Nervous, the worker answers, "No comprendo. No hablo Ingles."

The woman next to her answers for her, "She no speak English. She seventeen. She scared to be sent home. To Guatemala."

"How much are you paid?" Connie asks.

"Seven and twenty-five each hour. Minimum wage."

"All of you?" Connie gestures toward the whole line.

"Si."

She looks at the workers on the line, then at Misty and Lizzy. "God, can you imagine what would happen if one of these workers got sick, some awful virus or something. They'd all have it in a week." Connie turns to the line operator. "Does this thing have to go so fast?" He shakes his head, no. "OK. You can start it up again, but half speed." He smiles and nods and goes back into the booth. Connie continues, "OK, girls. Let's go up to my office."

The workers on the line watch the widows exit, then look at each other with cautious smiles.

As the three women stride toward the tallest building, Misty says, "That was appalling. I sure don't want to stop eating my country ham, but that can't be a good way to make it happen."

"I still love my prosciutto," Lizzy offers, "but not from this place."

"I had no idea how bad this whole mess is. I'm not going to give up my barbecue either, no way, but now that I'm in control I'm going to make some big changes. There's got to be a better way to grow BBQ." There is no mistaking her seriousness.

In the board room, the three uneasy men say little as Connie gives the orders. She summarizes, "Half as many pigs in the pens at any one time and check the conditions where they are raised. Slow all the lines to less than half the current speed, and all those on the lines get ten minutes rest each hour and twice as much workspace as they have now. Our minimum wage goes up to ten dollars an hour right away.

We can take a close look at the entire corporate pay scale later. In the meantime, we can see what our marketing people can do with our new philosophy and production standards. We might be surprised by what happens when these changes go public. Oh, by the way, how many of our workers are undocumented?" The three men all show varying levels of panic. "Don't worry. We'll work all that out later, I assure you. Good-bye, gentlemen."

Three bewildered men watch their new boss walk to the miniature car.

Back in the bug, riding toward a fading sun, Connie shakes her head and sighs, "That was worse than I ever imagined and embarrassing as hell." She pauses for a long time. Then she grins and looks at the other two, "Vegetarian tonight?"

From the back seat, the resounding answer is, "No way!"

Night Moves is playing on the radio.

It's Wednesday morning. The Sheriff has been informed without warning that DCI Chief Hinman is making a trip to Tripoli, and there is a battlefield level of tension among the five people at the Sheriff's office. Nelda has just cradled the phone. She turns to the others, wide-eyed, "That was the Big Chief. Said he wants to see how we are getting on with the investigation. Said he just turned off the interstate. Should be here in half-hour."

Shawn gets up and moves toward the door. "Think I'll go back into the field. I want to spend some more time looking around the timber where Craven's horse disappeared. It can't just vanish like that. It's got to leave some kind of evidence it was there."

"Oh no, you don't. You stay here, Shawn, I'm gonna need you here," Patrick sighs. "He's gonna want to know about you, and he'll probably go through the roof when he finds out we made you deputy. We're gonna need all the troops we can get."

For the next ten minutes, they play at looking busy, trying to make themselves believe they are doing something worthwhile. Patrick shuffles papers on his desk; Nelda takes great pains to make sure the wall has all the information that is supposed to be on it. They all jump when they hear and then see a long black Suburban with deeply tinted windows crunching gravel in the parking lot.

"That's a big fuckin car," Bill says.

"Musta been goin 80 to get here so quick," Phil says.

They watch as the driver, Deputy Chief Captain Elizabeth Orchincross, exits. She stands at relaxed attention as Charles Hinman, all six foot four inches of him, uncoils himself through the back door.

Hinman enters the office first, takes a good look around, and extends his hand to Kavanaugh "Sheriff."

Patrick takes his hand "Chief."

Nelda, anxious to get in the act and to diffuse any uneasiness she can, steps up, "This is the Nachawinga County Sheriff's Department, Sir. Well, we have two other part-time deputies who are off today. I'm Nelda Womble, dispatcher and office manager and about anything else they need me for." She laughs. Hinman doesn't. "This is Phil Dill, deputy."

"I'm Bill," Bill says.

"Right, right, Bill Dill." She turns to Phil, "And this is Bill, no, no, Phil Dill. Deputy. And this," She turns to Shawn, hesitates. "This is Shawn Gallagher, part-time volunteer deputy."

Shawn steps forward with a nervous half-smile and extends his hand, "It's a genuine pleasure, sir."

Hinman pauses, his eyes narrow, "Shawn Gallagher? I've heard that name? Shawn Galla...good God, Shawn Gallagher. You're the pigman."

Shawn answers with exaggerated shame and deference, "I cannot deny it, sir." He sighs. "I'm the very one."

Hinman looks slowly at the five of them, then to Kavanaugh, "What the hell is going on here, Sheriff?"

Shawn's early unease has somewhat given way to amusement at the situation. He says with a full grin, "They needed the help, sir."

"This man is one of our most important suspects, in fact, a prime suspect," Hinman by now is sputtering, "and you hire him as a deputy to work on the case. You got a jail here, Sheriff? That's where he should be."

"He volunteered. Anyway, I can't get a warrant and arrest somebody for acting like a fool." Pat says, "And that's all he's done. Besides, we checked him out. There's nobody seen him outta his woods before or since that stunt he pulled at the EPC meeting, which took place after the murders happened. And there's a whole town full of character witnesses here who will testify for him. I'll keep him around just in case, so we can keep an eye on him. We'll know where he is if we need him. He's a big help. You know we're understaffed."

Hinman blows out a mouthful of air. "Well, you're running this thing, Sheriff, whether I like it or not. Just don't let him out of your sight." He looks at Shawn, "I did get a laugh at what you pulled at that meeting. Those SOBs deserved what you gave um." Stern again, he goes on, "But you're still a suspect as far as I'm concerned and if you people here don't wrap this up before I'm in charge again, you will have a lot more questions to answer. Now, what have you found out about that woman north of here and the three wives? If Gallagher here is not a suspect, that's about all you got left."

"Marilyn Jacobson, she's the woman up in Franklin Township," Patrick answers. "She not only wouldn't slap a mosquito, she has a hard enough time just walking. There's no way she could have set up all that stuff with the pictures and all unless she did it virtually or something. I'm not sure she even owns a cell phone, let alone a computer."

Hinman is wearing down. "Doesn't seem like the three wives will help us much. You need to talk to them, but their alibis are pretty close to iron-clad."

"You're right. The timeline just doesn't work out. That man, Sanchez, who heard um talking about murder when they were in the hot tub? The robberies and murders had probably already happened when he heard that. I don't guess wishful thinking on their part is evidence that they had anything to do with the killings. I don't think we got a thing we can hold them on."

Hinman takes a deep breath, exhales, "So where does that leave us, Sheriff Kavanaugh?"

Long pause. The Nachawinga County posse look at each other. Tentatively, the Sheriff indicates the wall. There is a picture of Shawn Gallagher—crossed out. There are pictures of Misty Wooten, Connie Schittman, and Lizzy Birdseed—crossed out. There is a picture of Marilyn Jacobson holding a Stop Factory Farms sign—crossed out. There is a picture of an old, very old, International Harvester pickup truck—not crossed out. Patrick looks at Hinman, reluctant to continue, "See that pickup there? People have been spotting that old truck all over the county. Each time they spot it, it's in a place that has something to do with this case. They've seen it where the bodies were discovered, where the vehicles driven by the victims were found, and on and on. They see it, then the truck just disappears—no sign it was ever there, no tracks, no nothing. We've been on that, checking on these sightings, where people have seen it. Shawn has been looking at these sites, and he's found, written in the snow, the messages you see up there."

Hinman is incredulous, "You're telling me you're trying to track down a pickup truck?"

"It's not just the truck, it's who owned it."

"Well, who the hell owned it?"

Patrick hesitates, "A man, uh, named Craven Snuggs. Farmed north of here. Owned that truck for about as long as anybody can remember. Hated big agriculture as much as a man can hate anything. He could get pretty mean when he was riled up. Would of purely loved to see those big shots done in the way they were."

Hinman rubs his eyes, resigned. In a measured cadence, "It seems to me, Sheriff Kavanaugh, you should get this Craven Snuggs in here for questioning."

"There's a small problem, Chief," Patrick hesitates again, then goes on, "Ya see, Craven Snuggs is dead."

"Dead?"

"Been dead—fifteen, maybe sixteen years."

"So," Hinman seems to have grown a couple of inches, "the only remaining suspect is this Craven Snuggs, who has been dead for fifteen or sixteen years?" Hinman looks at his Vice Chief who is looking at the ceiling, "Holy fucking shit, the only suspect we've got left has been dead for over a decade-and-a-half?" He looks over at Nelda before she can admonish him, "Pardon my language, Ms. Womble."

"Well, Sheriff Kavanaugh," Hinman continues, "I think it best that I leave your jurisdiction and allow you to continue your pursuit of the ghost of Craven Snuggs. I will return to Des Moines and protect our terrified Guv and hope to hell I can find his damn portrait so I can get my division back to some real work. Then maybe we will come back to Nachawinga County and help you find some living suspects and put this case to bed." He signals Vice Chief Orchincross, who precedes him through the exit and opens the back door of the Suburban.

Pat follows him to the exit and shouts, "Shawn saw Snuggs's horse, too."

Without looking back, Hinman climbs into the big black car. Elizabeth Orchincross starts the engine and digs two long ruts in the gravel as she pulls out.

Shawn looks at Patrick, mimicking a child, "Now can I go look around my timber where that horse disappeared, Boss?"

The Sheriff throws his hands into the air.

Later that day, the Yellow VW, headed east, crosses the Possum River bridge on SR 70 into Nachawinga County. Conversation since the three riders had left Connie's farm had mostly centered around food. When they had commented on the quality of the sausage and bacon they were served for breakfast, the housekeeper told them that JJ Schittman never ate pork from his own packing plant. He always sent her to get it from a small farmer who sold meat and veggies at the Ames farmers' market. They had also been enthralled by the braised locally raised lamb at a small restaurant called *Relish* in a little college town they'd passed through the night before on their way back to Ames.

When she notices the county line sign, Lizzy says, "We're close. GPS says we turn left on the next road, then half a mile. That should be where my egg factory is."

Five minutes later they are in front of a gate with a sign that reads, *Freebird Poultry. Whatever You Want From A Chicken, We Can Get For You.* After Lizzy explains who she is to Alejandro Gutierrez, who is in charge of the gate, and thanks him for his condolences, they drive in and are met by an uneasy, overweight plant manager with a yellow complexion and a truly creative comb-over. Lizzy is all business, brushing off expressions of sympathy and turning down an offer of coffee and a guided tour. "We'll just poke around on our own, thanks. You can wait here for us, and we will talk when we're done." Although it is not much above freezing, drops of sweat run down the manager's forehead as a result of Lizzy's answer.

The building the three women enter is about the size of a regional airport terminal. Again, the stench is difficult, but after Patriot Pork they are getting used to foul odors, although the aroma of chicken shit is decidedly different from that of pig manure. They are greeted by rows of thirty-inch-square wire cages on racks seem crowded with dirty, white, beakless hens. Under the cages, a conveyer belt moves, catching eggs and carrying them to machines that crack them and do a marginal job of separating the shells from the liquid inside, which is then dumped into large stainless-steel tubs, mixed, and poured into tanker trucks to eventually become the key ingredient of various brands of egg muffins and sausage biscuits.

Noting the scarcity of employees, Lizzy remarks, "Looks like the hens are doing all the work. Wonder if they're making minimum wage, too."

She walks up to a young woman sitting at the moving line, watching the eggs go by. Occasionally the woman shines a light on one. "How many people work here?"

"Maybe seven, eight."

Lizzy looks up and down the line, amazed that almost everything is done by machines and hens. Most of the people she sees are either cleaning up broken eggs or watching for them. "And what are you looking for?" she asks the young woman.

"Bad eggs."

"Bad eggs?"

"Si."

She looks at the other two women. "I wonder if they are looking in the right place?"

Back at the office, the manager's mouth is agape as he listens to a very serious new owner and CEO's instructions. "To start with, I want only two hens per cage. Those cages look as crowded to me as the women's restrooms at an NFL game half-time. We'll investigate new cage designs later, but I want my hens to be comfortable until we decide what their new quarters are going to look like. By the way, what kind of retirement plan do you have for these workers? What happens when the chicks become old hens?" All three of the women are aware of the irony in this question, which goes right over the manager's head.

"Uh, we, uh we, well, we grind up the edible parts for chicken nuggets—we sell it to fast food companies. Whatever we can't get rid of that way goes to schools for lunches," the distraught and confused manager answers. "Everything ya can't eat goes to fertilizer." Then, with an attempt at pride, "Nothing wasted."

"Hmmm." Connie is having fun. "We'll work on that." She glances at the other two women and winks. "And what about the human employees. How many are there?"

"They're eight on each shift. We run three shifts of ten hours each," the now-heavily-perspiring manager replies, "three ten-hour shifts to make the hens think there are thirty hours in a day. Makes um lay more."

"Must be a little confusing for the humans. And how much do these humans make?"

Now the manager is unsure of whether he should be proud or ashamed of his answer, "Minimum, uh, minimum wage--if, uh if they're documented."

"And if they're not?" Her expression makes it clear that proud is not what he should be.

Now he's pretty much unsure of everything. "Well, uh, if they're, uh, not, we pay by the job."

"We will give them a thirty percent raise beginning tomorrow. Wait till we're gone so they'll think it was your idea—they'll love you for it."

The bewildered manager, having destroyed his comb-over by scratching his head, continues scratching as he watches the three women pile into the VW and drive through the gate.

Back in the car, Lizzy sighs, "Oh, my Lord." She gestures as if she is dusting her hands. "Well, two down and one to go."

Underway, Misty says, "I think we're getting pretty close to Franklin Township and my pig factories that are causing so much trouble there. Y'all know that's where Hubert wanted to put in two or three or twenty more of um. Sounded to me like he was going to fill the whole place with his pigs. We'll just drive around a bit and see what things look like. Then we'll go and see Miz Jacobson, Marilyn. I called her last night, she's the one who sat in a wheelchair in front of a bulldozer to keep it from starting a new building. She's expecting us."

143

"GPS says we are in Franklin Township as we speak." Lizzy, serving as navigator, squints at her cell phone. "About half-mile from 3202 Bourbon Street. That's the address you gave me, Misty. Nice name for her street."

Franklin Township is in a hilly part of Nachawinga County—mostly rolling, bare, harvested land. Beige cornfields with rows of foot-tall stalks mark where plants as tall as pro-basketball players stood three months earlier. Beanfields, mostly grey, with little lines of four-inch-high stubs, the remains of the lush soybean plants that covered the ground in the summer. Here and there, interrupting the complete monotony of harvested fields, are small pastures, still green, sprinkled with scatterings of cattle, mostly black, looking from a distance like fresh-ground pepper on pesto pasta. There are trees. Cottonwoods in gullies, oaks on hillside savannahs, cedars on neglected pasture, and a mixture of box-elder, mulberry, and elm along the banks of French Creek, which bisects the township. Most of the trees have lost their leaves at this time of year.

"Looks like some kind of settlement ahead," Connie says as they approach one of the higher hills they have seen. "There's Bourbon Street." They turn off the blacktop onto a gravel road up the hill. A few houses are visible, mostly turn-of-the-twentieth-century farmhouses, with a couple of nineteen-fifties vintage brick ranch houses. A neatly hand-painted sign simply reads, *Franklin, Population 87. Unincorporated. Established 1843.* When they reach the crest, the three are stunned by what they see. It's as if that whole hillside has been scalped. Instead of grass fields and scattered trees, there is an astonishing array of yellow machinery, what appear to be foundations for very large buildings, and the scattered detritus of the earth-moving and construction process. Dozers and Bobcats are chewing up ground and belching black smoke, and men in hardhats holding clipboards are marching around, giving orders, trying to accomplish as much as possible before the end of the day. No more than fifty yards on the downside of the disturbance are a white wooden church, a filling station/grocery, a large house surrounded by a white picket fence with a sign that reads *Maria's Day Care,* and an old one-room schoolhouse that has *Library* over the door.

Connie stops the car, and they just stare in silence for a very long moment before Misty says, "I'm pretty sure this mess is all the Wootens' fault. Let's drive around a little and see what other crap I am responsible for. Then we'll go see Miz Jacobson before I come back and stop this shit."

They continue down a line of buildings, three of them finished and full of squealing, grunting piglets, with lines of fans in the windows blowing out acrid fumes. Between each finished confinement, backhoes, ditch diggers, and other construction machines have dug into and leveled the deep black dirt, pushing trees over and eliminating any sign of grass or flowers. It looks like the plan is to extend hog houses through the middle of the village, cutting Franklin in half.

Misty looks grim, "Let's get out of here and go have a talk at 3202 Bourbon Street. Looks like I got a lot of restoration to think about."

Thirty-two-o-two is a large but unpretentious, Victorian-style farmhouse that looks to be about a hundred and twenty-five years old. It is in perfect shape, new powder blue paint trimmed in dark blue—window casings, door frames, railings, and gingerbread. The walk is lined with dormant flower plants, as are the house borders. Two large oaks dominate the front yard, with crab apples, plums, and bushes scattered around the rest of the lawn. The front door is bright red. Marilyn Jacobson is waiting for them on the wrap-around porch. She appears to be about eighty, give or take five years. She stands, with her cane, perfectly erect, emphasizing her height, unusual for a woman of her generation. She is wearing a thick, hand-knit maroon sweater. With a remarkable smile, she waves them in.

"I knew who you were when I saw that little yellow car driving around the village. Ain't much use for cars like that around here, specially with winter coming." Marilyn Jacobson walks to the edge of the porch stairs. "Please, come on up. Which one of you is Miz Wooten?"

Misty extends her hand, "Misty. Just Misty. This is Lizzy Birdseed and Connie Schittman." Misty indicates the others. "They go by first names too."

"And I'm Marilyn. Just Marilyn. Pleasure to have you here. Now, you ladies come on in the house. It's not too bad of a day for November but still nippy to be standing outside."

They follow her into a large living room that might have been unchanged for the past hundred years—a perfect match for the outside of the house. The style is consistent—upholstered wing-back chairs with wooden arms, a matching sofa and love seat, lamps with fringed shades on small tables. The furniture is used but not worn out. A fireplace, framed by an oak mantlepiece, is set in the interior wall. Dusty-rose Chantilly curtains hang in the windows. The only thing in the room that seems out of place is a large modern desk facing one of the front windows, cluttered with papers and various journals and a twenty-seven-inch Apple computer. Marilyn Jacobson's walker stands folded, discretely tucked away in the hallway leading to the stairs. Sadly, shattering the total tranquility of this setting is the inescapable, pervasive, oppressive odor of pig manure.

A man in one of the chairs stands when the four women come in the front door. About the same age as Marilyn, he is short and thick but not fat. He is wearing denim bib overalls, a blue chambray work shirt, and wool socks. He has left his work boots by the front door. He holds a green John Deere cap in his hands.

"This is Ezra Gustafson, ladies, but he wouldn't know you were talking to him if you called him Ezra," Marilyn indicates the man. "Been Gus long as I can remember, since before he could walk." Gus chuckles. "Misty, you said you wanted to talk about raising pigs, so I thought Gus might have a few things to add to the conversation. Maybe a little history. Gus, these are Misty, Connie, and Lizzy."

Gus nods. "Pleased to meetcha."

Marilyn gestures, "I think we got enough places to sit. Can I get anyone something to drink?"

Lizzy looks at the others, then, "We're good. Thanks." They all sit.

Misty begins, "I think I should start since it looks like it's the business I've inherited that's been hurting people around here. I think you are probably aware that our three husbands have recently met rather dramatic and, should I say, timely ends."

Marilyn and Gus start to speak. Misty stops them.

"Please don't offer your sympathy or tell us how sorry you are. None of us is suffering one bit from the misfortune that befell those three gentlemen. However, the three of us now have these businesses we have to figure out how to run. That's what we are doing and that's why I'm here. Connie and Lizzy have been to Patriot Pork and the Birdseed chicken factory, and they have ideas about changes they want to make. I want to hear from you about what changes you think Compassionate Family Farms should make."

Marilyn smiles, "Thank you, Misty, for coming here to listen to us. You are being very generous. We've been trying for almost three years to have a conversation with your hus—your late husband about what his business is doing to our way of life, with no success. He refused to talk to us. I'm not going to presume to tell you how your business should be run. But I can tell you how the way it is being run now is affecting our lives."

"And that's what I want to hear," Misty says.

Marilyn pauses, takes a deep breath, and continues. "Franklin Township is a community, has been for over a hundred and fifty years. We've been through the good and the bad, we've got real good folks and not-so-good folks, we've made some mistakes and we've made some good decisions. Even though we disagree on a lot of things, we talk. And we have always looked out for each other. But now it seems our little village is in real trouble."

She stands so she can see out of the window.

"Four years ago, give or take a month, Lyle Holmgren—he has a little farm on the east side of the township—started to put up a building. Nobody knew what it was at first. Residents hadn't gotten any information from the Supervisors or the DNR about any kind of permit, but it soon became obvious that it was going to be a CAFO. Folks went over to talk to Lyle about what he was doing. He said he was just going to build this one, a little one. Said he was having trouble making ends meet, what with corn and bean prices taking a dive and all. Said a Mister Wooten contacted him and promised if he would put up a building, Compassionate Farms would furnish pigs and feed for him to finish them out. All he would have to do would be to clean out the building, haul the manure away, watch them grow, and sell them back to him, Wooten, for a big profit. But a couple of years later, two more buildings went up, bigger ones. This time Mr. Wooten himself was building them, the one you saw west of the church and one over to the east, close to Miz Barber's elder-care business. We met with the Supervisors to object to the new ones. Holmgren's lot was already starting to make quite a stink. But they said all the rules were being followed and their hands were tied. We are peaceful people. We believe in rules. But following them or not, when these two lots started feeding pigs, the quality of our lives began to go downhill. Then, all of a sudden, work on new buildings started going on all over the place—looked like they were going to fill up the whole township. Still, the people who live here, the people who have to put up with these lots, had no recourse. Now Lyle says he's not making money on his pigs because Compassionate Farms sets the price he gets and he's barely meeting expenses. And he's out fifty thousand for his building. We've tried to get help from the DNR, and they say they have no authority—their hands are tied. 'Rules are rules,' as if we weren't sick and tired of hearing that. We formed a little action group and sent a petition to the state Environmental Protection Committee to stop the new construction, but the meeting has been postponed. We are not very hopeful it will do any good."

She turns toward the widows.

"Take a deep breath—it's obvious, isn't it? What the problem is? I think if people could've found buyers for their houses, most everyone around would have sold out and moved by now—even folks whose parents and grandparents built their homes in the first place. But real estate, houses, have gone down fifty, sixty percent since the first confinement went up. Still, nobody wants to buy um. Folks with breathing problems are suffering, their problems getting worse. Kids from here say their classmates don't want to be close to them in school because of the way their hair and clothes smell. On a warm day, it's impossible to get away from flies. We don't sit on our porches, don't cook in our backyards, don't even stand around and talk after church. Not many swimming pools in Franklin, but there is a little one behind that house you can see down the road to the south. They can't use it. Drained it two summers ago. They're going to fill it in, maybe plant a garden.

"I was born in this house, Misty. So was my mother. My Great Grandfather built it. My family has taken care of it like a precious jewel. I left Franklin when I was 18. Went to college and nursing school. Then my husband and I got all the traveling we wanted when we were both in the military. We dreamed of coming back to Franklin, to this house. He didn't make it. But I did, and there was no place else in this wide world that I wanted to be." The level of her voice rises dramatically. "I'm here, and I'm going to do everything I can to save this village even if I have to get run over by a damn bulldozer to do it. I won't have this township destroyed because somebody wants to make a lot of money off a bunch of fucking pigs." Then, quietly, "I won't ask you to excuse my language. It's the only way I know that can clearly express what I feel."

No one speaks for a long time. Gus looks at his feet, then his hat, then at the four women, then back at his feet, unsure of whether to be embarrassed or proud of Marilyn.

Misty gets up and walks to the window and stands by Marilyn. She looks at the construction going on along the road and down the hillside. "I should have paid more attention. I guess we all should have." The other two widows nod in agreement as she goes on, "I was so focused on getting my own back, what I thought I had coming to me. Once I got that, I didn't pay much attention to what was going on around me, didn't care. I had what I wanted, at least what I thought I wanted. It never occurred to me that what I thought of as my good fortune might be causing discomfort or pain to others. I had no idea, and I'm truly sorry for it."

Marilyn smiles, then looks at Gus. "I asked Gus to come to tell you how he produces the best pork in the Midwest, maybe the country. And maybe give you an idea of what it used to be like. I can tell you, the way he raised them, nobody ever complained about his pigs."

Gus looks up from his hat, "Well, I don't raise many of um no more. Never did, really, compared to what's in them buildins. Used to be, before the big boys come in, I'd turn over maybe three, four hundred head a year. That many, along with my beef and chickens, brought in all the income me and the family needed. Sold most of um local. Weanlings to farmers around who wanted to feed um out. Lots a folks would buy a finished hog or go in with their neighbor, then I'd take it to Watsons' locker over to MacDuff where it'd get cut up the way they wanted it. I had a pretty good reputation. Lots a folks come over from Des Moines, Cedar Rapids. Had one customer clear up to Rochester. That's in Minnesota. Then they was buyers would take the pigs that wasn't spoke for. But they ain't no more buyers around. Big guys do it all now— farrow um, feed um out in them prisons they keep um in, kill um, pack um, and sell um. No room in that chain for the little guy, like me. I still raise a few for my old customers, but if the wife an me still had our family to support we'd be in trouble.

"I love pigs. I've loved um since I was a little kid. That hillside over yonder that you can barely see, that pasture and little piece a timber, that's my place. Sows would farrow on that pasture."

Lizzy, looking puzzled asks, "What's 'farrow,' Gus?"

Gus smiles, "That's when the sows have their young'uns. See them shelters? Well, ya can hardly see um, but they's one a them little houses for each pig family. They live on that pasture and some corn I feed um till the acorns fall. Then I put um in the timber, let um clean up the acorns. They love them acorns. Folks say its acorns gives um that special flavor they cain't get anywheres else. Winters they go over to Watsons' locker, them that's spoke for. Nowadays I sell um person to person, farm to table. I surely do love them pigs."

"How many acres on your place?" Misty asks.

"147, more or less. Dad bought the place back in the early forties. Him and mom raised me an six others on it. Moved here from Minnesota, come down here on a wagon. Bought a old farmhouse a mile east a here, moved it to our place an fixed it up."

"Could your family live off a hundred and forty-seven acres back then?"

"We was fine. We was poor but we didn't know it. Six kids—all graduated college."

"Could you live off it now?"

"Maybe me an the wife an a dog—not a family."

"Did you ever think about putting up a confinement?" Lizzy asks him.

"Over my dead body." Gus's booming laugh fills the entire room. The others' laughter blends in.

"Thank you, Gus," Connie says to him. "It sounds like I should put my name on your list for some of that famous pork."

Gus smiles and nods, "I'd be pleased."

"Now," Marilyn says, "I hope you three won't turn me down when I invite you to supper tonight. When you told me you were coming, I got one of Gus's tenderloins out of the freezer and it's been slow roasting with my famous rub on it since morning. No excuses now. Will you do me the honor?"

The widows smile at each other, and Connie answers, "We'd be delighted."

Marilyn looks at Gus, "Won't you stay too?"

"Thank you, better not," he shakes his head. "I'm sure the wife's gonna have supper waiting for me. To tell the truth, I can hardly stand to eat um anymore. As matter a fact, I've almost become one of them there vegetarians. Don't mind other folks eating um—that's what they're here for, and that's what I raise um for. I give um a good life, a hell of a lot better than they git in them concrete prisons, and they give me a livin and they give good meals for lots a folk, and I sure hope people enjoy um. But I can see them little uns bouncing around on that hillside and I just never did have no appetite for um."

Marilyn gets up and turns to the widows, "I imagine that tenderloin's about ready to come out of the oven so I'll take care of things in the kitchen. Won't be long." All three of the widows offer help which she waves off as she goes into the hall toward the back of the house.

Gus is flustered at being left alone with the widows three. After a long silence, comfortable for the women but not for Gus, he stands, picks up his hat, and bows. "Well, I guess I best be getting on towards the house. Missus'l be waiting. Sure was nice to meet you all. If there's anything else I can do for ya just tell Marilyn." He puts his hat on and almost runs out the door.

Connie and Lizzy join Misty at the window. The reddening sun begins to drop behind a copse of aspens west of the house, signaling early dusk. They walk out on to the porch and look at the sunset-bathed hills. Misty turns to Connie, "You're right. Iowa is a beautiful state." She wrinkles her nose, "but right here it sure does stink."

152

They quickly retreat into the house and close the door just as Marilyn comes out of the kitchen. "I believe everything's ready. Let's go into the dining room."

The large oval table is covered with a lace-edged tablecloth and set with sterling silverware and blue willow china. There are dishes of vegetables, biscuits, and relish, and a large pitcher of iced tea, but the star of the table is a steaming pork tenderloin with a wonderful fragrance that has almost managed to overpower that of the pork outside.

With a mouth half-full, Misty turns to Marilyn, "What could the township do with some large concrete slabs?"

Marilyn looks at her for a long moment. "Tennis and basketball courts come to mind. I won't be using them much," She laughs, "but there are those around who would."

Misty smiles, "Looks like that should be possible. I'll be back in the morning to talk to the construction manager about a change in building plans."

"Now, excuse me, but I'm not going to let you ladies drive all the way to Ames after supper and turn around and come back in the morning...." Marilyn is emphatic. "You'd be wasting your gas and your time. I got enough bedrooms in this house to put up the three of you and more. I function as a kind of unofficial bed and breakfast here in Franklin. If there's a wedding or funeral and folks need putting up, Franklinites turn to me, so the rooms are ready for you. And besides, we got a lot more talking to do and you got to go see the Sheriff tomorrow." The widows' objections are half-hearted. Misty speaks for them all, "Marilyn, we'd be much obliged."

And talk they do, until well after midnite, about big agriculture's takeover of rural Iowa, about the death of small farms and small towns, about the dearth of local control, or local input, into decisions affecting the wellbeing of local citizens. All this over glasses of Marilyn's homemade wine. Late in the evening when Connie was asked how she liked the wine, she whorled her last sip around in her glass, sniffed it, and paraphrased an old Leon Redbone song, "It ain't French but it ain't bad and French ain't here." They all laughed and filled their glasses once again.

Seven o'clock Thursday morning and the town of Tripoli is under orange alert. Breakfast and coffee time at the Morning Brew is abuzz with "D'ya really think they are really coming here?" and "Are they still suspects?" and "D'ya think they done it?" and "What time are they coming?" and "Where?" Merchants in the few remaining downtown businesses are refusing to leave their storefront windows for fear of missing something, and the two members of the fire department are sitting in chairs outside the station, despite the early morning chill, on alert for any strange vehicle that might show up. Father O'Shea, trying to appear as if he is cleaning the front steps of St. Patrick's, is actually looking north up the highway in hopes of being the first one to spot three strangers. The three widows are coming to Tripoli.

Four pickups, two SUVs, and a sedan are already parked in front of the sheriff's office, doors closed, motors running, passengers inside, waiting for events to unfold.

Patrick is looking out the window, agitated. "I know what they're out there for. Who the hell let the word out those women were coming to town this morning?" He addresses Nelda and Shawn, also in the office. "I thought I told everybody to keep a lid on it." Shawn lifts his palms and shakes his head. Pat goes on, "Can't keep anything secret around here. Next thing ya know there'll be cars parked from MacDuff to Sears City." He turns slowly and frowns at Nelda, who tries to look innocent. "Only person I told was my sister, Shirley. I told her on pain of death to keep it to herself."

"Jesus, Nelda," Pat blows out his breath. "Telling Shirley, pain of death or not, is like telling CNN. Might as well of put up a sign on the courthouse. No wonder the parking lot's filling up like we were giving away free breakfast." At that moment, the Van Gorp rendering truck pulls into the lot, taking up three of the remaining parking places and leaking God knows what out of its bed. Luke gets out and Travis pries himself from under the steering wheel. "And look at that. What the hell are they doing here all the way from Onky?"

Luke and Travis walk into the office. Luke fishes around in his coverall pockets and pulls out another dirty sack, this time with Hardees on it, which he hands to Patrick.

"Hell's this?" Patrick looks in the sack.

"Another piece of that feller. Ain't gonna say what it looks like. Found it after we brought you them other pieces when we was emptying the truck again. Thought you'd wanna see it."

Patrick sniffs the sack, makes a face, then rolls the top shut. "You boys just gonna keep bringing this stuff in every time there's something going on you want to stick your noses into?" Shaking his head. "Well, thanks anyhow. I guess you boys need to get back to work. I do appreciate the, uh, the whatever it is." He hands the sack to Nelda who hands it to Shawn who hands it back to Patrick who throws it on the desk. Nelda, picking it up gently between her thumb and forefinger, takes it over to the green trash container and drops it in.

Travis lowers himself slowly into one of the folding chairs against the wall. "We got a little time to kill. Thought we jus might visit fer a while. Don't want to miss seeing um."

Patrick sighs, "Who?"

"You know."

"I don't know."

"You know. Wives a them dead dudes."

"What makes you think they're coming here?"

"Hell, Pat," Luke says. "Every damn body in this county an the next knows they's coming here today. Knows they was at the chicken factory yesterday; knows they spent the night to Marilyn Jacobson's an knows they's on their way here now. Thought you knowed." He is enjoying himself. "Heard they was hot looking. Me an Travis jus wanna see fer ourselves."

"Well shit, just make yourselves at home. Sit as long as you want," Pat is defeated. "Welcome to the Nachawinga County reality show. Sorry we don't have refreshments. Shawn, are our other two part-time deputies gonna be here today? We might need um to direct traffic in the parking lot."

"You're out of luck, Pat. They only work weekends."

Back at the Jacobson 'B&B,' Marilyn's guests have just finished a generous breakfast of Gus Gustafson's eggs and bacon, fresh-baked bread, and homemade blackberry jam. They were too stuffed to do more than taste the sausage gravy and biscuits. Misty gets up and says, "That was truly wonderful. Don't think I should eat again for a week but that's just not in my genes. I see the neighborhood "improvers" are back at work. I think I'll go have a little talk with the man in charge."

Marilyn, Connie, and Lizzy watch Misty exit the side door and walk along a narrow boardwalk to the construction headquarters trailer. They see her knock on the door and see a very handsome young man, in the neighborhood of thirty-five, come down the trailer steps. They notice Misty's obvious pleasure that, by her standards, at any rate, this boss is head and shoulders (literally and figuratively) above the other bosses they have encountered on their sojourn thus far. They see conversation they can't hear, but by gesture, it seems that construction should stop, that two large concrete slabs, probably built as floors for future CAFOs that will not be built, might be repurposed for something else (Misty gestures as if she is hitting a tennis ball and shooting a basket). They see cordial nods during another ten minutes of conversations and handshakes at the end. Misty pats the construction manager on his arm as Connie says to herself, "please don't pat him on the butt, at least not while Marilyn is watching."

Back at the table, Misty pours herself a final cup of coffee and, in true southern fashion, laces it liberally with cream and sugar. "Well, that was lovely. He was a little worried about his contract with Compassionate Farms, but I assured him we would honor his contract, only what he would be building would be a little different. Turns out, Marilyn, he is from around here and he hated seeing those CAFOs going up in the first place. He was tickled pink when I told him they were going to be community projects. His name is Barney. And I know you all noticed, he sure is good-looking. Marilyn, he's going to research the proper surfaces for those courts you wanted, and for the rest of that ground that's been chewed up. You know, at some point it might be a park. I told him to consult with you on everything. I predict that real estate and house prices will double when word gets out about what's gonna happen here, but nobody's gonna want to sell."

By the time they finish breakfast, it is nearly eleven and the temperature has climbed close to seventy, almost unheard of for Iowa in November. "Well, girls," Connie says, "let's load up the wagon and turn ourselves over to the sheriff and his posse and see if they're going to put us in jail for supposedly murdering our husbands. Want to come along, Marilyn?"

"Oh my, no. Thanks for the invitation but I think not. They might want to jail me as an accessory, and if not that, I've done enough disturbing of the peace for them to lock me up to keep me from doing more. I just want to say that what you ladies are thinking about is nothing I expected. You don't exactly look like the sort who would be so kind and understanding about our predicament here. Whoops, I didn't mean to say it like that—but I think you know what I was trying to say."

"We do indeed," Lizzy answers, "and thanks to you for giving Misty and me one of our best Iowa days yet."

Connie moves toward the front door, "All right ladies, we're on the road again." The three widows each give Marilyn Jacobson a hug and walk onto the porch. "You know, I think it's warm enough to put the top down and ride to Tripoli in high style."

The yellow Volkswagen, topless, three scarves flying in the wind, picks up its first vehicle follower at the south edge of MacDuff. By the time it reaches the Tripoli city limits, it has picked up at least a dozen and a half more and now looks like a homecoming parade without cheerleaders or a funeral procession without a hearse. As they pass the Kum and Go, Connie brakes to ask for directions to the Sheriff's Department. A man walking south at a very brisk pace points, "Straight ahead, Ma'am. Right under the flag." A multi-car pile-up behind the yellow bug is narrowly avoided, mainly because the speed of the parade has slowed to a crawl. Still, a small Honda and a large GMC have to swerve into the wrong lane to avoid rear-ending the vehicle in front, causing some cursing through rolled-down windows and at least one extended middle finger.

When the three reach the parking lot, Phil, who had to flip a coin with his brother for the privilege of being the first to meet the 'suspects,' leads them to the one remaining parking place, empty only because a large garbage can has been placed in the middle. Phil moves the can out of the way as Connie maneuvers the little car into the opening. He trips over himself opening doors and leading the three women into the office, as the spectators in the other parked cars look on and those standing by the door part to let them through. By now pedestrian onlookers have gathered on the corner as well, gossiping, smoking, and gawking.

The office is as crowded as the parking lot with folks who managed to think of some excuse to see the Sheriff. Luke and Travis elbow their way toward the women, wide-eyed. Travis tries to tell them about finding the bodies, Nelda manages to stop him. Pat, beside himself by now, trying to look as official as he can, shouts to the crowd, "Dammit folks. We got official confidential business to attend to. We need to talk to these ladies in private, so I'll have to ask all you folks to leave for now. The office is closed except for department personnel until at least two this afternoon." Travis and Luke, who have managed to hang back until the very end, almost fall down the steps as they leave, looking backward. Their parting words whispered, but loud enough to be heard by most everyone, "Sumbitch, them's sumpin." They continue talking and gesturing, now out of hearing, as Nelda slams the door behind them.

When Travis and Luke finally make it to their truck and the parking lot begins to clear out, Patrick turns to the suspects, trying as best he can to appear professional, "Welcome to our little town of Tripoli. Sheriff Kavanaugh here. My deputies, Phil and Bill Dill, and Shawn Gallagher. Our dispatcher and office manager, Nelda Womble. Of course, she's the one who really runs the place—couldn't function without her." Nelda, not at all impressed by Pat's attempt at flattery, treats the three women with a decidedly icy smile and three unenthusiastic handshakes.

"Why, Sheriff Kavanaugh, I am—we are— so pleased to meet you," Misty turns to Connie and Lizzy, in a clearly audible stage whisper, "I thought county sheriffs were supposed to be fat and dressed in shirts that are busting their buttons. This one is downright cute with that glitter on his hat and that six-gun on his belt. He can protect me anytime."

This time, with no smile at all, Nelda turns to Misty, "If you think Patrick is cute you should see his three kids. Two boys and a girl—they are a-dorable." She pauses, "His wife's not too bad either."

Phil, Bill, and Shawn are only partially able to hold back laughs as Pat's blush lights up the office.

Misty continues undeterred, "and that deputy over there, Shawn, I'd like to have that lawman as my body gaaad."

Nelda, in what has turned into a sparring match, looks at Shawn. "I think he's got another body in mind he'd like to gaad." She speaks the last word with an exaggerated, but not very good, southern drawl.

Shawn adds another blush to the room, astonished at Nelda's perception.

Pat regains his composure, somewhat. "Well, we better get down to business. Nelda, I guess I should sit at the desk. You can pull up a chair on the side there. I'd like you to take some notes."

Nelda vacates the chair with an unmistakably grumpy expression.

"Bill, you fix the chairs over there by the wall for the ladies." Bill lights a cigarette and starts to move the chairs. "And then step outside with that cigarette."

Bill, astonished at Pat's delicacy, moves the chair, frowns, and starts for the door. Phil lights a cigarette and joins him, and they make their exit like a car burning oil, leaving a trail of smoke behind them.

Everyone sits, including Shawn, who takes a chair beside the front window. Pat, trying to seem as official as possible, starts again, "I, uh, believe I need to read you your rights," he begins looking through the desk drawers, "Let's see," he opens another drawer, "that Miranda thing in here somewhere. Nelda, where did you put...?" Before he can finish, Nelda opens the last drawer, pulls out the frayed yellow poster, and hands it to him.

He takes it. "Ohhh kay, this is it all right." He reads off the poster, "Anything you say here can be used against you," then he quickly adds, "but you have the right to remain silent."

Lizzy chuckles, "That'll be the day when these three gals remain silent." They all laugh. Even Nelda smiles.

The Sheriff continues to read, "You have the right to have a lawyer to represent you, and the county will appoint one for you if you can't afford..."

Misty interrupts, "Honey, we can afford any lawyer we want, but I don't want to have anything to do with most of the lawyers I'm acquainted with."

Pat turns the poster over and sees it is blank, "Ohhh kay, I guess that's all your rights."

"Sheriff Kavanaugh," Lizzy says, "I can assure you we've got a hell of a lot more rights, but there's no need to go into all of them right now." Laughter again, this time Nelda joins in.

A little flustered, Pat continues, "Ohhh kay, we will begin the questioning. "Will you please state your names." They do so with exaggerated formality. "And are each of you, oh, hell, I mean were each of you married to one of the deceased?" He looks at his notes. "Hubert Wooten, Donald Birdseed, JJ Shittman, Jr.?" Nods from the three. "Do any of you have any knowledge pertaining to the deaths of any one of the aforementioned individuals? Anything whatsoever that will help us with this investigation?" Solemn negative headshakes this time. "Did any of you hire or offer some reward, money or, uh," he searches for a word, "uh, something else, to any person who might be willing to kill one or all of your late husbands?" Head shakes. "Do any of you know of anyone who might have wanted one of your husbands dead?"

They all burst into laughter at his question. Lizzy answers, "Let's start with the three of us." More laughter. "Aside from that, how long do you want the list to be? You don't have room in this building for all of um."

There is a long pause as everyone in the room smiles. Pat, embarrassed, looks at his desk wondering if there is something else he should ask. "Ohhh kay," Pat looks at Nelda, Shawn, and Phil and Bill who have re-entered the office. "Any of you have any further questions for these ladies?" Phil and Bill have come back into the room. They all shake their heads.

Pat sighs his relief at being finished. "Well, it looks like we don't have any more questions. To tell the truth, I can see no reason for holding you ladies at this time. Since you have all been very cooperative, you can go as you please. You will need to keep us informed of your whereabouts until we have finished with the investigation. If we need any more information from you, we will be in touch. Thanks for coming in."

Pat straightens his desk. Connie stands and looks at the wall, "I guess those pictures will be coming down, but if you put um back up I can give you a better one of me. The one you've got up there is terrible. Now that we're off the hook, it looks like you're out of suspects, except for that old pickup truck. What's that up there for?"

"Long story. Belonged to a man named Craven Snuggs. Seems like that pickup's been showing up almost every place that had anything to do with your dead husbands. People see it, then it disappears. At the hog lots, and the egg factory. Where they found the cars. One fellow even saw it in Denver, at your headquarters there, Miz Birdseed."

"An it don't leave no trace behind," Phil says. "Been seen around so much we figgered we needed to put its picture up too."

"Marilyn Jacobson told us about this man, Craven Snuggs," Lizzy says. "Sounds like he would've liked to see our husbands eliminated in the worst sort of way. But she said he's been dead for years. Burned up in a house fire that the sheriff at that time refused to investigate."

"That was a problem," Pat says. "We had a pretty good idea who might have started that fire. People who didn't like Craven fighting hog lots and big ag. But that sheriff wouldn't push it. Looked into it—for a couple of weeks. Then called it a cold case, accident, and let it go.

Nelda, now in a slightly warmer mood than when the widows first arrived, gets up to pause the conversation. "Let me interrupt here. It's lunchtime, folks. Yolanda's? We can talk more there."

Shawn addresses the three, "Join us? It's the best, in fact, the only, restaurant in town, and maybe the best Mexican in the state. Just around the corner."

"I'd be happy to come along, young man, if you'll let me sit next to you." Misty leers, "helps my digestion to be seated beside a handsome lawman. Work for you girls?"

They nod and everyone heads out the door.

Yolanda's set a new record that day for the number of customers that came through the door. The whole town seemed to be jostling for seats and tables to watch the goings-on of the three mysterious murder suspects.

The lunch was a huge success. Nelda, Lizzy, and Misty managed two margaritas grande each, Nelda becoming downright cozy halfway through her second one. Connie abstained as the designated driver, deciding it wasn't a good idea to drink huge drinks in front of the sheriff then get in a car and take off for her farm. They talked about Nachawinga County and Tripoli. They talked of little towns, little farms, the beautiful Iowa they had seen. The Sheriff complained about the county supervisors and their refusal to replace the department pickup truck with three hundred and twenty thousand miles on it, and their falling-apart Crown Vic that was useless on snow or mud. Nelda complained about her ten-year-old computer and bragged about her grandkids. Shawn talked about the harmfulness of large livestock operations and how it might be possible for the widows to reorganize their operations to produce meat that was better for people, better for animals, and much tastier. They also talked a lot about Craven Snuggs.

It is almost four as they all make their way through the few people still waiting to get a look at them and back to the Sheriff's office. Shawn zips up his jacket, "See ya later, folks, I'm gonna spend tomorrow in the woods. I want to see if I can find any sign of Craven's horse. Nice to have met you. Don't forget about my suggestions. Let me know if you want to talk more."

The widows climb into their little yellow bug and, waving as they leave the parking lot, point it into the sunset toward Ames. On the trip back, when they weren't talking about reorganizing their businesses, they were singing along with Bob Seger on the radio, *Give me that old-time rock and roll. That kinda music just soothes the soul. I reminisce about the days of old. With that old-time rock and roll.*

Shawn's timber is not very large. Sixty acres more or less. But it is adjacent to Buckthorn State Park, which straddles the southern county line, almost 1800 acres, little used because it has no electric hookups, no playgrounds, no lakes, and no gift shop. This means that Shawn's woods and the park combine to make up the only truly wild area around, and one of the few in the state. Iowa, the state in the union most altered from the way the native people used it and the settlers found it. Iowa, the state in the union with the fewest acres of public land. Altered by digging, draining, plowing, overgrazing, tiling, bulldozing, herbaciding, and anything else that might squeeze one more soybean or grain of corn from the ground, one more nickel from the land. But this woodland (too small to be a forest but close), has been left alone, with its meandering creeks, limestone bluffs, and deep gullies choked with tall grass and blackberries, making any kind of profit extraction too costly and difficult to be worthwhile. The few oak trees worth cutting and dragging to a sawmill have been cut and dragged, though many have come back as twin or triplet re-growths that have gained considerable size, along with the uncut hickory, elm, aspen, and hackberry. Now, in autumn, almost bare trees create lacy webs against the sky. Cedars wear the only green left aloft, but the ground that can be seen in spots where snow has melted is covered with overwintering green plants and a riot of colored leaves, looking like some kind of tweed fabric that has gone out of control in the weaving. Wild things—deer, turkeys, rabbits, pheasants—have retreated into this sanctuary after a gluttonous summer gorging on corn and beans and alfalfa in the outlying fields. They have been followed by foxes, coyotes, bobcats, and such, which have been gorging on them.

It is Shawn's favorite time of year. The time when he can see the culmination of natural processes at work: consumption and storing of summer's bounty. Nuts, fruit, seeds, buried in the ground and carried into hidden dens, fat stored on the bodies of prey then transferred to bodies of predators, all making living through the hard winter possible for those strong enough to survive it and eliminating those that are not. As a scientist, he marvels at nature's experiments, replicated year after year, with only careful changes that fit into the process without consequences that disrupt the whole, without taking anything that won't be paid back. It feels right to him to be a part of the process, taking venison for himself and a friend or two each year, along with pheasants and turkey, to be cooked with the morels and asparagus gathered during summer months. Also, Shawn is convinced that food can best be produced for humans following this same process. That this production of food can take place alongside the natural processes without disrupting and finally destroying both nature and itself. This was Shawn's work at State, and it is on his mind as he enters the woods on this morning. He wonders how he could have wasted over a year on what he now views as total foolishness—dressing up like a pig, sending insulting but pointless letters, writing articles for journals and magazines to be read only by people who think like himself. He misses the research he was doing and continually tries to figure a way he can pick up where he left off without having to give in and follow the orders of people he doesn't trust.

As he enters the woods, walking through the damp leaves that make it possible for him to move almost as quietly as the creatures that are watching him, there is something else that he is thinking of, something it seems he has not been able not to think about for at least the last four or so years. Amie Greene. Amie, who seems to be woven, sprite-like, in every cedar tree. Amie, atop every boulder, like the White Rock Ginger Ale fairy. Amie, behind every rise, sprinting away as soon as he sees her, always almost hidden by mist, always just out of reach.

What is wrong with me? I've rehearsed the words I want to say to her a thousand times. I've even written them down on paper that I have then thrown into the fireplace for fear someone might find them. I LOVE AMIE GREENE. Have since the day she walked into my office. Have for four years. Why can't I just say that to her? The professor/advisor stuff is over and done with. But I'm still paralyzed.

Suddenly he realizes he has just shouted, "I LOVE AMIE GREENE" at the top of his lungs for everyone around to hear. Of course, there is no one around to hear. He also realizes he needs to try to concentrate on what he supposedly is here for. And, truth be told, this seems almost as absurd as his stint as a pig impersonator. Looking for the horse, or the truck, or any sign of a dead man? A ghost?

He moves deeper into the timber, trying to imagine where a saddled horse might hang out, or to remember a lane or opening where an old pickup truck might hide. He has to shake his head. He is well aware that Craven's truck probably can't just cruise around by itself looking for a spot to be out of sight for a while. He sits and slides on his rear-end through the snow into a ravine, getting his butt wet. He crawls up the other bank on his knees, getting them wet, using exposed roots for hand-holds. Then he does a belly flop into the leaves when he reaches the top, getting a lot of the rest of him wet and not caring. He walks toward an edge of shrubs and looks out onto a large opening, thick with rust-red dormant big and little bluestem and the white puffballs of gone-to-seed goldenrod and blazing star. He picks seed from a milkweed pod and releases the parachutes into the breeze. He wonders, as he often does, what this land, this county, this whole state would have looked like two hundred years earlier, before it was changed before it was fucked up. What would it have looked like if he were the first human to have seen it? Of course, he knew that just by seeing it he might have begun the process of fucking it up.

He straddles a fallen hickory tree, wide as a saddle, and thinks again of Craven's horse.

This is idiotic. Craven's horse? Even if it did wander around in the woods after he let it out of the fire, the horse would be long dead by now. Hell, that horse was fifteen when I used to go to his farm. We're all completely crazy, thinking some dead man had something to do with killing those three big shots, much as we know he'd have been mighty happy to see them done in when he was alive. But he's dead now, and his horse is dead, and his truck is rusting away in some gulley somewhere, and we're all seeing things. Those three men? They were just unlucky. Some kind of bizarre coincidence. Two of them got drunk and fell into their hog lots. Those hogs were happy for a little change in their diet. Fate doing the right thing. Don't know about Birdseed. But there's bound to be some sane explanation for that too. Maybe it's just divine will.

He is thinking seriously about going back to Pat's office and telling the posse how stupid the whole thing is, telling them to call it off before they all become a laughingstock. He looks through a tunnel in the brush and sees Amie sitting on a stump. Then she disappears. No, it's just a stump. See? You can see things you want to see—even if they're not there.

Shawn's cell pings. He doesn't usually look at his texts right away, doesn't like to be yanked around by his phone, but this time he looks. From Amie Greene: to Shawn Gallagher, Sheriff Kavanaugh, Nelda Womble, Tim Taylor. "I've got the rest of the afternoon off, and I want to do some more deputy work. Where should I go?" Responses come back right away from Pat, Nelda, and Tim, almost as if they were just waiting for this message, all with pretty much the same directions, "Go help Shawn. He's looking for Craven's horse."

Shawn can't believe what he sees. He reads everything again. Finally, he thumbs in his answer, "I'll meet you at my cabin as soon as you can get here." He takes a deep breath, dismounts from his hickory log steed, and again shouts Amie Green's name into the empty, snowy woods.

Amie doesn't even drive to her designated space behind her building, she just stops her Prius in the no parking zone at the front door and, two steps at a time, sprints to her apartment. She is in danger of destroying her teacher outfit as she tears off her blazer and climbs

167

out of her wool slacks, pulls on heavy socks, a fleece sweatshirt, and flannel-lined jeans. She starts to put Shawn's flannel shirt on, she's worn it every day since he loaned it to her, then thinks better of it, holds it to her face, takes a deep breath, and stuffs it into a brown grocery bag along with extra socks and sweatshirt. Pull boots on, grab gloves, shrug into down puffer jacket, and head for the door. Halfway through, she stops, goes into her bathroom, picks up her toothbrush and a tube of toothpaste, and drops them in the grocery bag. Out the door, slam it locked, down the steps at dangerous speed. Once seated in the car with the brown bag beside her, she picks up the toothbrush and looks at it.

C'mon Amie. What in the world did you bring that for? Wishful thinking? He's had every chance in the world to ask me to stay over at his cabin, and I freeze up when I think of making the first move. My professor, my advisor. Right now, the two most mournful words in the English language: 'good friends.' I guess I'll spend the rest of the day walking around the woods looking for a dead man's horse and truck with a ;good friend.' Well, dammit, could be worse.

As the little red Prius pulls off the exit ramp onto I-80, the first light snowflakes of the afternoon land on the windshield and melt. Amie heads east to the accompaniment of Dylan singing *Buckets of Rain* on XM. It takes her an hour and a quarter to get to Shawn's turn-off, and another ten minutes to get to the cabin.

Meanwhile, Shawn has straightened things up, made his bed, put water on the stove for tea or hot chocolate. He checks to see what he might offer Amie for dinner if it looks like she might stay that long, and he can get up the nerve to ask her. He gets two deer steaks out of the freezer, looking out the window every two minutes in hopes he might see her car appear. It appears. For a moment, Shawn doesn't know whether to run out the front door to greet her or flee out the back into the woods. He chooses the former but doesn't run, trying not to completely lose his cool.

Amie watches him cross the porch and wave. *This time's going to be it, I'm sure. At least a little hug—or maybe a peck on the cheek. I can just feel it. He's not my professor anymore. Dammit. If he doesn't do something, I'm just going to throw my arms around his neck and jump up and hug him with my legs.* She waves back.

Shawn walks down the steps and crosses toward her. He tries to control his breathing. *OK. I'm not her advisor. I'm not her professor. I'm going to quit being a timid wuss. Just one big hug. If she likes it that's just great. If she doesn't, that's the breaks. At least I'll know.*

She steps toward him, brown bag in her left hand. "Water main broke. Flooded the halls. They called school off at eleven. I couldn't wait to get back to my deputy job." She smiles.

He smiles back. "Didn't find anything this morning, but if there's a horse in these woods, we should at least find some sign this afternoon."

They stand, looking into each other's eyes. The silence seems like long minutes to both of them. He sticks out his hand. "I'm really glad you're here."

She hesitates; takes it. "Me too."

They shake hands.

Amie. *Dammit.*

Shawn. *Shit.*

After another long moment, Shawn says, "We don't have a lot of daylight left," as they walk into the cabin. "Looks like you're dressed OK for looking for a dead man's horse and truck. We can put that bag inside and get on with the search."

The two 'good friends' descend the porch steps and enter the woods.

Two hours later. By now Shawn has expressed his misgivings about the possibility of finding a horse or a truck or, for that matter, whether either one even exists anymore. But Amie reminds him of the messages in the snow, now melted away. She stops and takes a slow look around from where they are standing. "Anyhow, it's a wonderful walk." She watches as an oversized leaf from a sentinel sycamore, carved like lace by the diligent chewing of some hungry insect, floats down and lands in a small pool of snowmelt. "It is really beautiful in here."

Shawn, looking up at a few crystal flakes that are working their way through the bare tree limb canopy, "I hoped you'd like it. As far as I'm concerned, it's the most beautiful place I know of. No mountains, no ocean. But its beauty screws its way into your heart and becomes a part of you. Dad bought it when I was in grade school. Then had to sell it when the Walmart opened in Newlin, and his hardware business fell through the floor. I was heartbroken, but I still used to sneak out here and spend hours walking and watching and listening. The man who bought it knew what I was doing, but it still seemed like it was mine, so it never seemed right to me to have to ask his permission. I just kept sneaking in. I knew this place by heart by the time I graduated. When I got a job, had money coming in, I called that man every month to see if he would sell it back. On one of the calls, he said he would, said he had fallen in love with it too, wanted to keep it from being 'improved.' Said he'd sell it back if I put it in a conservation easement. I think he was just holding me off to make sure I really wanted the place and would take care of it. Used almost all my salary, from the time I had one until I got it paid for. Put it in that easement to keep it from ever being changed. It's saving my life now."

They look around into the fading light. He leans slightly toward Amie, moves his hand an inch, two inches toward hers. She doesn't see, but she feels his movement and a pull toward him as if there was some kind of force at work. They freeze, almost losing balance and falling into each other.

Then, Shawn breaks the silence. "We're losing light. We can pick this search up again tomorrow or not, depending on what Pat thinks. Maybe wrap it up one way or another. Can you make it?"

"Sure. After all, I'm a deputy. Gotta do my job."

"I, uh, when I got the message you were coming, I got out a couple of deer steaks, I hope that appeals. I've got some carrots and potatoes, French bread and olive oil. And I found a bottle of pretty good Italian wine. Will, uhm, will you stay for supper?" He holds his breath.

"Oh, sure, I'd like that." She hopes she didn't shout or answer too quickly.

They walk slowly through the disappearing light toward the cabin and climb the stairs, each trying to hold down their excitement.

Inside, Shawn throws some small split logs into the fireplace and stirs what remains of the fire. They stand for a while, rubbing their hands and watching as the embers begin to lick flames around the new wood. Amie hangs her jacket on a hook by the door and breathes in the fireplace smell. "Is there anything I can do to help?"

"Oh, no thanks, I'm good. I get nervous when anybody pays too much attention to my cooking. You just relax and keep an eye on the coals, keep um even. When I get the veggies in the oven I'll put a grill in the fireplace. I can do the steaks in there."

She watches as he sets up the grill. Venison, roast veggies, and Italian wine. *Who do I check with to make sure this isn't a dream—and to whom do I pray to make sure I don't wake up?*

Shawn and Amie are sitting on the sagging sofa, warm, full, both with a little buzz on. Neither knows if it's from the wine or each other. The sofa's sag has slowly moved them closer together. They have talked on and on about things that are most important to them—the land, the air, the water, their state, the beauty of it all—and of ways the harm might be stopped.

Amie, putting it off up to this point, looks at her watch. "Oh Lord, how could it have gotten so late? I really must start back."

Shawn is as reluctant to break the spell as a school kid is to get out of bed on a Monday morning. The only answer he can think of is, 'But baby it's cold outside.' He resists the temptation to say it. She grabs her coat, hat, and scarf. When he opens the door, they are hit by a blast of wind and snow. They had been paying so much attention to each other, they had paid no attention to the outside. The snowfall is so heavy they can't see the porch rail, even though the light is on. His mixture of glee and guilt makes him sound like her advisor again, "In all good conscience I can't let you drive back to Des Moines in this. I'm not sure you could even make it to the gravel road." He pauses, trying not to sound too seductive, "And anyway, there is a third of a bottle of wine left." Amie looks at him with absolutely no argument.

Their discussion of who sleeps on the bed and who sleeps on the couch would make almost as perfect a sitcom episode as their first meeting in his faculty office.

Shawn. "I'll take the couch. I wake up early."

Amie. "No, no, I'll be fine. My own bed is not much more than a couch."

Shawn. "Amie, you are, after all, my guest. I can't make you sleep on a couch."

Amie. "I don't want to shove you out of your bedroom."

Shawn. "No argument. You're in the bedroom."

Amie. "But—OK."

Shawn. *Why can't we both sleep in the bed?*

Amie. *Why can't we both sleep in the bed?*

Shawn. "I've got an unused toothbrush in the bathroom."

Amie. "I, um…I brought mine."

They look at each other. Long pause.

She picks up her paper bag and walks into the bedroom. He gets his sleeping bag out of the closet and unrolls it onto the sagging sofa.

Amie undresses in the warm bedroom, gets Shawn's flannel shirt out of her bag, puts it on very slowly, and climbs into bed. She pulls the quilt up to her chin and sighs. *Why can't we both sleep in the bed?*

Shawn worms his way into his sleeping bag without unzipping it. He puts his arms around himself and curls up like a caterpillar in a cocoon. *Why can't we both sleep in the bed?*

They sleep.

Amie is not sure if it is the smell of coffee, the sunlight beginning to reflect off the snow, or the sound of Shawn's tiptoeing in the kitchen that wakes her. She is sure that it is warm, she has Shawn's shirt on, and she doesn't want to get out of bed. For a moment she thinks of unbuttoning the shirt and lying there half-covered until he has to come in to see if she's OK. She loves the thought and keeps it until she realizes that he has started to make more noise than necessary and that must be the way he is going to make sure she's awake. She does one last cat stretch and dresses. This time, Shawn's shirt stays on.

After coffee, fruit, and big cinnamon buns, she says, "I can fix sandwiches for lunch if you've got the makings."

He looks a little guilty, "Not much here, but there's bread on the top shelf. You can use anything else you find."

Ten minutes later, after he has washed and stowed the dishes, she puts four sandwiches in a bag, "PB and J it is." He puts the bag in a small backpack, they get dressed for the outside cold, and the two 'good friends' walk into the timber.

It's one of those glorious mornings when it doesn't matter that it's as cold as northern Siberia. There is not a hint of a breeze. The sky as clear as water in a glacier lake; you can't tell with certainty how far away an object—a tree, a bluff, an eagle riding a thermal—is. The early-night wet snow, cemented to trees and bushes by the thirty-degree temperature plunge, has made the woods look like decorations on one of those glittery Hallmark cards—cheesy on paper, but stunning in real life. They say almost nothing as they wander, overcome by their closeness to each other. After three hours or so, they realize that their tracks in the snow, along with those of the animals that live there,

173

have pretty much covered the entire timber floor. However, nothing made by a horse, or an old pickup is in the mix. They haven't seen anything but a small herd of six deer, a couple of wild turkeys, and a fat possum with a missing tail that paid them absolutely no mind.

"Hungry?" Shawn looks at Amie.

"I thought you'd never bring that up," she answers.

"We can sit over there." He points to a huge oak tree recently blown down by an August windstorm.

They sit. The sandwiches disappear. Shawn gets up and takes a few steps. "I think this is a wild goose—no, a wild truck chase. What d'ya say we zigzag our way back to the cabin and if we don't see anything, I can pull your car to the gravel road and I'll follow you to Tripoli. We need to tell Patrick we're wasting our time and taxpayer dollars. Taxpayer dollars. That'll be a big deal when the supervisors decide whether or not to approve his budget for next year.

The zigzag is pretty slow. They are enthralled by the refracted sunlight off the crystal tree limbs, a rabbit erupting with a small puff of snow from under its log cover, a barred owl dropping from an oak and weaving its way through the tree trunks. They can see the cabin but are reluctant to leave the woods. As they look back from where they came, both of them feel some urgency to get to Tripoli and report the non-success of their search. One more step toward the cabin— and it appears. A twenty, thirty, forty-year-old International Harvester pick-up is parked behind the Jeep and the Prius, the bright sun reflecting off the windshield making it impossible to see inside. Neither of them moves or even breathes. Finally, simultaneously, they take a step toward the vehicle.

"Hold it. No closer. Just listen," a voice speaks through what appears to be a rolled-down side window. "Turn around and look back the way you come. That big tree bout a hundred yards in, that wolf oak yonder. The biggest tree you can see. On the west side, there's some names scratched in the snow, bout the only patch a snow you two haven't tromped over today. Take a picture of them names. Make sure you can read um cause they'll be gone when I'm gone." They stand frozen, too astonished to move. "I want all them folks whose names are there to come to this spot where you're standing next Saturday night, four hours after sunset. That'd be about nine o'clock. I don't want nobody else to show up. Nobody. And I don't want you to say nothing about this outside the Sheriff's office. If you do, it's all off. I ain't gonna solve this case that all of y'all been running around trying to figger out. But I am gonna put an end to it. I'll give that half-pint Guv his picture back. I'll fix it so that big chief Hinman can go to work on what he thinks are more important things. The Nachawinga Sheriff's Department can get back to writing traffic tickets and breaking up bar fights. Amie, you can keep doing the good stuff you're doin at that school. And you, Shawn, can figger out a way to get your real work started again an forget about pig suits and chicken suits and that mess. You can put the investigation to bed. It's gonna be the biggest cold case in the history of this state and that's the way it should be, a cold case. Them three that's dead deserve to be dead. This county and this state's better off without um and all of you are gonna leave it at that. Let the newspapers try to explain it for the next fifty years."

Amie takes a step toward the truck, "But who are…"

"Don't come no closer and don't talk. I ain't gonna answer no questions, and I ain't gonna wait here forever. Now git over to that tree do what I said."

The two are unable to move until the voice says, "Go on now before them names melt." They go to the tree and a patch of undisturbed snow about the size of Shawn's living room. There are no tracks, only the names. He takes pictures just in time as they watch the names disappear into the rest of the melting snow. Quickly they walk back toward the truck, but there is nothing there. Only a red Toyota and a beat-up Jeep. All the snow around is undisturbed—no ruts, no tracks—nothing.

Amie looks at the place where the truck had been. "They're not going to believe this."

"You don't expect us to believe this." Sheriff Kavanaugh is looking at the list of names in Shawn's snow picture, downloaded onto the department's old computer. "He told you to take the pictures and then he disappeared? This is a joke, right? Shawn, the comedian. The funny pigman."

Nelda, Phil, Bill, and Tim are also staring at the picture on the computer screen. Tim breaks the silence. "Come on, Amie. Did Shawn talk you into this?"

"I kinda wish it was a joke," Amie says, "but I saw the same thing he saw. I tried to take a picture of the truck, but when I looked at my phone there was nothing there but a blank screen. Shawn's telling you what happened, what we saw and heard."

Pat takes his hat off, scratches his head, and puts it back on. "So, we're all supposed to be in front of your shack at nine on Saturday?"

"That's what he said, all. The seven of us, and Hinman and the Guv." Shawn looks at Phil and Bill.

Phil says, "Damn if I want to go out in the woods to meet with no spook."

"Whoever was talking to us out of that truck said all the names that were in the snow. He was clear on that. And yours was in the snow," Shawn says.

"You boys'll be just as safe as you'd be here. Maybe we can get that Big Chief Hinman to hold your hand." Pat says.

Amie takes off her knit cap and shakes out her hair, "And no word gets out. He said that absolutely no one else was to know about this. No one. If it gets around town the whole thing is off. This has to be top secret."

Slowly, they all turn toward Nelda, who puts her hands up, "Not one word. This time I promise—no word." She crosses her heart.

Pat takes a breath and squinches his eyes shut. "We got one big problem, folks. How in bloody hell are we gonna get the Guv and Big Chief Charles Hinman to stand around in front of Shawn's porch with a bunch of people they think are hayseeds waiting for a ghost. The Guv won't go anywhere without the whole damn Highway Patrol with him, and if I try to get Hinman to buy in, he'll have a big laugh and shove me out his office window."

"I'll work on the Guv," Tim speaks up. "I'll see him all next week so I'll have time. He's so convinced he's in serious danger until that picture is recovered that he'll probably go along with anything that might get it back. Of course, he'll be scared to death without his eighty-man bodyguard, but he's even scareder as long as that portrait is gone."

"And Hinman sure seems anxious to get the Guv off his rear end so's he can get back to his usual job and feel important again," Nelda says. "You can go over to Des Moines and talk to him, Pat. He should be willing to give it a try."

"Peace officer to peace officer," Shawn grins.

Phil lights a cigarette. "And what if this ghost don't show up? What if we end up standing out there up to our elbows in snow with the Guv and that Hinman feller an nothing happens? What are ya gonna do then?"

"I guess we'll just have to deal with that when it happens." There is uncharacteristic tension in Pat's voice. "We don't have anything else to go on, have we? And get your ass outside with that damn cigarette, Bill."

"I'm ..."

"Just do it."

The sound of car wheels in the parking lot causes them all to look out the front window as a familiar yellow Volkswagen pulls to a stop, followed by two spotless, white and gold Sheriff's vehicles—one truck and one sporty ATV.

Pat lifts his hat. "What the hell are they doing back. Wonder if they got in some kind of trouble and some Sheriff from somewhere brought um here for us to lock up? What kinda Sheriff's department can afford them fancy vehicles."

Connie exits the VW and glides through the office door, followed by Misty from the ATV and Lizzy from the truck. She opens her crocodile Coach handbag, pulls out some papers, and puts them on the desk. "We've been doing a little car trading for you folks. Everything's in order. All you've got to do is sign these titles for the County and take those piles of junk on wheels you got parked out back and sell them to some scrapyard somewhere if they'll get that far. Or maybe you can auction them off as classics. Anyhow, make sure the supervisors put the money back in your budget and not in theirs."

Lizzy winks at Pat. "We don't want this to look like we're bribing you. But since it looks like we're off the suspect list, we thought that such a classy posse should be carried around in classy vehicles and not have to worry every time they went out on a call if they were going to have to hitchhike back to the office."

"Seriously," Misty speaks up, "we feel like our dear departed hubbies have ripped this county off for so much, we'd like to begin paying a little of it back. This is a start. Now get out there and have a look at your new motor pool."

They all file out into the parking lot and walk around the new vehicles. The insignia on the doors are perfect: 'Sheriff, Nachawinga County,' in gold lettering outlined in black with the county logo emblazoned above. To the rear of the lettering is a small, tasteful red heart with the initials, CS, MW, and LB in it. Misty points to one of them, "And under no circumstances are you to remove the hearts. If you do, we will return and remove the vehicles."

Phil opens the door of a GM Sierra 2500 Denali and begins pushing buttons and pulling levers. "Bells and whistles. Ain't they gonna be amazed at the state Sheriffs' convention when we pull up sitting in our heated leather seats, listening to the steereo." Meanwhile, Bill is checking things out in a Ford Bronco Sport, turning on the flashing red and blue lights. Suddenly the siren blasts. Nelda jumps. "Turn that damn siren off, Phil or Bill or whoever you are, you scared the living daylights out of all of us."

The men continue fawning over the vehicles, opening and closing doors, looking at the engines, and kicking tires. Kids under a Christmas tree. Finally, Connie breaks it up. "Well, for one, I'm hungry. What do you say we go over to Yolanda's, best Mexican food north of Laredo, and we bereaved ladies can make one more contribution to the County and buy you dinner? We're spending the night in Franklin at Marilyn's B & B to talk over some plans she has for the village and the township and see what we can do to help her out."

On the walk over, Misty leans toward Pat and says, "I still think you're probably the cutest sheriff between Montana and Maryland." Nelda comes close to losing her good humor again but then grins as she pokes Misty in the ribs.

And a good dinner is had by all. They each try something new on the menu and, as before, Connie decides that, in front of the Sheriff, she should limit herself to one drink, unlike the other two. As Nachawinga's finest once again watches the VW depart, Pat takes off his hat. "Wow! What do you think of that?" After a moment's thought, "I sure as hell don't look forward to going to see Hinman, but it's gonna be a lot more fun than I thought it would be driving that big ol' truck to Des Moines. There's not gonna be much to do for the rest of the week. I think we should all meet at Shawn's at about five on Saturday and get ready for the big event? Or should I say the big fiasco?"

"I'll make a pot of chili," Shawn says, "if somebody'll take care of the salad."

"We'll make that for you, "Phil and Bill speak at the same time.

"Bread here," Nelda says.

"And I'll bring cookies," Amie finishes off the menu.

"I guess that covers it." Pat smiles rather weakly. "At least that gives us one thing to look forward to."

Sheriff Kavanaugh hasn't slept very well for two nights and he is still trying to get the courage to pick up the phone and make an appointment with the Chief of the State Department of Criminal Investigation to try to convince him that he has to come to the middle of Nachawinga County in the middle of nowhere in the middle of the night to meet with a ghost. Pat's wife, Margie Deane, just back from taking the kids to meet the school bus, comes to the breakfast table with a fresh pot of coffee and tops off his cup. "You're worried, aren't you? You been tossing around so much the last couple of nights I can tell you haven't got much sleep cause I haven't got much either."

"Sorry, hon." Pat looks at his half-eaten breakfast, scrambled eggs and toast gone cold. "It's just that most people think of us as a bunch of hicks any way. It's not gonna help any if it gets around that we think this case rests on the cooperation of a ghost and it turns out to be some kind of hoax. Or worse, that we just been fooling ourselves thinking we could bust this case open by chasing an old truck. Sure isn't gonna make next year's election any easier. I may be looking for another job."

Margie Deane tries to make her smile as warm and encouraging as she can. "Well, speaking of jobs, I better get on over to the bank and get behind my teller's window or we'll both be looking for a job."

"I kind of think I ought to forget about getting Hinman down here and just go with the guys and see if there is anything to this pickup business. I don't think he'll go along in a hundred years anyway, an if he does come down for nothing we won't ever hear the end of it."

Margie Deane puts on her coat and kisses Pat on the mouth. "Do what you think's best, my darlin. But if it does work out, you're not gonna have to worry one bit about next year's election." Just as she closes the door behind, her Pat's cell rings. He puts it on speaker.

"Sheriff?"

"That's me."

"It's Tim. Deputy Tim. It wasn't easy, but I got the Guv on board. He's scared shitless, but he said if he can ride with Hinman in his official car, and if you guarantee his safety, he'll do it to get the picture back. Now, you just have to convince Hinman."

Pat takes a deep breath and blows out a puff of air. "Well, I been thinking about that Tim. Might be better if just the staff went over to the woods to..."

Tim stops him, "No way, Sheriff. Both Shawn and Amie heard the voice, and it said all nine people. We don't want to screw this up now."

Pat is embarrassed. "OK, Deputy Taylor. I guess I better call and see if I can get an appointment."

"I made one for you," Tim Taylor answers. "Ten O'clock. You got two hours. You know how to get there?"

"I got the address," Pat says. "I think if I punch it into this fancy truck it'll do everything but walk me up the steps to his office."

"You don't expect me to believe this." Chief Charles Hinman draws himself up to his full NBA power-forward height and glares at Pat. "Who was it had this encounter with a spirit truck? Shawn Galla-gher, the pigman, comedian extraordinaire? He is pulling our chains. He's probably sitting somewhere over his third cup of coffee laughing his butt off."

Pat, wishes he was anywhere in the state other than this third-floor office, surrounded by windows with a view of the entire city, in front of a desk that's big enough to play ping pong on. He wonders why he ever thought he could talk this man into coming to his back-woods county for an audience with a truck.

"He wasn't the only one there, Chief Hinman. Amie Greene was with him. You've probably heard of her. She's the teacher who won all those awards at Cohn middle school. She wouldn't have gone along with a prank. I'm sure they both saw something. And besides, they took pictures."

"Well, you're not gonna catch me in the woods somewhere in the middle of Nachawinga County in the middle of the night waiting to see if some damn phoenix rising from the ashes is gonna drive his truck up and end this case for us, and that's the goddam end of it."

"The Guv has signed on." Pat is pleading. "And whoever or whatever it was in that truck said he'd tell you where you can find that picture. It'll get the Guv off your ass."

Hinman looks out the window toward the capital, then turns toward Pat. "Nobody gets on my ass, Sheriff." He is about to continue when his phone rings and he picks it up. "OK. Put Tim Taylor through."

Pause. "Mr. Taylor."

Pause. "I have a pretty good idea where you are."

Pause. "How about you just tell the Guv to go fuck himself. No, I know you won't tell him that."

Pause. "He says he'll let me go back and do the job I came here to do if I will just go, no matter what happens? Are you sure, truck or no truck, picture or no picture?"

Pause. He glances at Pat. "You tell him I will be at the back door of his mansion at six-thirty on Saturday night. And if any of this, I mean one shred of this, gets leaked, I'm heading back to LA Hell, I might just head back anyhow."

He continues to look for a long moment at the Capital surrounded by state patrol cars. He shakes his head. Then he slowly turns to Pat and sighs. "We'll be there before nine. And you heard what I said, Sheriff Kavanaugh. If word ever gets out about this, you'll be lucky after the next election to get a job mopping vomit off your jail cell floors."

This time Pat looks Charles Hinman directly in the eye. "Shit Chief, I already do that."

On the way down, he takes the steps three at a time. He can't wait to get his butt on those heated leather seats, get Willy and Waylon on the Bose speakers, and cruise the long way back to Tripoli.

It is a dark and snowy Saturday night.

The Nachawinga posse are gathered on the porch of Shawn's cabin, waiting for the Chief, the Guv, and The Truck. The supper was convivial—warm fire, steaming bowls of chili, Amie's warm giant chocolate chip cookies, good Chianti—but hardly relaxed. Now that they are outside, the fifteen-degree cold is starting to creep into the many layers of clothing everyone is wearing, and, with the help of a stiff wind, chasing away any lingering effects of the wine and the fireplace. Also, the tension level is getting even higher.

Pat paces back and forth on the porch, descends to the driveway, paces back and forth in the snow, climbs back up the steps to the porch, and paces some more. Nelda mutters behind him, whispering, but making sure she is heard. "Might not be the dumbest thing we've ever done, but it's pretty damn close."

Pat stalks back down the steps, takes off his hat, and scratches his head. "Hell, the Guv and the Chief might not even show, let alone the truck." He squints at Shawn and Amie and puts his hat back on. "Something better happen with that damn truck, or we're gonna be up shit creek and it frozen solid."

"Pat, we just told you what we saw and heard," Amie says. "Just be cool and hang in there. That truck and whoever was in it is going to show up. I'm sure of it."

"Tim's driving the Guv and the Chief. He'll get um here," Shawn adds, "He told me …." He is interrupted by the sound of tires spinning in the slush and headlights turning the snow into glitter as the big black Suburban slides to a halt beside the shiny new Nachawinga Sheriff's Department fleet. Tim gets out on the driver's side. "I sure hope we can get out of here when whoever or whatever is supposed to show up is done with us."

Chief Hinman, immaculate in his usual black suit, white shirt and tie, with his black wool overcoat, is reluctant to step into the slush with his city shoes on. The Guv is huddled in the far rear seat with a plaid wool blanket over his knees. Hinman rolls his window down, stares around slowly, noticing the Sierra and the Bronco, "Your department must have hit the lottery, Sheriff Kavanaugh. We don't have anything like that in our motor pool." Pat starts to answer but then just raises his eyebrows and slightly tosses his head upward as if to say, No big deal.

Tim opens the rear door for the Guv who pulls his blanket a bit higher and turns his overcoat collar up. "Just keep the motor running, I'll stay in here."

Hinman steps carefully through the slush, joins the others on the porch, crosses his arms, and continues to stare into the blackness. No one speaks.

Five minutes, then ten minutes pass.

Pat looks at his watch.

Nelda looks at her watch.

Shawn looks at his watch.

Tim looks at his watch.

Hinman looks at his watch and recrosses his arms. "Five minutes till nine." He continues to stare.

Four minutes pass. No one speaks. Hinman pushes up his sleeve to look at his watch again.

At first, there is just a blue-green glow at the edge of the timber, flickering, like a light from a welding job. There is no sound. The flickering lights form an arch where they reflect off the surrounding mist. A pair of headlights appear, as if from a vehicle that had been sitting there for a long time. This light, bouncing off fallen and falling snow, illuminates an old International Harvester pickup truck, faded green, rust spot shaped like a wild turkey visible on the door, melted snow running down the doors, but completely intact, with panels of wooden slats extending the sides of the bed upward. The driver's window is open, but it's impossible to see inside. The effect, looking at the truck through the crystal proscenium, is that of a perfectly lit stage setting.

No one knows how long those on the porch stood gaping at the scene waiting for an actor, a line, for the show to begin. No one knows if anyone moved.

Finally, from the truck, "You're about as quiet a bunch as ever I seen." No one speaks. The voice waits. Then, "Guess you ain't gonna say nothing, so I'll get things started. I am proud you all showed up. Lemme see, is everybody here?

"Sheriff Pat Kavanaugh. Good to see ya, Pat. I can remember you from when you was no mor'n a little puppy dog, know'd your mom an dad an the rest of your family. Come a long way. Glad when you got elected and glad you got elected again. Looks like you're gonna make a good sheriff. Keep it up. You're gonna have some work to do before we get done here." Pat glances at the others to see how they are reacting to what the voice is saying.

The voice continues, "Hmmm, I suppose you must be Chuck Hinman." Hinman stiffens noticeably at being called 'Chuck' but has no idea where or to whom he can object. For one of the few times in his life, he is at a loss as to what to say or do. "I hear you're doing good things for this state, heading up one of the few departments that finally seems to be running like it should. You need to straighten your boss up a little bit. You know a lot more about what you're doing than he does so, don't let him push you around. I'll have more to say to you later." Completely non-plussed and immobile, Hinman simply continues to frown.

"Nelda Womble. If you hadn't been happily married twenty years ago, I'd have tried to talk you into running away with me. You sure were a hot little number then and you've held up mighty good since. But that's a little beside the point. I called you here because I know you're the engine that keeps this little Sheriff's department running on its track. They're going to need you to keep doing that.

"Miss Amie Greene." Amie and Shawn have slowly moved toward each other while the voice was speaking. Amie moves even closer when it calls her name. "Miss Greene, I called you here partly because I just wanted to see you. I know about you at that school in Des Moines and you've become a hero to me. I'm mighty proud of what you're doing. A few more like you and people might begin to realize what's happening to our land and prairies and waterways and begin to do something about it, even if it's just a strip of ground in a bad neighborhood. I surely believe you've already had a influence on the folks standing on this porch with their mouths hanging open, and maybe they can all start turning a thing or two around and give you a little help for a change." Shawn smiles at Amie. Neither has realized that they are holding hands.

"Shawn Gallagher, you and I go back a pretty long ways. We had a lot a good talks before we both left town. Talking about what a mess our way of making food has become and how it's bound to collapse on itself in another generation. And we talked about how animals can be raised right, without hurting um or the people around um. I was real happy to see you become a star at State and begin to work on ways to bring some kind of common sense to our agriculture. But you've kind of got off track, boy, in the last year or so, making a spectacle outa yerself and carrying on with all sorts of foolishness that ain't gonna get ya nowhere. I think you should just drop all that stuff and pick up where ya left off. Stop wasting yer time. See if you can't figure a way to get us outa this mess that farming has come to that we can all live with. And I think that young gal whose hand you are holding might make a good person to partner up with."

Shawn and Amie pull their hands apart, then gently rejoin them. There is beginning to be a slow relaxation on the porch as all those present seem to be waiting for further instructions. The voice continues from the truck, "Let me see now, seems like we're missing one of the characters from this little play we're putting on. Who might that be? Ain't we supposed to have the Guv of our fair state present? Can't we get him up there on stage with the rest of you? Mr. Taylor, can you help us with this? I believe you're the one who talked him into coming. You tell him it's his cue."

"I...give me a minute." Tim walks down from the porch and opens the door of the Suburban. Whispering can be heard in the back seat. "I don't want to go out there. Don't make me go. Do I have to?" More whispering. Finally, the Guv steps out of the car, his Snoopy pilot's hat pulled over his ears and his plaid lap rug around his shoulders.

"Well, Guv." From the truck. "You can get on up there on the stage with the rest of um. This is yer big scene."

With Tim's help, he does so.

"I guess you're one a the big reasons we're all gathered here. I understand you're anxious to recover a portrait that you were so proud of, so it won't end up in a hog lot or garbage truck along with another corpse. You can be sure I understand your concern."

The Guv is trying to pull the fur-lined aviator cap down over his shoulders like a shy kid on his first day of school. He settles for the blanket, wrapping it tightly around himself, and reluctantly joins the others.

"I believe most anybody would worry a little if four portraits of four egotistical big-shots went missing, and three of um were found alongside their dead subjects, particularly if he was the person depicted in the unrecovered fourth one. I believe, however, I can help you with its recovery, but there are a few conditions for every one of you."

Those on the porch begin to whisper.

"Just hush up and listen." The volume of the voice rises a bit. "First of all, I want you lawmen to understand there ain't gonna be a discovery of a guilty person or persons to wrap this case up nice and neat. Chuck, I know you don't like to have a case like this left hanging. The last thing you want is something that just goes on and on, but that's the way it's gonna be, and you're just gonna have to work that little problem out for yourselves. There was a cold case here in this county some years back. I think most a you might know about that one. It seems that particular case resolved itself. Accidents can be a good thing sometimes if they happen to the right people. By now you've probably got a pretty good idea who, or what mighta made all this happen. But nobody's gonna believe you if you try to tell um. Anyway, you need to figure out how you can put this one away without ruining the reputations of what appears to me to be two fine law officers, a promising A.G. candidate, a good scientist, and a mighty fine young woman. I'm pretty sure you can do it.

"Now for you, Guv." The Guv, bent over like a sick chicken under his cap and shawl, turns toward the truck. "C'mon, my man, straighten up. You look like you just lost a election. You don't have to worry about that. How long have you been in office? Three terms? Ten? You're in a state where folks keep reelecting their governors because the voters are much too nice to throw um out. You got locks on the office for life, so start fighting for the right things and stop following along after the big money people like an underfed dog. Lead, man. Lead. I want you to see to it that the skim-milk rules you have that reg-ulate animal feeding operations are completely overhauled, and the DNR has the money and personnel to enforce um. Fine the hell outa the lawbreakers until they run out of cash, then put um in jail. And while you're at it, overhaul that joke of a Environmental Protection Committee. Kick out the pigs that are feeding at that trough and fill it with Amie Greenes and maybe a Shawn Gallagher or two. There's lots more that you can figure out on yer own—just use yer brain and yer heart. Chief-of-staff Taylor can help you out. Pay attention to him. His head's in the right place. He might get yer job one day when you finally decide to hang it up and move to Arizona. Why else do ya think he would put up with you all this time? Help him out along his way. Now, you better get on it if you don't want your picture to turn up in a unpleasant place. An you've seen what that can lead to.

"I ain't forgot you, Bill and Phil—or Phil and Bill, whatever it is. You might not get much attention, but you're good deputies, so keep helping Pat. He needs it. You might also tell him he needs to start buying his own cigarettes. And help Nelda get yer names straight.

"You nine up there on that porch can make a change. This place is worth saving. You've gotta show people how they can stop looking at our land like a bank account that they can spend down to nothing, then move to someplace warm. It's as alive as you are, and you gotta stop people from killing it.

"Now Guv, get on your hotline to the State Patrol. They're all hanging around your house now, wondering what the hell they're supposed to do. Tell um to get back on the road and start doing what they're being paid for before all the teenagers in the state turn I 80 into a drag strip. Ain't nobody gonna hurt you if you do what yer told. Taylor, you get in touch with the staff at the Guv's mansion and tell um they have tomorrow off. I want the Guv's mansion to be empty and I want you all to be under that row of pictures, where one portrait is missing. Be there at eight o'clock in the morning. You folks get started now. And don't waste any time starting on what I've told ya to do. Hell, it,s gonna take you an hour to get that big black bus turned around and back to the county road. An you all better hope you don't have to deal with me no more."

Slow fade. The stage, the set, the whole show recedes into the starkness of the black trees at the edge of the timber. Each spectator in their own way feels as if they are coming out of some sort of a dream.

The Guv scurries back into the official car. Pat turns on a flashlight and moves toward the spot where the 'scene' took place. Hinman and Shawn do the same. The beams illuminate the 'stage,' sweeping front, back, side to side. There is nothing there. No truck, no tracks. Only fresh, white, undisturbed snow, reflecting bright light into their faces.

And it does take them about an hour to get the Suburban to the county road, with everyone giving directions and solutions at once. Tim starts behind the wheel. From everyone, "Rock it—back and forth." "No, no, don't let the wheels spin." "Try four-wheel low." "Wait, stop. You're up to the floorboards."

From Hinman, "Let me behind the wheel."

From everyone, "You're going the wrong way, you're gonna hit the porch."

Finally, from Amie, "We got tow-chains, don't we? Let's hook them to the front and back. We can spin this big boat around."

That's what they do, and it works. After just about an hour they get the big Suburban turned around, the Guv all the while back in his safe spot in the rear seat. Tim and Hinman get in front and Patrick tows them to the gravel with his brand-new truck.

Hinman rolls down his window. "Eight o'clock."

Pat slogs through the snow to the window with a wicked grin. "Eight o'clock. Will we be calling you 'Chuck' now?"

Hinman's scowl deepens as he rolls up his window without comment. Then he changes his mind, lowers the window, and says with the hint of a smile, "What do you think?"

He closes the window as the big car, with some wheel spinning, but adequate traction, heads toward Des Moines.

For the past five minutes, Shawn has been trying to figure out a delicate way he can suggest that Amie might stay at the cabin rather than try to drive home at this late hour in the snow, and Amie has been hoping he would do just that. They are holding hands again when Nelda, the uber arranger, says, "Pat, you and the boys can take the truck. Amie, you don't want to drive home this late. I've got plenty of room, so you can stay with me. I make a great breakfast. We'll take the Bronco."

Shawn, hoping for a different arrangement, can only think, *shit*.

Amie, still holding Shawn's hand, turns toward the others. "Thanks, Nelda. I'm staying here. We'll both see you all in the morning."

There is a hint of a smile on Nelda's face as she raises one eyebrow and says, "Right."

Shawn and Amie watch as the flashy new vehicles splash down the slushy two-track.

All of their tension seems to leave them as they step into the cabin and shed their coats. Inside, they look at each other for a long time. Then Shawn says, "if you're hungry, there's chili left. Maybe I can find some wine."

"Not yet," Amie says. She walks toward the fireplace and unbuttons her borrowed shirt. She catches it as it falls from her bare shoulders and hangs it on the mantlepiece. "It's lost some of its smoke smell, needs to be recharged." Everything has slowed down as she moves toward Shawn. She helps him out of his sweater and shirt. Her snow-cloud grey eyes are wide as she looks into his. "I'll take that hug now."

No red lights. No sirens. No screeching tires. No hurry.

After a long kiss, they shake hands. Then, without letting go, they walk toward the bed on pillows of laughter.

The next morning when the Nachawinga County posse drive up in their new fleet, the deserted surroundings of the Guv's mansion seem spooky. Gone are the patrol cars lined up along the street in front and on the parking area in the back. Also missing are the uniformed and plainclothes officers shivering on the frozen grounds. As they pull into two empty spaces, Tim and Hinman appear at the back entrance and motion the arrivals in. They walk through the modest service doorway and Tim greets them. "Don't know if we've been conned or not. We checked out the main hall for his picture. There's still a big

191

empty spot on the governor's portrait row where it ought to be. No change there. I sure was hoping it would show up."

Hinman's frown has returned with double intensity. "I don't know how, but I think we've been taken for a ride—completely bamboozled. If any of this gets out ..."

"Guv's upstairs in his apartment," Tim interrupts. "He doesn't want to come out. Let's all go up to the conference room and I'll go in and talk to him. He should be able to get his nerve back now that we're all here"

They take seats in the conference room, with the exception of Hinman, who is rigid and pacing. If it weren't for his footsteps echoing off the high ceiling, the room would be, like the rest of the mansion, as quiet as Craven's burnt-out foundations.

Finally, some muffled conversation can be heard behind the apartment door and, as they all turn toward the sound, the Guv enters in his blue velour bathrobe and dual allegiance slippers with Tim behind, trying not to appear to be pushing him, but gently urging him along.

"OK, you people go on down and see what you can find," the Guv is almost whispering. "I'll go back to my apartment and wait for you. You let me know right away if you discover any trace of that portrait. Sheriff, maybe one or two of your deputies should stay with me."

"You will come down these stairs with us right now," Hinman half-closes one eye and raises the other eyebrow. It is clear to everyone who hears him that this is an order. "You're the main actor in this little play, and we are not going to get to the final curtain without you. Now let's move." This last is said with military officer finality, but in spite of his bravado, Hinman, along with the rest, moves down toward the main hall with some trepidation.

When they reach portrait row, the Guv is the first to speak, wide-eyed and beside himself with excitement. "There it is. Look, by God, there it is. Son-of-a-bitch, there it is, bigger'n life. Don't I look pretty?

No, no…we gotta get that picture down. There's a ladder around here someplace. I want to take it down right now and we can burn the damn thing. I want to be rid of it once and for all. We can take it right downstairs and throw it in the furnace and…"

"You leave that ugly thing right where it is." The voice seems to come from the balustrade directly behind the group as they turn around with dance team precision. "That thing stays there until they's some reason for it to disappear again, and Guv, I don't think you want that to happen."

"But I, I…," the Guv looks around. He doesn't know in which direction he should speak.

"No buts." This time the voice seems to come from someplace under the floor. They all turn in that direction but see nothing. "If that thing comes down, you an me both are going to be real unhappy."

Confused, they all try to locate the voice. "You all remember what I said you need to do," comes from behind them again. "I want each one a you to raise yer right hand." They look around. Hinman and the Guv seem reluctant. "Chuck, Guv, do it." Slowly they all raise their hands. "Swear you will all try yer dead-level best to do what I told ya. And also swear that you will never tell anyone, ever, what has gone on for the last two days." They mumble inaudible oaths. From yet another part of the room, near the ceiling, "Swear." More mumbling. Finally, from outside the large front door, this time with great volume, echoing throughout the building. "Let me hear you, SWEAR."

Bewildered, with hands raised, they again mumble their oaths. Silence. Slowly they look around, then at each other. They move to the ornately decorated entrance and look down on the street. At first, there is nothing. Only a few crows. Then they see what appears to be a puff of exhaust smoke. Through the smoke and fog, they can see an old International Harvester pickup truck with wooden sides on the bed and a rust spot shaped like a turkey on the door slowly heading east. Toward Nachawinga County. It stops briefly at a light, then, followed by the crows, turns left toward the interstate, and disappears into the haze.

THE FANTASY

Three weeks later, on the front page of the *Des Moines Register*:

DEATHS OF THREE AGRI-BUSINESS EXECUTIVES DEEMED ACCIDENTAL

A joint news release from the State Department of Criminal Investigation and the Nachawinga County Sheriff's Department has ended over three weeks of speculation about the circumstances surrounding the deaths of three chief executives of three major meat-producing corporations operating in Iowa. In an interview, DCI Chief Charles Hinman stated that after an extensive investigation by the two organizations, no evidence of human-instigated foul play has been found on the bodies of any of the three deceased. He stated that the owners of the two swine CAFOs, Mr. Hubert Wooten of North Carolina and Mr. JJ Schittman, II, of Ames, seem to have accidentally fallen into their confinements, where they were killed and partially consumed by their pigs. Mr. Donald Birdseed, of Denver, Colorado, was mistaken for a garbage bin on a particularly foggy day and was killed by being baled in a trash compacter. Both Hinman and Sheriff Patrick Kavanaugh commented on the fact that the timing of these accidents was an extremely bizarre coincidence, but the Sheriff said, "This sort of thing happens all the time in law enforcement." Each officer was highly complimentary of the other's work. The DCI Chief went on to say…

The next month, from the *Tripoli Independent*:

FRANKLIN TOWNSHIP OFFICIALS TELL OF PLANNED COMMUNITY IMPROVEMENTS.

There are major changes in store for the village of Franklin and Franklin Township. Marilyn Jacobson, the spokesperson for the Trustees of the township, outlined a number of planned community improvements made possible by a generous grant from Compassionate Family Farms. Ms. Jacobson said that tennis and basketball courts are to be built utilizing building foundations that were to be used for large animal confinements, and construction has begun to modify a sewerage lagoon into a public swimming pool. Confinements that are currently in use will cease operation and the structures will either be destroyed or repurposed for the community. The new CEO, Misty Wooten, told reporters that Compassionate Family Farms expects to change its corporate structure and image and make major changes in the way it produces its products. Lyle Holmgren, a local farmer, will be converting his swine operation to a radically new method (or, from what this reporter understands, he might be reverting to a radical old method) as an experimental project with a grant from the corporation. "I haven't been this excited since my first 4H project," a jubilant Holmgren said. " Finally, I will be able to…"

Six weeks later, from OINK, *The Weekly Newsletter of the Central States Pork Producers Association*: MAJOR CHANGES EXPECTED IN MIDWESTERN PORK, CHICKEN, AND EGG PRODUCTION.

Although details are still sketchy, OINK has learned of a huge merger that will likely shake the foundations of the meat production industry in the heartland. It appears that the widows of the former CEOs of Patriot Pork, Compassionate Family Farms, and Freebird Poultry, who are the new chief officers of the three corporations, plan a merger that will form one umbrella organization. Also, this reporter has learned that there will be major changes in the way their animals are raised, the way packing plants are designed and operated, and the working relationships between small producers and the corporation. The corporation will be headquartered at CLM Farms (formerly JJ Farms) where CEO Connie Schittman and COO Lizzy Birdseed will reside. The third officer, CIO Misty Wooten, will work out of North Carolina, where she plans to handle public relations and the corporate charity foundation, oversee Carolina operations, and continue her education. At this time OINK has been unable to contact the three officers for further comment but…

Three months later, from the *State University Alumni Magazine*:

SHAWN GALLAGHER, Animal Studies graduate and former Assistant Professor of Biology, has been named head of the newly formed Craven Snuggs Center for Research in Sustainable Animal Agriculture. Construction has begun in southwest Nachawinga County on a state-of-the-art campus, which will include a headquarters building and extensive laboratory facilities. Discussions are underway regarding the use of the laboratories for teaching and research by several colleges and universities in the state, including our institution. It is expected that research faculty and staff will eventually number from forty to forty-five individuals. The focus of the work will be on techniques that will lead to sustainable and humane production of pork, beef, and poultry products and…

Eight months later,

From: wooten.misty@clmindustries.com.

To: Connie; Lizzy

Great seeing y'all last month. Everything on this front as far as the business is concerned is peachy. Lots of national publicity about our production modifications. I understand orders for sustainable country ham, sausage, and other specialties are over the top. Continuing negotiations with the Food Bear grocery chain to use our products exclusively. Nibbles from Hardees and McDonalds (ha). Positive changes are taking place in our N.C. units. People from N.C. State have contacted me about internships and post-docs at the Snuggs Center. Also, UNC. (Go Heels). I'm super excited about being back in school. They gave me enough credits (I guess for being old) to graduate in two years if I go to summer school. The professor in my

Faulkner seminar is soooo cute. He said he can't date a student while she's in his class, but when the semester is over, he wants to take me to dinner. Says he knows a fab BBQ joint. Glad you two are happy living there together. I know you both told me you had had it with men for a spell, but I don't believe I can go quite that far just now. I miss you. More later. See y'all in a couple of …

Nine months later, from the Buzzzz section of the *Tripoli Independent:*

We have learned of a private celebration that was held at the Des Moines apartment of Mr. Timothy Taylor to celebrate the marriage of our own Shawn Gallagher and Miss Amie Greene of Des Moines. The impressive guest list included the State Guv; Charles Hinman, Chief of the DCI; Lizzy Birdseed, Misty Wooten, and Connie Schittman, agribusiness executives; and the members of our own Nachawinga County Sheriff's Department.

Both bride and groom were dressed casually as well as the attendees befitting the informality of the ceremony.

Future plans for Mr. Gallagher include employment as director of the new Craven Snuggs Center for Research. Although Ms. Greene has been offered a full-ride scholarship and teaching assistantship in the Environmental Studies graduate program at State University and also a high position at the Polk County School Board, she has elected to remain at Cohn Middle School where she says she loves her teaching and has important projects to complete.

The bride and groom will reside in the woodland cabin…

Twenty-nine months later, from the platform at the graduation ceremony of East Carolina University, delivered by the Chancellor:

"Misty Wooten. Bachelor of Arts in American Literature. Magna Cum Laude. The Chancellor's Medal is awarded each year to an individual for outstanding achievement…"

Thirty-three months later, from the *Wall Street Journal*:

Notes From Iowa

In an unprecedented move, the Governor of Iowa, a Republican, running unopposed for his fifth term, has endorsed Mr. Timothy Taylor, a Democrat, for State Attorney General. As a result, the Iowa Republican Party will not nominate a candidate for the office, and it appears that Mr. Taylor will also run unopposed in his party's primary. This is the first instance …

Thirty-six months later, from *Iowa Outdoors*, a publication of the Iowa Department of Natural Resources:

There have been no permit applications for new CAFOs in the State in the past three years.

THANKS

To the Tuesday Night Pandemic Zoom writers' group: Janet Carl, Chris and Judy Hunter, and Betty Moffett for enduring my early stumbles while at the same time making me believe that I might be able to finish a novel and for laughing when I read it to them.

To more readers than I can list here for their keen eyes and ears, their suggestions and criticism.

To Mark Baechtel, Harley McIlrath, Kelly Yenser, and Dean Bakopoulas for going beyond reading to editing and, in the process, teaching me to be a better writer.

To Steve Semken and Ice Cube Press for taking a chance on a budding old writer.

To my son Ruben for making me know his appreciation was genuine.

The Ice Cube Press began publishing in 1991 to focus on how to live with the natural world and to better understand how people can best live together in the communities they share and inhabit. Using the literary arts to explore life and experiences in the heartland of the United States we have been recognized by a number of well-known writers including: Bill Bradley, Gary Snyder, Gene Logsdon, Wes Jackson, Patricia Hampl, Greg Brown, Jim Harrison, Annie Dillard, Ken Burns, Roz Chast, Jane Hamilton, Daniel Menaker, Kathleen Norris, Janisse Ray, Craig Lesley, Alison Deming, Harriet Lerner, Richard Lynn Stegner, Richard Rhodes, Michael Pollan, David Abram, David Orr, and Barry Lopez. We've published a number of well-known authors including: Mary Swander, Jim Heynen, Mary Pipher, Bill Holm, Connie Mutel, John T. Price, Carol Bly, Marvin Bell, Debra Marquart, Ted Kooser, Stephanie Mills, Bill McKibben, Craig Lesley, Elizabeth McCracken, Derrick Jensen, Dean Bakopoulos, Rick Bass, Linda Hogan, Pam Houston, Paul Gruchow and Bill Moyers. Check out Ice Cube Press books on our web site, join our email list, Facebook group, or follow us on Twitter. Visit booksellers, museum shops, or any place you can find good books and support our truly honest to goodness independent publishing projects and discover why we continue striving to "hear the other side."

Ice Cube Press, LLC (Est. 1991)
North Liberty, Iowa, Midwest, USA

Resting above the Silurian and Jordan aquifers
steve@icecubepress.com
Check us out on Twitter and Facebook.
www.icecubepress.com

Celebrating Thirty-One Years of Independent Publishing

To Fenna Marie—
fellow adventurer, and
roundabout traveler, as well as
the right person, at the
right place, at the right time.

Sandy Moffett, Emeritus Professor of Theatre at Grinnell College, joined the faculty in 1971 and continues to teach and direct plays on occasion, serving as utility infielder for his department. An avid outdoorsman and conservationist, he spends most of his time restoring prairie on his small farm, writing songs and stories, playing guitar and mandolin in The Too Many String Band, and catering to the whims of his three grandchildren. His writing has appeared in *The Wapsipinicon Almanac, Rootstalk, Saltwater Sportsman,* and other publications. This is his first novel.